TO HEL1

MW01050441

TO HELL AND BACK

Book 3 of the Lily Harper Series

H.P. Mallory

TO HELL AND BACK
Book 3 of the LILY HARPER Series
By
HP MALLORY

Copyright ©2019 by HP Mallory

Acknowledgements:

To my family: Thank you for all your support!

To Jenny Harrington: Thank you for entering my "Become a character in my next book" contest. I really hope you enjoy your character! You were LOTS of fun to write!

To my beta readers: Evie Amaro and Jessica Love, thank you for all your input and your help!

To my editor, Teri, at www.editingfairy.com: thank you for an excellent job, as always.

"Let us descend now unto greater woe."
– Dante's *Inferno*

ONE

Tallis needed me.

That was the only thought in my head.

"Lils," Bill, my guardian angel, started as he shook his head and a frown contorted his doughy, round face. "There's no way in hells I'm gonna let you go after that overgrown Scottish ape on your own." He bit his lower lip like he was about to cry and studied me with narrowed eyes as he shook his head again. Then he sighed. "Not that *I'm* signin' up to go after him neither, 'cause I'm not. As I see it, Tido freakin' took off an' left us in the dust back there at the tavern so whatever shiznit he's gotten himself into now, he freakin' deserves." Taking a long breath, he faced the third person in our party, Delilah Crespo, who was staring at both of us with wide eyes, shock still obvious in her vacant gaze. Her surprise was, no doubt, based on the fact that she'd just narrowly escaped the third level of the Underground City in which she'd nearly been killed by Plutus, the wolf demon.

"Bill," I began, having already rejected the notion of taking Bill and Delilah with me to help Tallis out of whatever quandary he was currently in. No, it was imperative that I go to Tallis by myself because I sensed that whatever state Tallis was in, he wouldn't welcome visitors. He probably wouldn't even be happy

1

to see me. Yep, knowing Tallis and his less-than-friendly personality, three would most definitely be a crowd.

"No-sir-ee, Billy Bob," the rotund angel continued, shaking his head slowly from side to side. "We need ta just keep on movin' an' get ourselves outta this messed up forest, and get us the hells home. I've had enough of this Halloween shit ta last me all ..."

"Bill," I interrupted again, but he immediately speared me with a cross expression. Then he folded his arms over his man boobs. "I have to go back," I insisted in a tone of voice that forbade any further arguments.

"Nope, Lily Harper, you ain't about ta convince me otherwise, even *with* your serious voice. I ain't fallin' for it, nips." Taking a deep breath, he glared at me. "What you're talkin' 'bout is pure craziness, girl." He glanced back at Delilah who still couldn't manage to utter a sound. "Nope, this is most definitely a case of chicks before dicks."

"What?" I demanded, frowning at him as frustration began to gnaw inside me.

"The female version of bros before hos," Bill responded with a shrug like the answer was obvious. "An' in this case, Tido's the dick." He looked over at Delilah again. "Ain't that the truth, though?"

Delilah just looked back at him blankly.

"Bill, I know it sounds crazy, but ..." I started.

"Do I gotta remind you of what's gonna happen as soon as you start walkin' through this screwed up hate-forest alone?" He continued to nod like he already had the answer to his question. "It's gonna trick you out an' make you lose your way. Then, when you're all good an' confused as shit, it's gonna send one o' them man-sized spiders ta finish you off; or you're gonna get raped by one o' those freakin' trees just like in that *Evil Dead* movie. An' if you're thinkin' Bruce Campbell's gonna pull some zombie killin' super-

2

coolness, think again, Lils, 'cause this ain't no classic movie. This here's real life." Then he glanced over at Delilah and nodded sullenly. "The struggle is real, yo."

"Bill," I said, my tone hinting at my growing irritation.

"For reals," he said, nodding his head emphatically. "This forest is full of some crazy ass shit that I ain't gonna be no part of. 'Specially not for freakin' Conan who don't give a rat's ass about good ol' Billy."

"Should I remind you that if it weren't for *Conan*, I wouldn't still be here?" I replied glumly. And that was the truth. Having been so ill-prepared for my first two visits to the Underground City, if not for Tallis, I would have lost my life not once, but twice. "And who knows where you would be!"

Bill continued to shake his head as if the past were of no consequence to him. "Billy's had just about enough of demons an' wolf men an' Alaire an' haunted, rapin' trees. An' I've fo sure had more than enough of He-Man an' his Frankenfood he tries to pass off as real grub!" He faced Delilah and raised his eyebrows. "Dee, we gotta get ourselves the hells outta here and into In-N-Out so's we can forget about this bad frickin' trip over some triple-triples." He faced me again. "An' you, honey mounds, are comin' with us."

"No, Bill, I'm not," I answered with finality.

Our argument had only been going on for a few minutes, but I was already exhausted. Even though I couldn't deny that it probably was complete insanity for me to even attempt to make my way back to Tallis alone, I also knew it was the right thing to do. Tallis had stood by me too many times for me not to return the favor. And even though I had no idea where he was now, or what sort of trouble he was up against, I only hoped I could help him.

The first hurdle would be navigating the haunted forest, known as the Dark Wood, in order to find him.

3

That might not sound like much of a feat, but Bill was right, the Dark Wood was almost as dangerous as the Underground City, itself. The forest was alive in its own right and seemed to have a vendetta against travelers; i.e., if you were unlucky enough to find yourself lost in the Dark Wood, you *were* as good as dead.

"Tallis needs me," I continued. "And I can't tell you why or how, but as far as this forest is concerned, I know my sword will protect me and keep me safe." My voice began to waver since my statement sounded ridiculous even to my own ears.

"Your sword is gonna protect you and keep you safe?" Bill repeated, in a tone of obvious disbelief as he stared at me with both eyebrows reaching for the dark sky.

"Yes," I insisted.

"Nips, I hate ta break it to ya, but no magical Care Bear is just gonna show up and break out a can of demon whup ass with a rainbow, some hearts and a super annoying song."

I decided to ignore his comment. "When I touched my sword just now, I received the distinct impression that Tallis was in trouble and needed me. It was almost like he was using the sword to communicate with me." Tallis had forged my sword with his own hands and since he also possessed Druid magic, I figured it wasn't much of a stretch to believe that he'd endowed the sword with some level of mystical capability, or even magic. "And along with the information that Tallis needs me, I also am pretty sure that I'll be safe if I go after him."

"This sounds like crazy talk, yoze," Bill said as he shook his head before cupping the back of his neck with his sweaty palm, looking as if he were frustrated beyond belief. He glanced over at Delilah and sighed heavily. "Nips has lost her damn mind!"

4

"Oh," Delilah said as her eyebrows knitted in the middle of her forehead and she looked like she was about to cry.

"I know it sounds crazy," I admitted with a nod, hoping my admission would remove all doubt as to whether I still possessed all my marbles. "But I know what the sword showed me and how it made me feel." Of that, there was no doubt in my mind. "I know that Tallis is in trouble and I have to go to him."

Bill sighed again. "Then I guess it's three for the road."

"No," I almost snapped as I interrupted him. "Bill, I have to do this alone." I took a deep breath. "I have to … go alone."

"Lils, as you know, I'm your guardian angel, but I can't do much guardin' if you're here in this horror forest an' I'm not!" Bill argued. Truth be told, he wasn't much of a guardian in the first place. It was strictly his fault that I'd been killed in a car accident several weeks earlier. Apparently, Bill had been paying more attention to seducing some random woman than he had been to ensuring that I was safe. Consequently, I'd died.

Because Bill was employed by Afterlife Enterprises, the company responsible for sorting out the recently dead and sending them on to the Kingdom (think heaven) or the Underground City (think the opposite of heaven), they were the ones who were ultimately responsible for my untimely passing. Since the manager of Afterlife Enterprises, Jason Streethorn, realized I'd basically had him between a rock and a hard place, he'd offered me the option of living again. The only alternative available to me was spending the next hundred years in Shade, which was a holding area for souls before they could move on to the Kingdom. In Shade, there was nothing to look forward to, although there was also nothing to not look forward to. Shade just was. To me, though, Shade sounded like my own personal hell, so I'd opted to live again. But as with most things involving the afterlife, nothing was ever what it seemed …

Due to a glitch in the Afterlife's computer system during Y2K, souls that were meant to go to the Kingdom ended up in the Underground City, and vice versa. The whole thing ended up being one giant cluster f#$%. Hoping to avoid numerous afterlife lawsuits, Jason Streethorn employed a team of "Soul Retrievers." Their main responsibility was locating misplaced souls and returning them to their proper location. So where did I enter into this happy little equation? When Jason offered me the chance to live again, admitting that my death was indirectly the fault of Afterlife Enterprises, he offered me life with one condition—that I become a Soul Retriever. At first, I thought I'd gotten the better side of the deal, and I readily agreed, only to discover I was assigned to retrieving souls in the Underground City, which was basically hell by another name. Even though I did have a guardian angel along for the ride, in the grand scheme of things, that didn't amount to much.

Why? Because Bill wasn't exactly what anyone would imagine when it came to angels. Instead of a beautiful, glowing entity with white wings, Bill looked more like the love child of Jack Black and Zach Galifianakis. Anyway, after my whole untimely death episode, Bill was put on probation. Because Jason Streethorn wasn't sure what to do with him, he decided to send Bill to me. Even though Bill wasn't much of an asset, since he couldn't protect me in the Underground City or the Dark Wood, he had quickly become my best friend. So on that front, I was grateful for him.

"Bill, you know you can't protect me here; so you being my guardian angel is really a moot point," I said with a glance at Delilah who was becoming paler by the minute. I faced Bill again. "You need to get her out

6

of here and back to the earthly plane, before she goes into real shock." From the looks of it, Delilah was maybe no more than a couple steps away from a complete breakdown. Not that I could blame her. This was Delilah's first mission into the Underground and she was as unprepared as I was my first time around. "Take her to our apartment and teach her everything you know," I continued. "Then, both of you just wait for me. As soon as I make sure Tallis is okay, I'll head home."

"How long is that gonna be, Lils?" Bill demanded, his lips turning down into a worried frown.

I shrugged. "I don't know." It was an uncomfortable feeling. I didn't know what was wrong with Tallis, or how long he needed me to tend to him. "Give me a week," I finished, hoping a week would be enough time. For all I knew, Tallis could already be dead, in which case, I'd be home a lot sooner ...

No, don't even think that! I said to myself. *Tallis isn't dead, you know that. He can't die.*

It was true. Tallis was immortal due to the spirit of the warrior, Donnchadh, who resided inside him. But Tallis's immortality was both a blessing and a curse. It promised his ongoing health and vitality, but it couldn't offer him absolution, which was what Tallis ultimately yearned for. "I will try to contact you if I'm able to," I finished, wondering how that would even be possible as soon as I said it.

"Here," Bill said as he fished out his cell phone from his shorts pocket and handed it to me. "You'll need this more than I will." I nodded and accepted the phone, which was currently held together by duct tape. I unzipped my fanny pack and pushed the phone in, re-zipping it as I faced my friend.

"Everything is going to be okay," I said in a soft voice as I smiled at Bill and then at Delilah. I could only hope I was speaking the truth.

"Don't you go dyin' on me," Bill replied in a cracking voice as he opened his arms wide and I fell into them. I forced myself to hold my tears back, while banishing the idea that there was a very good chance I might never see my friend again.

Be strong, Lily, I told myself.

"I'll be fine," I mumbled while pasting on a big smile. "The only thing we have left to fear is fear itself," I finished, quoting FDR.

"I knew your inner nerd was in there somewhere," Bill said with a sad smile, his eyes shining.

I nodded as I pulled away from him, and thought I should probably hug Delilah, but feared I might succumb to the wave of emotion that was already cresting inside me. I waved to her instead. Then I picked up my sword, and turning on my heel, headed back into the haunted wood.

***

For as bad as the Underground City was, the Dark Wood was no walk in the park. It was a haunted forest with a mind of its own, which was usually bent on making you lose your way so you could fall prey to one of the many hideous creatures that lived inside its perimeters. But, luckily for me, I'd already experienced the Dark Wood a few times so I knew what to expect. I also had my sword to help lead the way.

I'd been walking for maybe an hour, holding my sword out in front of me like it was some sort of homing device. Ridiculous as I might have looked, it did seem as if the sword knew its way around the forest. Every now and then, it would incline itself in either an easterly or westerly direction, and so I followed whatever direction it indicated.

The wind picked up and blew its icy breath through the leafless branches of the dead forest that surrounded me. "Dark Wood" was an appropriate name for the forest because it was far removed from anything light and airy. The Dark Wood bordered the Underground City, so it existed in perpetual darkness, which made traveling through it difficult because I never knew what time of day or night it was. I also never had any idea of how long I'd been walking because there was no sun moving in an arc through the sky, signaling the onset of the afternoon or dusk. There was only the darkness of night. The most off-putting part about the Dark Wood, however, was the nothingness. No birds were singing, there was no foliage or greenery to speak of, nothing but dreariness and seemingly never-ending dead tree branches that obscured the sky like myriad sharp spears.

I felt something buzzing from my midsection, and my breath caught in my throat. Seconds later, I realized it was just Bill's phone vibrating with what I imagined was an incoming text message. I paused and glanced around myself to make sure I wasn't about to be waylaid by some hideous creature. Not finding anything suspicious in the immediate vicinity, I unzipped my fanny pack and pulled out Bill's phone. I flipped open the top and noticed it was, indeed, a text. It read:

I have not heard from Ms. Harper. Am I to believe that she is thus declining my dinner invitation? By nature, I am not a patient man. Please advise.

Even though there was no name associated with the text, I immediately knew who it was: Alaire, the Master of the Underground City.

"Ugh," I said to myself out loud as my heart joined my stomach in dropping down to my feet.

Alaire had texted Bill a few hours earlier, inviting me to dine with him. I wasn't sure why, but Alaire harbored some sort of odd fascination with me. Tallis made it sound like Alaire was more enthralled with my innocence than he was with me, but I couldn't be sure where my innocence ended and I began. It seemed we

9

were one and the same. As to Alaire, he was the very antithesis of anything wholesome, which was probably the chief reason he seemed to be so taken with me— being, as he was, so unaccustomed to innocence in the Underground City.

Regardless of the reasons why Alaire was interested in me, the important factor was that he basically had me right where he wanted me. He'd threatened to report me to Afterlife Enterprises when I'd offed one of his demon wolves during my last trip into the Underground City. As far as the wolf was concerned, I'd just been defending myself against its attack, but Afterlife Enterprises wasn't much concerned with the reasons why certain events took place. Instead, it seemed like Jason Streethorn had his nose stuffed right up Alaire's, ahem, backside, because whatever Alaire wanted, Alaire got. Which meant if Alaire pressed charges, and I was convicted of murdering one of his employees, I would be punished by an infraction. And two infractions were a ticket to Shade for the next hundred years.

I inhaled deeply and texted back:

This is Lily. I thought you said I had until tomorrow night at ten p.m. to respond to your invitation?

I flipped the phone closed just as it hummed again, alerting me to a new text. I flipped it back open and read:

I have since changed my mind. I expect a more prompt response.

I was surprised by Alaire's quick reply, but then figured he probably didn't have much else to do in his high-rise office building, manned by no one save himself.

How about I respond by tomorrow at nine p.m.? I texted back as a smile curled my lips. Even though I knew I had to accept Alaire's dinner invitation, or run the risk of earning my first infraction, I wasn't about to let him off the hook so easily. Alaire, as Master of

10

the Underground City, expected to get his way, which made him cocky. And those were two attributes I found incredibly irritating in any man.

Very funny, Ms. Harper, he texted back a few seconds later. *I expect your response immediately.*

As in posthaste?

I find your sense of humor vexing, to say the least, he replied. *Shall I remind you of the infraction that awaits you?*

So now he was going to threaten me? I swallowed hard and felt my eyes narrowing as irritation began to spiral through me. *Should I suppose that dinner with you means the infraction is no longer on the table?* I typed back hurriedly, then added: *No pun intended.* The thought that I should be more aware of my surroundings flashed through my mind, and I glanced up and scanned the perimeter of the forest, although I found nothing untoward or suspicious. I returned my attention to the broken phone screen. Alaire hadn't responded so I continued. *Because if the infraction is non-negotiable, then my reply to your dinner invitation is no.*

If you agree to be my dinner guest, you have my word you will receive no infraction.

I sighed before typing my next message. *Should I trust the word of the Master of the Underground City? I confess you don't strike me as being very trustworthy.* I knew it was a risky thing to say, and it definitely wasn't a good idea to incite his anger, but I was worried that he wouldn't keep his end of the bargain. Not that asking him if he was trustworthy would prove otherwise, but anyhow ...

Indeed, you should. I value honesty, Ms. Harper, and as such, you will always know where you stand with me.

And there it was. I didn't know what I was expecting from him, but hoped his word was truly his bond. *Okay,* I wrote back. *Next Tuesday evening at eight p.m.* I shook my head and wondered what I was getting myself into. But having already made my bed, there was no turning back now. *Am I still to meet you at the gates of the Underground City?*

Yes. He texted immediately. *I will send a car to ensure you are unharmed by my employees.*

I found it somewhat ironically eerie that Alaire referred to his demons as his employees, but c'est la vie. *Okay,* I texted back before something occurred to me. *One last request ...*

And what request might that be? I realized he was flirting with me, a realization that made me sick to my stomach.

Due to unforeseen circumstances, I will be stuck in the Dark Wood for a while, and as I'm sure you're fully aware, it's impossible to tell the day from the night. Well, as long as I was in the middle of the Dark Wood, anyway. The sun did shine where Tallis lived, on the periphery of the Dark Wood, but I wasn't sure how much time I'd be spending there, if any time at all ... *Right now, I have no idea what day or time it is ...* I accidentally clicked the "send" button even though I wasn't finished typing.

It is Friday at midnight.

Just as I started to type my response, the phone suddenly rang. I jumped in surprise as soon as the shrill ring met my ears. "Hello?" I answered in a dubious tone, having a good idea of who might be on the other end.

"My fingers were beginning to cramp," Alaire explained, although I was sure he was exaggerating. "As to your request," he continued in his slight Scandinavian accent, "I imagine you would appreciate it if I alerted you when you are due to arrive at the gates of my city?"

"Yes," I answered immediately as I started walking again. I figured I shouldn't loiter in the haunted forest where God-only-knew-what was probably preparing to ambush me. It was bad enough that my attention was now focused on a phone call. "Otherwise, I have no way of knowing when Tuesday at eight p.m. rolls around." But then I remembered it would probably take me some time to make the trip to the gates of the Underground. "Maybe you should text me at the beginning of each new day because I'm not sure how long it will take me to reach the gates."

"Where, exactly, are you in the Dark Wood?" Alaire inquired, sounding bored. I could hear the tapping of his fingernails against his desk.

"I don't know," I answered with a sigh as I glanced around myself. "The terrain here all looks the same."

Alaire tsked me a few times as if he were disappointed with my retort, which I found exasperating. "Not a very wise choice to be lost in the Dark Wood, now, is it?"

"Well, it's not as though I planned to get lost!" I railed back at him. I held my sword out before me and it pointed in an easterly direction. "And for your information, I'm not lost," I snapped back, not wanting it to sound like I was ill prepared for the trip. "My sword is doing a great job of leading me wherever I have to go."

"And just where would that be?" he continued, his tone of voice now sounding amused.

"To where I'm going," I spat back, not wanting him to know that Tallis could be in trouble and I was trying to find him. I had a feeling that information wasn't safe in Alaire's hands. Even though Tallis and Alaire appeared to share a long history, well, as far as I could tell from the last time we were in Alaire's office, anyway, it didn't seem as if their history was a friendly one. And any non-friend of Tallis's was a non-friend of mine.

"Is your lover with you?" Alaire asked, going for disinterested, but not quite succeeding.

"He isn't my lover."

13

"Perhaps not yet, although I daresay he would quite like to try the role on for size?"

I inhaled deeply, then exhaled just as long. "No comment."

Alaire was quiet for a few seconds until all I could hear was the even cadence of his breathing. "And the angel?"

"What about him?"

"Is he with you?"

"No," I answered, immediately thinking better of it.

Alaire exhaled slowly, the only sound on the other line the tapping of his fingernails. "As I understand it, then, you are lost in the Dark Wood and all alone?"

"No and yes."

The cadence of his fingernail tapping increased. "As the Dark Wood is not part of the Underground City, I am *sadly* unable to protect you."

"Then I guess I'll have to protect myself," I responded haughtily. "I definitely wouldn't want my death to be the reason for missing our dinner date." I couldn't help my acidic laugh.

"Nor would I, my lady, nor would I."

"And on that happy note, I'm going to hang up," I said quickly. "I should be paying attention to my surroundings, rather than this conversation."

"On that subject, we shall agree for once," he answered. "Please do be careful, my dear, and one word of advice if you will welcome it?"

"What?" I grumbled.

"Enable your phone's flashlight capability if it has one—the light will keep the creatures of the Dark Wood at bay."

"Okay," I answered, thinking his advice was surprisingly sound. "Good-bye, Alaire."

"Good-bye, my dear Ms. Harper."

I clicked the button to end the conversation and then clicked on the settings icon and located the flashlight button. I turned the flashlight on and

14

immediately felt more comfortable as soon as the phone brightened the path in front of me. If there was one good thing about the Underground City, it was that it was surrounded by a strong electric force field that enabled anything electrical, which meant Bill's phone would maintain a full battery. At least, that's what Tallis had told me. I could only hope the same rule applied in the Dark Wood.

I plopped the phone back into my fanny pack and felt a tug on the end of my sword, which indicated I should make a sharp right. I did as instructed and felt energy beginning to vibrate up the cold metal. I was suddenly overcome with the feeling that I had finally reached my destination.

I held the phone up and in the bright light, I tried to make out the lines of Tallis's cabin but was only greeted with the remains of a few gnarled tree trunks. I took a few steps forward and heard the unmistakable sounds of rustling in the undergrowth. And undergrowth, i.e., bushes, could only mean one thing—I had to have reached an area of the Dark Wood which nourished life. I felt elation begin to grow in my gut because the only section of the Dark Wood which boasted anything living was the same place where Tallis lived.

"I'm here, Tallis," I whispered.

"Already sinks each star that was ascending"
– Dante's *Inferno*

TWO

I wasn't sure if I should have knocked on Tallis's front door, or just opened it, or what. I lingered outside for another second or two before reminding myself that Tallis was in trouble, so timing was of the utmost importance. I needed to take action ... now. Clenching my sword in my left hand, I pushed against the door, which immediately swung open. I stepped back and watched the door close again while my Scooby senses went on high alert. Ordinarily, Tallis was much better about security. When living in the Dark Wood, one had to be overly conscientious about one's surroundings ... As a rule, Tallis's door was locked from the inside if he were home, or the outside if he wasn't. With my heart lodged in my throat, I leaned my right arm against the large, wooden door, which yielded immediately, making a whining sort of noise.

Inhaling deeply, I stepped inside, closing the door behind me. The inside of Tallis's humble abode was dark and eerily quiet. It didn't feel like the same place I was accustomed to. Usually, there was a fire burning in the hearth and the scent of hearty stew flavored the air. Now, however, the acrid odor of alcohol overwhelmed the small space. And there was no warmth from a fire. The air was crisp and cold. It caused goose bumps to ride up my naked arms and midriff. As luck had it, I was wearing nothing more

16

than a workout bra and a pair of tight yoga pants—
ideal for sparring with the creatures of the
Underground City, but not so perfect when warding off
the cold.

"Tallis!" I called out as I took another step
forward, finding it hard to make my way in the pitch-
black darkness. Then I remembered Bill's phone and
the flashlight application. Pulling his phone out from
my fanny pack, I clicked the icon for the desktop and
had to squint at the brightness of the screen. I clicked
the lightbulb icon and held the phone out so I could
see where I was going. The odor of whiskey was so
caustic, I had to breathe through my mouth.

The flashlight lit up the log walls of Tallis's home,
imbuing them with a creepy glow. I shifted my
attention to the pieces of splintered wood that littered
the floor in front of the fireplace—pieces of wood that
were once Tallis's couch. My heartbeat started to race
as soon as I viewed the carnage. The roughly hewn log
table still stood in one corner of the room, but one of
the two chairs was broken and discarded. The other
chair was lying on its side and didn't look damaged, as
far as I could tell. The straw mattress that lay in the
far corner of the room was still intact, but the only
things atop it were a few animal furs that Tallis used
as rugs or blankets. There was no trace of Tallis.

He isn't here, I told myself and felt my heart drop
all the way to the dirt floor.

I turned and did one final inspection of Tallis's
house before reaching the conclusion that he most
definitely wasn't home. I took another tentative step
forward as I tried to figure out why my sword had led
me here if Tallis wasn't. My attention returned to the
splintered pieces of wood strewn about the room as
panic began to spiral through my body.

If he isn't here ... I thought and then gulped,
shaking my head as I tried to figure out my next

17

course of action. *Maybe he was here a little while ago, but got attacked and had to vacate the place?*

But where would he have gone? I argued with myself. *And how in the world will I find him now?* I started to chew on my lower lip, not at all comfortable at leaving Tallis's house to venture into the merciless territory of the Dark Wood again. *Maybe he's outside or planning to return soon? You know what they say— it's better to wait for someone who's lost to come to you than to go searching for him ...*

Was that true though? Because it really didn't make much sense ...

Hmm, I couldn't be sure. But if Tallis were somewhere out there, lost in the Dark Wood, I had basically zero chance of finding him. Especially since my sword clearly wasn't as good at navigating as I'd assumed.

With disappointment and frustration coursing through me, I turned on the ball of my foot and held Bill's phone up so I could light the way back to the door. It felt like the weight of the world had fallen on my shoulders because I didn't have a clue of what I should do next. As soon as my attention settled on the door, I felt an icy-cold, iron grip around my ankle. A scream that started in my throat never made it past my lips before I felt myself falling backward. I released Bill's cell phone at the same time as my sword. Suddenly surrounded by the bleak darkness, I could only make out the sound of my sword when it clattered against something metal before landing on the dirt floor. I was quick to follow. I hit the back of my head against the ground and winced in pain. The fall knocked the wind right out of my lungs. My eyelids clenched tightly shut on their own.

"Who are ye?"

I heard Tallis's voice, but it sounded different somehow—foreign. The acrid scent of whiskey now fully overcame me and it took me a few seconds before I realized it was on his breath.

Even though he'd asked me a question, I found it difficult to talk. In fact, it was difficult even to open my eyes. I wasn't sure whether it was because I couldn't breathe, or it might have been from hitting my head so hard, but I felt very dizzy. I couldn't concentrate on anything except the incessant pounding between my ears.

"If ye dinnae answer meh, Ah'll rip ye in two, straight down yer middle," Tallis threatened in an uneven voice that reeked of stale alcohol. As soon as the words left his mouth, I felt the cold iron of a blade pressing on my throat. Instinctively, I opened my eyes. My reward was a brief flash of pain inside my head. Ignoring my discomfort, I found Tallis looming above me, staring down at me through alien eyes. They were eclipsed by black, much darker than their usual midnight blue, and he was illuminated by a pale, bluish light. At first, I thought he was glowing, but I soon realized it was just the flashlight application on Bill's phone which was now shining directly on him from where it lay on the floor.

Tallis was just as stunning as I remembered him. Wearing only a kilt, his naked chest was ... impressive. The span of his shoulders prevented me from seeing anything beyond him, not that I was interested in whatever was behind him. Instead, my attention was riveted on his sculpted muscles which covered his body like a suit, only eclipsed by his imposing size. The guy had to be nearly seven feet tall. Despite his mouth-watering, awe-inspiring body, it was Tallis's face that always kept me captivated. His was the face of a warrior, one that most women would not have described as handsome. A huge scar bisected his cheek, running from the tip of one eyebrow and ending at his jawline, giving him the appearance of someone who had truly weathered a storm. The lines of his

19

square, chiseled jaw and cheeks were heightened by the shortness of his hair, which was as black as his eyes were presently.

He pushed the tip of the blade against my throat again, reminding me that I should have been paying attention to whatever it was he'd said. *Answer him! He's going to gut you, you moron!* I reprimanded myself internally, suddenly growing irate for becoming so awestruck at the very sight of him. Especially when he clearly didn't recognize me and, consequently, intended to do me in.

"T ... Tallis," I managed, in a small, insignificant voice. There was no expression of recognition on Tallis's face. It was blank. With my heartbeat racing, I wondered why he had no idea who I was. Then I realized he couldn't see me. The flashlight was solely focused on him, which kept me obscured in the darkness.

"A lass," he responded in a voice laced with surprise and doubt. The knotted furrow between his eyebrows settled and he leaned back on his haunches, albeit clumsily. He was clearly intoxicated. If the smell on his breath wasn't proof enough, his uneven movements betrayed him. He reached for the flashlight and shined it on me, temporarily blinding me as he shone it from my head down to my thighs, which were currently playing prisoner to his. "Och aye, ye are ah lass," he repeated, setting the flashlight down beside me until it caught us both in its bright stream of light. Even though his eyes still appeared to be just as dangerous as they were moments earlier, a smile now played on his lips.

"Of course I am!" I railed out, finally finding myself. I brought my right hand to my head and rubbed my temples, praying that my throbbing headache would cease. Tallis's eyes narrowed on me as he studied me with cold calculation. Despite his murderous gaze, I was relieved he no longer held my carotid artery hostage to the tip of his blade.

As soon as I took another look at him, warmth suffused me. I was suddenly overwhelmed with the need to reach out and touch him. I wanted to revel in the fact that he was here and safe, rather than lost somewhere in the Dark Wood. But there was something in his eyes that stopped me, something that didn't seem to fit. "Tallis?" I said again, my voice a bit stronger. I tried to free myself, but his thighs clamped tightly around my middle. "What," I started, the words stinging my throat. "What happened here? Wh ... Why is all your furniture broken?" I inhaled deeply and scanned the room, taking in all the broken furniture again. "Are you okay? Did someone attack you?"

I reached out to touch his face even though I knew it was a risky thing to do because Tallis didn't like to be touched. I couldn't help it though—he was the main reason I was still alive. Without him, I never would have survived the Underground City or the Dark Wood. Tallis was my protector and he was my friend.

As soon as I made contact with his cheek, he slammed my arm to the ground and forced his blade back to my throat. The air hitched in my lungs and a whimper escaped from my lips as pain traveled up my arm.

"Who are ye?" he demanded again, his eyes narrowing into mere slits. "An' whit dae ye want?"

My eyebrows knotted in frustration as my heartbeat began to pound louder. Okay, so it wasn't a good idea to touch him, but his violent reaction seemed a little over the top ..."What do you mean, who am I?" I repeated, frowning at him, my voice sounding panicked. "I'm Lily," I continued slowly, attempting to sit up. He pushed me, none-too-gently, back onto the dirt floor, pinning me between his thighs again.

21

"Ah dinnae know ah 'Lily,'" he answered as his eyes perused my face and moved lower still, to my bust. "Boot ye are ah lass, which means ye are nae threat." It struck me that his Scottish accent was a lot stronger now, more pronounced than I remembered it. "Nae," he continued as a smile appeared on his mouth again. But it wasn't a smile I'd ever seen on Tallis before. Not that Tallis smiled much, but in the few times I'd had the pleasure of seeing an expression of mirth on his face, it looked very different from this. No, this really couldn't even be considered a smile at all— it was too libidinous, too lecherous. "Ye are nae threat," he repeated. His brogue was definitely much more audible than usual.

"You sound different," I replied, then hesitated as I wondered if it was just the alcohol's effect on him. "You've been drinking too much."

"Ye cannae bevvy tae mooch," he responded as his gaze settled on the junction between my thighs and my breath caught.

"Tallis," I said again, feeling suddenly sheepish and uncomfortable under his lustful gaze. He didn't respond, but I noticed that when I said his name, he did nothing to show the slightest acknowledgment. I might as well have been calling him someone else's name for the reaction I received from him. "Why are you acting so … so weird?" I asked, shaking my head. "Why don't you know who I am?"

Maybe he hit his head during whatever altercation happened here? I wondered as my attention returned to the splintered furniture. *Or maybe it's the alcohol that's clouding his mind? Whatever it is, he's acting really … strange. He's not acting like himself at all.*

"Less talkin'," he grumbled as his eyes scanned my body again, resting on my thighs. He pulled the blade away from my throat and gently trailed it down the center of my chest, then farther still until he reached my fanny pack. He studied it with curiosity

22

for a moment or two but then simply slipped the blade beneath the band and yanked upward, severing the band in two.

"Hey!" I yelled at him angrily. "What the hell is wrong with you? I needed that!"

But he didn't pay me any attention. Instead, he tore the fanny pack from me and threw it unceremoniously into the corner of the room. Before I could further argue, he brought the tip of the blade back to my belly button. He paused there momentarily, drawing lazy swirls around my belly button with the tip of the blade.

Even though I knew something was off, that something wasn't right between us, I couldn't help the excitement that was already starting from deep within me. Tallis just had this reaction on me. Sure, he and I had argued plenty of times, and there were several occasions when I might have said I hated him, but I couldn't deny that we shared a mutual physical connection. Yep, I had to admit that Tallis turned me on. A lot.

"You're drunk," I started, thinking I didn't want to do anything sexual with him if he were intoxicated. Not only had I never had sex with Tallis before, I'd never had sex with anyone before. Period.

He responded by dragging the blade from my belly button down to the waistline of my yoga pants. He slipped the blade beneath my waistband and held it there, as if it were a threat. "Tallis," I repeated, my tone of voice lower, emitting a warning of its own. There was an expression on his face that I'd never seen before and it scared me.

"Ah dinnae care," he replied, pulling the blade forward until I could hear the sound of the material ripping beneath it. I pushed against his bulky arms with both of my hands as real fear began to snake through me. But I might as well have been pushing a wall for all the good it did. His thighs felt like iron manacles as he tightened them around my middle. I shivered in the cold air that suddenly invaded my most vulnerable of places. Glancing up at Tallis again, I found his eyes fixated on the junction between my thighs.

"Tallis," I said, my voice now coming out as only a whisper. "You're scaring me."

But Tallis didn't respond. Well, not in words anyway. Instead, he pressed the cold blade of the handle up against the sensitive nub between my thighs. I bucked up against him but with his thighs pinning mine to the floor, I didn't get very far. "What are you doing?" I shouted at him, the pounding of my heart deafening.

"Ye ask tae many questions, lass," he replied before rubbing the handle against me, up and down. Even though my mind insisted something was wrong with Tallis, and I needed to find out what *it* was, my body couldn't resist him. I instinctively arched up, loving the blissful feelings that were already raining down on me. I closed my eyes, reveling in the ecstasy, even though a small voice from within warned me not to lose myself.

Tallis chuckled and I opened my eyes, finding his riveted on mine. While staring at me unblinkingly, he continued rubbing the handle on me, the same lecherous smile still curving his lips. He had to be fully aware that even though my words might have demonstrated otherwise, I was enjoying this. It was pretty plainly obvious by my body's reaction.

"There's ah good lass," he whispered. A new wave of pleasure started to grow in the pit of my belly, reaching its fingers upward until the stinging sensation in my pelvis turned into an all-out burning.

"Tallis," I breathed out, barely able to say his name, trying my hardest not to completely lose myself in the moment. But there was a niggling doubt inside

24

me, warning me that something wasn't right, that something about Tallis was off.

"Joost keep quiet an' let meh dae wif ye whit Ah want," he said in a thick brogue. He increased the speed of his ministrations as my eyes clenched tightly shut of their own accord. I moaned loudly—I couldn't stop myself. In response, Tallis chuckled again. Seconds later, I opened my eyes when I felt the handle of the blade no longer rubbing against me.

Some of my sanity immediately returned. I opened my mouth, ready to argue why we needed to stop what we were doing, and why we shouldn't have started doing it in the first place, especially since he was two hundred sheets to the wind ... But the words slipped right off my tongue once I saw his eyes. They were entirely black. It looked as if his pupils had swallowed the whites of his eyes.

And that was when I realized why Tallis had not only failed to recognize me, but also didn't seem to know his own name.

"Donnchadh," I said. It was the name of the Celtic warrior who possessed Tallis, and thereby, imbued him with immortality.

Tallis's attention was instantly fastened on me. Seeing the expression of recognition in his eyes, it felt as if my heart stopped for the breadth of a few seconds. I now knew what all of this meant and it was a reality that bothered me, hugely.

Ordinarily, Tallis managed to control the spirit of Donnchadh, to suppress it. But now ... it appeared that Donnchadh had somehow taken charge of Tallis. That meant the spirit of the most powerful of warriors, one that Tallis had described as "brutal," was now controlling Tallis's body ... What that meant for Tallis's spirit, however, I didn't know.

I felt the handle of the blade at my opening and seconds later, he pushed it into me. Without thinking, I closed my eyes as a moan dropped off my lips. I could feel him pulling the handle out of me, only to push it in again, this time deeper. It took my muddled mind a few seconds to realize I didn't experience any pain which was answer enough to the question of whether or not the body I inhabited was a virgin. Once I felt him pull the blade's handle out of me and push it back in again, all thoughts of whether or not I was a virgin fled right out of my mind. Instead, I reflexively arched up again, even though I tried to resist the urges of desire that were already coursing through me. But it was impossible. I was too far gone, way too excited to respond with a rational thought.

"Och aye, good lass," Tallis crooned down at me. He slid the handle of the blade out of me and paused for the span of a few heartbeats, only to push it in again as deeply as it would go. Any arguments against what he was doing to me completely evaporated right out of my mind.

No, Lily! I heard my voice yelling at me from within my head. *This isn't Tallis! This is Donnchadh!*

Tallis, Donnchadh … what's the difference? I argued, rocking back and forth against the handle of the blade, pushing down hard on Tallis's hand when he thrust the handle up higher inside me. When he started rolling my nub between his thumb and index finger while the handle of the blade was still up inside me, I felt my hands fisting at my sides as pure bliss captured me.

Lily, this isn't the way it was supposed to happen with him! that voice screamed back at me. *If you're going to have sex with him, make sure it's with Tallis, for God's sake!*

As soon as the thought entered my head, Tallis, er, Donnchadh, pulled the blade's handle out of me and dropped it on the floor. I leaned up onto my elbows and watched him reach down and unfasten one of the two straps that held his kilt together. A cold dose of reality suddenly sunk into me as I realized what he intended to do. Pushing my legs together, and using my elbows as support, I thrust myself backwards. Donnchadh looked up from where he was unfastening the second leather strap and observed me curiously.

"Tallis," I said, in an uneven voice. "Tallis, if you're in there, please take control of your body again!" My voice went from breathy and soft to loud and slightly panicked. "Please, Tallis!"

"Lass, dinnae play games wif meh," Donnchadh said, turning his steely eyes on me as his jaw tightened. "Ye are nae match fur meh an' Ah will take whit Ah want." He grasped me around the ankle and yanked me back toward him. It was pretty crystal clear as to what was going to happen next.

Go for your sword, Lily! I commanded myself, realizing my sword was the only thing that could protect me. Rotating my body, I glanced back and spotted the shiny metal weapon where it lay, maybe a few feet from me. I flipped over onto my stomach and started to get up to grab the sword when I felt Donnchadh's arm around my middle. He yanked me backwards as I screamed.

"Ah prefer ta take ye oan yer hands an' knees," he whispered in my ear, his breath still reeking of whiskey. Even though it was Tallis's voice and Tallis's body, this wasn't Tallis. This was Donnchadh. He reached down and ripped my yoga pants off my hips, pushing them down to my knees. Then he forced me onto all fours, grabbing me around my waist and pulling me up against him. I could feel his erection against the inside of my thigh.

While focusing on the shiny steel of my sword where it lay on the floor, I clenched my eyes shut tightly. *Tallis,* I called out to the two-thousand-year-old Celtic warrior whom I considered my guardian. *I can't fight Donnchadh—he's way too strong! I need your help! I can't do this alone!*

27

I felt Donnchadh positioning himself behind me. I opened my eyes and focused on my sword with all the determination I possessed. *Tallis, I need you! Please! Don't let him do this to me!*

Donnchadh's breathing increased, clouding me with its pungent alcohol stench. With a squeal, I lurched forward when I felt his hardness at my opening. Chuckling, he gripped both of my shoulders as he pulled me back into place.

"Dinnae be afraid, wee lass," he whispered into my ear with a hearty laugh while palming a handful of my hair. He wrapped it around his hand, yanking my head up at an uncomfortable angle. "The pain will be quick, boot the pleasure lastin'."

Even with my neck craned awkwardly, I didn't take my eyes from my sword. Donnchadh reached down to reposition himself at my entry with the hand that wasn't gripping my hair.

Tallis! I screamed inside my head at the same time that Donnchadh thrust himself forward. I lurched forward also, and just barely missed being impaled by his anxious erection. He tightened his grip on my hair and yanked me backwards again, this time with more urgency.

"Dinnae make meh angry, lass," he ground out. "Ye willnae like the ootcome."

I didn't reply because I was too focused on my sword, willing it to come to me. Even though a part of me knew it was completely crazy to expect the sword to move of its own accord, another part of me insisted that the sword possessed some level of magic, so was it really too absurd to hope that I could somehow communicate with it? And, better yet, that it could somehow ... transport itself to me?

Tallis! I screamed out again mentally. *Please, Tallis, help me! I need you!*

Tears started to sting my eyes as I wholly focused on the gleaming metal of my sword where it lay in the dirt. As I watched it, the sword flopped a few times like a fish out of water. I briefly recognized the feelings of shock deep in my gut as I watched the sword fling itself forward, as if by an invisible hand. Extending both of my arms out as far as I could reach, I inched forward, but didn't make it very far. I felt Donnchadh's menacing grip around my midsection as he yanked me backwards again. But he was too late. The ice cold metal touched the palm of my right hand, and I wrapped my fingers around the hilt of my sword as I flipped over so my back was on the dirt floor. Then I held my sword up against Donnchadh, like it was a cross, or a garlic bulb, and he were a vampire. I had no idea what I was doing. I definitely had no script to follow. I just went with what felt natural and right.

He immediately pulled away from me and dropped his hands off my waist before his kilt fell down again and covered his erection, which was also rapidly on its way down.

Touch him with the blade, I told myself, not understanding why I was overcome with the urge to bring the blade to Donnchadh's skin. But I went with it anyway. Stabling myself with my left hand on the ground, I jumped up until I was standing right in front of the immense warrior. Then I thrust the flat side of the sword's blade against his chest with all my might, closing my eyes as I held the sword in place.

I heard Tallis shrieking, but I knew it was really Donnchadh. He took a few unsteady steps backward until he was pinned up against the wall. I didn't release my sword. I continued to force the flat side of the blade against his abdomen, and he just stood there, as if trapped, throwing his head from side to side while he howled in what sounded like agony.

Suddenly, everything went dark. It was as if someone had walked into the room and turned off Bill's flashlight phone, although, of course, no one had. I was aware that my eyes were still open but I couldn't see anything. I didn't have much time to worry about it, though, because before I knew it, a flood of images began to flash before me.

The first was one that I recognized, a castle that I'd seen before. Fergus Castle. It was the same image I'd seen the very first time I'd touched my sword. Tallis had explained to me at the time that it was his family's castle and had been in his bloodline for centuries.

As soon as the image of the castle faded away, it was replaced by one of Tallis, only he looked younger somehow or, at least, less experienced. He was on his knees, embracing an immense sword that had to be five feet long. He was chanting something, but the words were lost on the wind that whipped through his black hair which fell beyond his waist. Bonfires burned a bright orange in the background, contrasting against the dark night sky. I didn't know why or how, but I was suddenly imbued with the understanding that I was at the Samhain festival which celebrated the end of the harvest season and the beginning of winter's darkness.

I could suddenly smell the coppery scent of blood. I watched the vision Tallis glancing to his side and reaching down to a goat. Its throat was slit, and its life was starting to slip away as the blood leaked from the deep wound on its neck. Tallis reached over and ran his finger through the blood, smearing it across both of his cheeks. This illusion of Tallis was missing the scar that ran from his eyebrow to his jaw.

The soft sound of whimpering interrupted the stillness of the night and I watched Tallis look behind his shoulder. It was as if I were watching a movie playing behind my eyelids because I could suddenly see what my vision of Tallis was seeing—a beautiful blond woman who was maybe twenty years old. She was tied to a tree with her hands bound behind her. Her face was red and her eyes were swollen. It was obvious she'd been crying and judging by the wild look in her eyes, I knew she was terrified.

Tallis looked completely unconcerned with the girl. Instead, he bent down to his right side and retrieved a quaich, which was a traditional, two-handled drinking cup of Scottish origin. I watched Tallis bring the quaich to his lips, but he didn't drink from it. Instead, he continued to chant something that didn't sound like English, so I figured it was Gaelic. He closed his eyes and tipped the quaich up, swallowing the contents. That done, he dropped the cup and suddenly bent over, gripping his stomach as if he were in the throes of intense anguish.

I was reminded of the time Tallis told me how Donnchadh had assumed residency inside his body. The possession had taken place in Scotland, only it was such a long time ago that Scotland had been comprised of various warring tribes and it had been known as Alba. During the Samhain festival, Tallis had drunk some sort of tea brewed from the spores of the rye fungus. Apparently, after drinking the spores, Tallis could separate his body from his soul, and become one with the spiritual world which is exactly what he'd done. I could only imagine that same moment was now playing itself out behind my eyelids.

I watched the vision of Tallis wail out a horrible sound, like his insides were melting. He rocked back and forth as he clutched his stomach and shouted words and phrases I didn't understand. The whimpers of the woman who was tied to the tree became cries of terror. But it wasn't her cries that grabbed my attention. Instead, I swore I could hear the soft sounds of chanting. But aside from Tallis and the woman, no one else was present. As soon as I doubted whether or not I'd heard the other voices, the chanting began to grow louder. But, still, I couldn't see anyone besides Tallis and the woman. It was almost as if the voices

belonged to the spirits who joined the earthly plane
during Samhain.

The visionary Tallis lifted his head. He was
panting and sweat beaded on his forehead but it was
his eyes that held me captive. They were entirely
black, the surest sign that Donnchadh had entered his
body. Tallis started chanting again, his voice coming
out rough, and pained. For some reason, I could now
understand the words even though they weren't in
English. He welcomed the spirit of the great warrior
into his body, and celebrated the idea that this spirit
would help him prevail against the Roman threat. I
watched Tallis turn to face the woman who was tied to
the tree. Understanding immediately dawned on me.
She was intended as an offering to Donnchadh, a
sexual one. Seeing as how Donnchadh had been
trapped in the spiritual plane for thousands of years, I
supposed it made sense that the first thing he would
want to do upon inhabiting a human body again was
have sex.

Seeing Tallis's eyes which were now eclipsed
black, the woman began shaking her head and
screaming. I watched him approach her until he stood
directly in front of her. He reached forward, gripped
her gown in his large hands and tore it in two, straight
down the middle. Her smallish breasts bounced as she
struggled against the ropes that bound her to the tree.
Even though I knew what was happening—that Tallis,
with Donnchadh at the helm, was about to rape the
poor girl—I couldn't reconcile this man as the Tallis
Black that I'd come to know so well. Yes, Tallis *had*
admitted he'd been far less than a morally decent
person in the past. He'd allied himself with the
Romans after they'd bribed him with riches and power.
In allying himself with his enemies, he'd ended up
backstabbing his own people and in the process, the
Romans had massacred them.

32

While I was fully aware that Tallis had a terrible past in which he'd committed unspeakable crimes, he'd also spent a long time in penance, atoning for his past sins and wrongdoings. And it was that repentance that allowed me to look beyond his past transgressions and accept him for the person he now was. It was his inordinate sense of responsibility and regret that enabled me to care so deeply for him.

Luckily I was spared having to watch Donnchadh rape the girl. Instead, the vision faded and I found myself facing Tallis, the real Tallis. It took me a second or two to shake off the vision but when I did, I glanced down at my arms and noticed I was still holding him captive with my sword. He was pinned against the log wall of his home. As soon as I made eye contact with him, the blackness of his eyes yielded to the midnight blue I'd come to know so well.

"Tallis?" I asked in a breathless, hopeful voice.

He didn't respond, but instead, passed out.

"Loitering is forbidden"
– Dante's *Inferno*

THREE

When Tallis lost consciousness, I couldn't catch him because it would have been like trying to stop a boulder from falling off a mountain. I did, however, manage to push him against the wall, so he wouldn't do a face-plant on the dirt floor. Once his butt hit the ground and he was in a hunched-over position, leaning against the wall, I could finally take a breath. I inhaled and exhaled deeply, straining to convince my heartbeat to regulate. When it began to slow down, I considered what I needed to do next. I propped my sword against the wall beside Tallis before grabbing Bill's phone with the flashlight app. Crouching down on my knees, I shined the flashlight on the sleeping giant.

I wanted to make sure he was still breathing and alive. The gentle rise and fall of his chest assuaged my fears and I sighed long and hard. Now able to catch my breath and consider everything that had just happened, I shook my head as I thought about how close I'd come to having sex with Tallis. While that very topic had played through my mind more than once (okay, on numerous occasions), what I'd just been through wasn't exactly how I'd imagined it.

"I hope you're okay, Tallis," I said as I ran my index finger down the side of his face and noticed how clammy his skin was. I figured Donnchadh must've short-circuited once his spirit encountered my sword.

34

Then, maybe, Tallis's body just shut down—like a system overload or something. Who knew? Maybe the spirits of Tallis and Donnchadh were still fighting it out behind Tallis's otherwise calm exterior.

I glanced down at myself and sighed again, once I saw the state of my yoga pants. Even though I'd tried to yank them back up to my waist, Donnchadh had done a damn good job of slicing them in half, all the way to my crotch. I stood up, trying again to hike them up as high as I could, but my female parts were still fully exposed. But my dilemma would have to wait. For now, my prime concern was to make sure Tallis was really Tallis when he woke up. If he were still Donnchadh, I'd have one hell of another battle on my hands.

"Tallis, Tallis, Tallis," I tsked as I shook my head, relief still suffusing me. Holding the top of my hand to his forehead, I tried to determine if he had a fever. His forehead was covered in sweat, but he felt cold, rather than hot, which I figured was a good sign. I brought my fingers down the side of his face again, loving the rough texture of his stubble. He still reeked of alcohol, but I no longer cared. All that concerned me now was making sure that Tallis was in full control of his body; and that this fainting episode wasn't a sign of something worse going on inside him. As far as ascertaining whether or not he was okay, I wasn't sure what to do, or how long to wait for him to wake up.

Don't worry about that now, Lily, I reprimanded myself. *Just restrain him so if he does wake up and he's still Donnchadh, at least, you won't have to worry about protecting yourself.*

"I have no idea how, or why, Donnchadh took control of you, but you've got to keep him at bay, Tallis," I continued as thoughts of Donnchadh making a return appearance began to plague me.

Yes, I definitely needed to restrain Tallis so when he did wake up, he'd be slightly more controllable. I

35

glanced around the small house, but didn't find anything capable of holding back a Titan. Then I remembered the long lengths of fiber rope that Tallis kept outside the back of his house. He used the rope to tie up his demon pets, the Grevels, when he didn't want them trailing him through the Dark Wood.

Thinking the rope was exactly what I needed, I immediately started for the front door. Then I thought better of it after I pictured Tallis waking up with Donnchadh still at the helm of his body while I was outside. Since my sword had done a pretty damn good job of immobilizing him earlier, I figured it couldn't hurt to try it out again. Holding up my shredded pants, I went to retrieve my sword and then leaned it against Tallis's chest, between both of his legs. Just as I started to pull away, something on his chest grabbed my attention.

I held the flashlight-phone over him and noticed a reddish, triangular mark in the shape of a blade staining the skin between both of his nipples. It was the outline of my sword from where I'd pushed it up against him earlier, right before he'd passed out. It looked as if the blade had somehow branded him even though it hadn't been hot. "Interesting," I said to no one in particular, secretly wondering if, somehow, my sword might have forced Donnchadh back into the deeper recesses of Tallis's psyche.

Tallis and I should only have been so lucky ...

"You stay put," I said to the sleeping man who looked, in repose, about as threatening as a baby. But in this case, looks were absolutely deceiving. Using one hand to grab Bill's phone in order to light my way, I used my other hand to hold up my pants as I started for the front door. Upon opening it, the darkness that engulfed the entire wood surrounded me. But Tallis lived on the periphery of the Dark Wood, which meant the sun rose every morning and set every night. "Then it must be evening right now," I said to myself, sighing

36

with frustration. I could hear the sounds of the Grevels as they shuffled through the foliage; but the sounds were lost on me. I suddenly became livid with the darkness. The intense desire to see the sun again, and feel its warmth on my back was so overwhelming, it manifested itself as bitter anger that started in the pit of my stomach and climbed up to my throat.

Don't lose yourself, Lily, I warned myself. *Just focus on the task at hand. You'll see the sunlight soon enough.*

With a renewed sense of purpose, I hurried out the front door, being careful to close it behind me. Then I set off for the rear of the house, searching for as much rope as I could find. I could hear the Grevels behind me, but figured they weren't any threat. They knew who I was by now. Once I made it to the back of Tallis's home, I ran the flashlight back and forth in front of me until I saw the rope. It was looped around a large nail, sticking out at the top of the wall. Straining on my tiptoes, I reached for the rope with the hand that wasn't holding Bill's phone and yanked it off the rusty nail.

I could hear the Grevels dispersing into the undergrowth, no doubt figuring I was about to tie them up. "You're safe this time, guys," I said with a slight laugh as I started for the front door again, needing to yank up my pants when they started to sag.

I opened the door and went inside, immediately shining the flashlight beam onto the still form of Tallis where he leaned against the wall. I exhaled a relieved breath, seeing as how he was exactly where I'd left him and appeared to still be sleeping. Closing the door behind me, I approached him carefully and checked to be sure he was, in fact, still alive. He was.

"Looks like I'm going to have to tie you to your bed," I announced, only after realizing I had no other alternative. He was closest to the bed and there wasn't really anything else large enough to keep him immobilized once he decided to wake up. He was still a few feet from the bed though, which meant I had to move him, a feat in and of itself.

I grumbled something unintelligible even to my own ears, and placed Bill's phone on the edge of the straw mattress so that it lit up the two log posts at the end of the bed. I figured I could tie each of Tallis's hands to the posts. Yes, it would have been lots better, not to mention much more comfortable for Tallis, if I could manage to get him on top of the bed, but there was no way in hell I could lift him.

I inhaled and exhaled quickly as I shook my head and approached the enormous man. I reached down and gripped him beneath his armpits, shifting him so that his back was facing the bed. Then I pulled him toward the bed, but didn't get very far. He was so awkward and heavy, it felt like I was trying to move a three-hundred-pound bag of sand. Trying to get a better grip underneath his arms, I pulled him again, but only managed to move him maybe another two inches. I stood up and looked behind myself, measuring another two feet or so before he'd be close enough to tie him to the bedposts. Facing Tallis again, I suddenly wanted to cry. It also didn't help that the waistline of my pants had migrated down to the top of my butt.

Come on, Lily, you can do this! I cheered myself on.

He's impossible to move! There's no way ...

You have to do this! I interrupted myself. *Because if you don't and Donnchadh is still in charge of Tallis's body, he's going to attempt to rape you again as soon as he wakes up!*

Apparently, that thought was enough to motivate me, because before I knew what I was doing, my hands were back beneath Tallis's armpits. I began hefting and heaving with all my might. Releasing him

38

again, we managed to move another six inches or so. I breathed out a pent-up breath of frustration and anxiety. Meanwhile, I tried to ignore my pants which were now hanging around the center of my butt, which meant I had plumber's crack, and then some. I gripped Tallis's arms and yanked him backwards with every ounce of strength I still possessed. Feeling the burn in my arms, I released him, and looking back at the bed, realized I had maybe a foot or so left to go.

"You can do this, Lily Harper," I said out loud as I gripped my pants and yanked them back up to my waist. "Come on, you're almost there!"

I grabbed his arms again and pulled him backwards as hard as I could. In response, his body skidded along with me, his head bumping into the crossbeam that held his bed together. I immediately glanced down at him, afraid that ramming his head into the bed might have woken him up, but was relieved to find it hadn't. "Sorry," I said with a slight laugh, even though I figured he couldn't hear me.

I didn't give myself long to rest because I was too concerned that the head-ramming incident and all the jostling while moving him might have woken him up. Instead, I immediately went for the rope. I decided to use the two-column tie in order to bind each of his arms to the bedposts. Going for his left wrist, I brought the rope over his head and allowed his arm to lean against the log post of the bed which was closest to the wall. Lifting my sword from his chest, I measured about eight feet of the rope before severing it with the blade.

Thank God for my peasant training, I thought, referring to my previous life, when I'd belonged to a medieval reenactment club. As a newbie, I'd been elected into the peasant class where I'd had to learn lots of things, including how to make a fire from nothing but pieces of wood, as well as the basics in knot-tying. How ironic that back then I'd never

39

thought any of this information would have come in handy.

How wrong I'd been …

Folding the rope in half evenly, I wrapped it over and under Tallis's left wrist, and around the bedpost. I did the same thing another two times, making sure there was enough rope to hold him in place. Then I crossed both ropes and wrapped them around the middle of his wrist and the bedpost, cinching them tightly.

"Hmm, not bad," I said to myself once I finished tying the knot. I glanced at Tallis's unbelievably muscular arms and thought I should tie another knot or two on top of the two-column tie. I wanted to make sure the knot was as secure as possible. The last thing I needed was an irate Donnchadh breaking free and taking out his revenge on me. After binding Tallis's left arm to the bedpost, I followed suit with his right wrist and the other post of the bed.

As far as his legs were concerned, I couldn't find anything to tie them to, so I just settled on another two-column tie to fasten them together. I figured he wouldn't be able to get very far if he couldn't move his feet. When I finished binding Tallis's legs, preventing him from doing much of anything, I turned to the problem of my pants. They were now hanging halfway down my butt again. Seeing as how Tallis was very much at home with making his own clothing and shoes, I was convinced he had to have a needle and something close to thread somewhere.

I replaced my sword against his chest, figuring it was the safest place, before going to the opposite side of the room. Tallis didn't have a lot of possessions, which made searching through them relatively easy and painless. After a few minutes, I found a large needle and some narrow pieces of leather in a wooden box beneath his table. I threaded the large hole of the needle with the leather ribbons before setting to work on fixing the damage inflicted by Donnchadh on my pants.

It took me about ten minutes to sew up the rip, and once I finished that chore, I turned to my fanny pack, which Donnchadh had also severed. A few minutes later, I'd sewed the belt of the fanny pack back together as best I could.

My tasks completed, I faced Tallis and reached down, wiping the cold sweat from his brow. "Come on, Tallis, be okay," I whispered to him. "I need for you to be okay."

Of course, there was no response, but his even breathing continued to hint to the fact that from a medical standpoint, he was probably all right. As far as his mental health was concerned, however, I couldn't be sure.

With nothing more to do for Tallis, I faced the problem of how cold and dark it was in his house. I decided to light a fire in the hearth. Collecting all the broken wood from his couch and chair, I piled them into the fireplace and found the pack of matches Tallis kept in a small iron bowl beside the fireplace. He also kept a wooden box full of aged moss, which he used for kindling. I reached inside and grabbed a few fistfuls of the stuff, tucking it between the pieces of wood I'd already piled in the fireplace. Then I lit the match and watched the moss catch fire until the entire heap of wood burned brightly.

I glanced over at Tallis to make sure everything was copasetic with him, and it appeared it was. I faced the fire again, holding my hands in front of my body to warm them. That was when my stomach began growling, reminding me I hadn't eaten anything in who knew how long? The idea of satisfying my suddenly overpowering hunger left me aching with disappointment. Why? Because that was the part in the whole Survival 101, living off the land, etcetera, that I wasn't good at. In general, whenever I traveled with Tallis, he provided our dinner. Truth be told, I hadn't done any hunting at all.

I stood up with a groan and approached the front door, not even sure where I should start. I glanced back at my sword where it leaned against Tallis's chest, but I didn't go for it because I figured it would be useless. It wasn't like some random, savory animal was just going to throw itself on my blade.

"A bow and arrow would come in really handy right about now," I said out loud, and frowned as soon as I realized Tallis didn't own one. Well, as far as I knew anyway …

Deciding to do some investigating outside, I opened the front door and immediately noticed the carcass of something lying on the ground right in front of me.

Ask and ye shall receive, I thought to myself as a grin curved my mouth. Hearing the sounds of the Grevels in the undergrowth, I realized this hapless, bloody creature was a gift from them. "Thanks, guys!" I said cheerily while bending down to pick the matted thing up. Returning to the low light of the fire, I studied the carcass, trying to figure out what it was exactly. When I failed to reach a conclusion, I decided I wasn't that concerned over it. Instead, I took the carcass to Tallis's basin sink. I used a jug of water, which was Tallis's kitchen faucet, and did my best to clean the blood and dirt off the creature. I noticed that Tallis's paring knife, which was really just a piece of flint that he'd sharpened into a blade, was sitting beside the jug of water. Before I had a chance to pick the knife up, Bill's phone buzzed with an incoming text. Placing the carcass on the lip of the basin, I wiped my hands on my pants and glanced down at the phone. It read:

It is Saturday. Three in the morning.

It was Alaire.

I thought you were supposed to text me once it was morning? I responded.

It is morning, he texted back.

Ha-ha, Alaire. I meant you were supposed to text me at a reasonable hour. I was irritated and could feel myself frowning.

I was concerned that perhaps you were not still alive, came his response.

Sorry to disappoint you, but I'm alive and well.

I am not disappointed, my dear. Quite the contrary.

My stomach started to growl as I focused on the carcass again and thought to myself that the only thing standing between me and my dinner was Alaire.

I hate to end this conversation prematurely, but I have to figure out how to cook something that resembles roadkill, I typed. *So unless you have any recipes for unidentifiable, bloody carcasses, I need to get going.*

Of what species is your carcass, Ms. Harper?

I shook my head and shrugged, only then realizing he couldn't see me. *I don't know, but it's the size of a rabbit.*

Have you skinned it?

No.

Are you in possession of a knife or some type of blade?

I glanced over at the flint blade again. *Yes.*

Alaire didn't respond right away, so I figured whatever he was texting was long. I could only hope he'd just retrieved his Betty Crocker Cookbook and was texting me a recipe for braised rabbit with mushroom sauce ...

First, you will need to skin the creature. Do so by cutting a ring around each of its legs, just above the leg joint. Do not cut deeply. On each leg, make a single slice going up from the ring cut to the backside of the creature. Begin to pull away some of the hide, working from the ring cut at the foot joint down to the creature's genitalia.

Its genitalia? I texted back, figuring he was having a go at me.

What would you prefer I call it?

I could feel my cheeks coloring as soon as I realized he wasn't making a joke which made me sound like I was all of ten years old. I muttered something that even I couldn't make out, but texted back: *Never mind. Please continue.*

Very well, he replied. There was another lengthy pause during which I figured he was finishing his directions.

Make sure not to puncture or sever the bladder as you cut your way down the creature's middle. With both hands, begin pulling the hide from the body. It should slip off easily at this point. Quite like peeling a banana. Work your way into the sleeve of the hide where you find the creature's arms, removing its arms from the hide. This can be a bit tricky, so take your time. Then simply work the hide down from the upper torso to the head. Pull the hide to the base of the skull. Next, sever the head from the spine. The skin should entirely detach from the body. Next, clean and dress the flesh.

I was impressed. I couldn't help it. *Wow, so not only are you the leader of Hell, but you're also an expert hunter? You must have quite the resume.*

You are unimaginably witty, Ms. Harper, he answered, and even though we were conversing through text, sarcasm dripped off his words. *As regards my resume … If you recall, I informed you that I hail from Swedish lineage?*

I did remember. It was a conversation we'd had upon first being introduced to one another. *You said you were a Viking once upon a time.*

Quite so. And as I also informed you, that while I was not a noble savage by any stretch of the imagination, I was a savage all the same, which meant

44

I had to know the ins and outs of hunting and foraging for my supper.

That's great, I texted back, not really sure what else to say. My stomach began to growl again, reminding me how hungry I was. *Anyway, I'm starving so I need to get going. Thanks for your detailed instructions.* Then I thought better of ending the conversation too prematurely. I added: *maybe you should start writing a Viking cookbook ...*

Your flare for the humorous never ceases to amaze me.

I aim to please, I replied, not even realizing I was smiling until I felt my lips spreading into a grin of their own accord. Realizing Alaire was amusing me, I immediately forced the smile away and decided to get off the phone as quickly as I could. *This carcass isn't going to skin itself so I'm going for real this time.*

Very well. As always, it was a pleasure, my lady.

Just as I was about to put Bill's phone back into my fanny pack, Alaire texted again.

Please give the Yeti my regards.

The breath caught in my throat. "Yeti" was one of Bill's pet-names for Tallis. During our first introduction to Alaire, Bill had referred to Tallis as such, which had amused Alaire no end. But that didn't bother me. More concerning was learning that Alaire had figured out my mission through the Dark Wood had something to do with Tallis. That was information I didn't want Alaire to know. Of course, the more I thought about it, the more I realized it was fairly obvious that my errand had something to do with the enormous, brooding Scot, especially since I was in the Dark Wood.

I decided not to answer Alaire and, instead, replaced Bill's phone in my fanny pack. I returned to the carcass that would soon become my dinner and decided to put Alaire's explicit instructions to use.

"We crossed the circle to the other bank"
– Dante's *Inferno*

FOUR

Tallis was still unconscious.

I sat in front of the fire, after having eaten half of the creature the Grevels procured for my dinner. I was saving the other half for Tallis, in case he decided to wake up anytime soon. Even though I wasn't full, my stomach was no longer growling and was now contentedly digesting whatever creature I'd just eaten. For that much, I was grateful.

As for my insentient companion, I had a feeling he was returning to consciousness. It wasn't as though he'd suddenly opened his eyes and started talking, or anything obvious like that, but his demeanor was substantially different than it had been mere hours ago. Instead of remaining comatose, for the last hour, he'd been thrashing around, moaning and groaning, while straining against the ropes that held him to the bed. And his sweating had increased tenfold. True, these weren't necessarily *good* things, but I figured any sign of life was better than no sign at all.

"Donnchadh." Tallis's voice was a mere whisper but I could distinctly make out the name of the warrior spirit inside him.

It was the first time Tallis had said anything since my trusty sword had put him into this vegetative state. I immediately approached him, throwing all caution to the wind. Then, I remembered it might very well be Donnchadh at the wheel, rather than Tallis. As soon as that thought crossed my mind, I held myself back. I studied Tallis for a second or two longer, trying to determine whether or not it was safe to approach him.

He suddenly threw his head from side to side and a grimace distorted his face, suggesting that he was in serious pain. Beads of perspiration poured from his forehead, and another unhappy moan escaped his mouth as he struggled against his bindings.

"Tallis," I said in a soft voice, trying to reassure him but at the same time trying to reassure myself that this was, in fact, Tallis whom I was dealing with. Taking a few tentative steps toward him, I checked the ropes to be sure they were still holding him firmly. They appeared to be doing a pretty good job so I figured I'd probably be safe if it was Donnchadh who suddenly awoke.

"It's just me … Lily," I said, leaning down and placing my hand on Tallis's forehead. This time, he felt hot. Although I obviously wasn't a doctor, even I knew that hot wasn't good.

Previously, while zoning out on nothing in particular, owing to all the time I'd had, I'd noticed a scrap of fabric wedged into a hole in the wall just beyond Tallis's head. Standing up, I retrieved the piece of what looked like muslin and took it to the sink basin. Reaching for the jug of cold water, I doused the piece of muslin in the water, wringing it out gently. Then I approached Tallis again, hoping the cold compress might lower his temperature.

He was still groaning and mumbling incoherently, tossing his head from this side to that, but this time, his cheeks appeared pink, as though he'd been outside in the sun too long. Leaning over him, I ran the cold, wet compress across his forehead, sopping up the sweat that beaded along his hairline. As soon as I touched him with the wet muslin, he immediately quieted down and stopped thrashing. I couldn't help but notice the acerbic smell of whiskey which was now thicker in the air than it had been. I assumed Tallis must have been going through alcohol withdrawal and was now sweating it out and detoxifying. Well, that is, if immortals had to do that sort of thing ...

Tallis started to buck underneath me again, tugging against his ropes as he gritted his teeth and shut his eyes tightly together. I ran the damp cloth back and forth across his forehead again as he continued to struggle against the ties that restrained him. "Tallis, I'm here with you," I repeated, trying to soothe him. "It's Lily."

"Lil ... ly," he repeated and stopped fighting, but didn't open his eyes.

"Yes, that's right," I said as a big smile curled my mouth. "Can you hear me?" But there was no response. "Can you open your eyes, Tallis?"

Still no response. He appeared to be stuck in the border between sleeping and waking. He muttered something unintelligible, which brought my attention to his mouth. His lips appeared so dry and cracked, they reminded me of the fissures in a parched desert. Thinking he was probably thirsty and needed water, I returned to the sink and doused the muslin in more water, cupping my other hand underneath it to keep the water from dripping all over the ground. I returned to Tallis's side and got down on my knees. Leaning over him, I rotated his head toward me so I wouldn't have to reach so far to empty the water into his mouth. Then I pursed his lips together so they resembled a fish's lips and squeezed a few drops of water onto his tongue. At first, the water just seemed to pool there, but seconds later, he swallowed it.

"Good, Tallis, good," I encouraged him with a heartfelt smile, glad to be making some sort of headway. I squeezed more drops into his mouth and watched him swallow them. Then I stood up and retrieved the jug of water by the basin, returning to Tallis's side moments later. I submerged the fabric

48

directly into the jug and brought it to Tallis's lips again. This time, I squeezed more water into his mouth, which he eagerly gulped.

The sun was just starting to creep up into the sky, bathing both of us in an early morning blue. Tallis's scar that ran the length of one side of his face didn't seem as pronounced in the dawn's light and he appeared younger somehow. Or maybe it was just that I was accustomed to the scowl he usually wore, which seemed more pronounced whenever Bill was around. I smiled sadly while thinking how gratefully I would welcome that scowl now because it would mean that Tallis was back to himself again.

Glancing outside the two dusty windows, my whole being seemed to lift with the realization that I would soon see the sun again. With the dawning of a new day, I knew everything would be okay, that everything would work itself out. It was a silly feeling, really, because the sunrise couldn't guarantee anything, but I was so sorely in need of positive thoughts that I allowed them to run unchecked.

Looking at Tallis, I placed my hand on his forehead and was glad to discover he wasn't quite as hot as before, which I took as a positive sign.

"Tallis, I need you to resist whatever is going on inside you," I whispered. I dunked the muslin into the water again and transferred the water into his open mouth. "I know you can fight it, and I know you can fight Donnchadh," I continued, even though I had no clue whether or not he could hear me, let alone understand what I was saying. But the house was so quiet that I needed to hear someone's voice, even if it was only my own. "You're the strongest person I know," I told him. "I believe in you, Tallis. I know you can do this."

"Donnchadh," Tallis muttered. Moments later, his jaw went stiff. I looked down at his hands and noticed they were fisted at his sides. Clenching his eyes shut

49

tightly, he repeated Donnchadh's name. Then he started battling with his restraints, huffing and puffing with the exertion. I placed both of my hands on his wrists and tried to still him, if only to calm him down.

"Tallis, can you hear me?" I demanded in a loud voice.

He grumbled something that didn't make any sense, and I wondered if it was Gaelic.

"Are you Tallis or Donnchadh?" I asked.

He didn't respond as he started to thrash again, muttering while gnashing his teeth in such a way that conveyed extreme discomfort. I guessed it had something to do with his internal struggle with Donnchadh.

"Tallis, fight him!" I said in the same urgent tone. "Subdue him! I know you can do it!"

Hoping to help keep the warrior spirit at bay, I reached for my sword, which I'd previously placed beside him. With a deep and steady breath, I remembered only too well the effect my sword had had on him earlier, but I reached out and placed the blade against his chest anyway.

Immediately, a bolt of energy flowed up my arms, and it was all I could do to keep my sword positioned against him. The energy bolt left my arms and became a thrumming, pulsating hum that vibrated through my entire being. I tried to release my sword because I was worried that whatever reaction it was creating wasn't a good one, but I found I couldn't. I pulled on it with all my might, but couldn't release my hands.

When I looked down at Tallis, I noticed his whole body was slack, and he was sort of slouched against the foot of the bed. For all intents and purposes, he looked like he was dead. But I couldn't ponder that subject for too long because before I knew it, I was overcome with feelings that I didn't recognize as my own.

My entire body felt heavy, as if someone had just laid an iron cloak around my shoulders. My breathing only came in short spurts; and even though my eyes were open, I couldn't see anything but darkness. Seconds later, I was overwhelmed with new sensations that I couldn't place right away. After my muddled and shocked mind took another few seconds, I recognized the sensation as intense dread mixed with a rage I'd never experienced before. I could hear myself screaming, but my voice sounded far away, like I was listening to it under water. Then there was nothing but silence, matching the void of the darkness that surrounded me.

I tried to release my sword again, but I was completely immobilized. I couldn't move anything—not my hands, my arms or even my legs. I was rooted in place. Frightened by this sudden realization, I tried desperately to move my hands and, when that failed, my legs, but again, to no avail. I was paralyzed. Another intense wave of anger filled me as feelings of desperation immediately took its place. A searing pain that emanated from my back and threaded itself through my entire body struck me, and I winced in agony as it stitched itself through my every last nerve. Seconds later, intense nausea began in the pit of my stomach.

You're inside Tallis's body, feeling exactly what he's feeling.

The voice was mine and I heard the words inside my head, but the thought didn't belong to me at all. It was as if someone had just jumped inside my mind and spoken to me, using my own voice. There was a surety to the statement that I couldn't possibly have possessed because I had no idea what was happening to me, or why I was suddenly feeling the way I was.

Another wave of pain and nausea confronted me and I couldn't focus on anything else but the burning ache until it passed a few seconds later.

51

Tallis's body is polluted, the voice which didn't belong to me continued. *Donnchadh is contaminating him, and trying to force Tallis's spirit into submission so Donnchadh can usurp his own dominance and control.*

How do I stop Donnchadh? I found the will to ask the question right before another wave of agony overcame me, and then I couldn't concentrate on anything besides the pain.

You must release the pollutants from Tallis's body. You must rid him of the toxins caused by Donnchadh's possession of his body because Tallis cannot help himself.

And just like that, I was suddenly me again. The pain and nausea instantly vanished—nothing but a distant memory. I found myself on all fours on the dirt floor. I was panting, and my breath came and went in short little gasps that made me light-headed and dizzy. As soon as I regained my bearings, I sat up and faced Tallis, turning my attention to my sword, which still lay pressed against him.

While focusing on the shiny steel of my sword's blade, realization dawned on me. I was completely, undeniably convinced that my sword had been communicating with me. My sword had been the one to inform me what Tallis needed and how I could help him. I still didn't understand how it was possible, or why, but there was definitely an intense connection between Tallis and me and that connection was borne through my sword.

I took another deep breath and stood up as I tried to determine what I should do next. It was one thing to know what had to be done, and another thing to know how to execute it.

You must release the pollutants from Tallis's body, I repeated to myself, growing angry when the answer didn't appear right away.

"Release the pollutants? What does that even mean?" I yelled out, throwing my hands up in the air with unconcealed frustration. "What does that mean?" I repeated more softly as my gaze fell on Tallis again. He'd already fallen victim to whatever sleep had claimed him for the last five or so hours. I suddenly felt like I wanted to cry, because although I didn't like seeing him straining against his ropes and thrashing around, it was a definite improvement to the catatonic state he'd been in previously, and was now in once again.

Donnchadh's pollutants had to be contaminating Tallis, stealing whatever strength and will Tallis had left to defeat the warrior spirit inside him. I had to act and I had to act quickly …

"But I don't know what to do!" I screamed out loud as tears filled my eyes. I just felt so helpless, so completely useless, as precious seconds and minutes kept slipping past. Each second that elapsed meant Tallis was losing the fight, and there wasn't a damn thing I was doing about it.

But I don't know what to do! I repeated, this time in my mind.

My palms grew clammy as sweat began beading along the small of my back, tickling me as it dripped. I started to pace, searching for an answer, and trying to understand what it meant that I had to release the pollutants of Donnchadh. I paced forward and backward four times, hammering myself with the question of *how* to solve this riddle.

And then, like a beacon in the darkness, the answer appeared.

I remembered an instance a long time ago when I was walking through the Dark Wood alone. I'd stumbled across Tallis in the snow. He'd been sitting on his haunches with his black kilt hiding his lower half. His bare back with the Celtic tattoos on his upper arms and the image of the leafless tree which dominated the entirety of his back faced me. But, at the time, I hadn't so much noticed his tattoos as I had the blood which poured from the branches and roots of the tree on his back, making the tree, itself, appear to be bleeding. Tallis's blood had stained the white snow beneath him, but the snow hadn't absorbed it. Rather, it appeared that the snow had rejected Tallis's blood because it flowed into a single channel, which emptied into a small creek in front of him.

I recalled my utter confusion at seeing Tallis pick up a cat o' nine tails before he began flogging himself with it. I'd watched in horror as the multiple braided leather thongs, attached to silver blades, dug into his flesh, and his body bled out its response. Only later did I learn that this was Tallis's way of atoning for his ignoble past. What I'd failed to realize, until now, was that this same ritual was also responsible for releasing the pollutants from Donnchadh, pollutants that would otherwise disallow Tallis's spirit from predominating over Donnchadh's.

My eyes grew wider as I understood what I needed to do.

I can't do it to him, I thought to myself as I shook my head and felt sick to my stomach. *I can't hurt him.*

You have to! I chided back. *Because if you don't, Donnchadh's spirit will take over and Tallis will be lost.*

No ...

If you don't release the toxins that are suffocating him, you're allowing him to die, Lily. You can't allow Tallis to die! I reprimanded my other voice.

It took me another few seconds before I could accept the idea that I would have to whip Tallis in order to make him bleed out Donnchadh's pollutants. It wasn't a task that was easy to accept but once I'd made peace with it, I faced the problem of locating the cat o' nine tails. I turned around in a circle to take stock of my surroundings. But figuring it wasn't as though Tallis would flaunt the thing by hanging it up in clear sight, I imagined I'd probably have to search through his belongings. That wasn't a daunting job

54

because Tallis didn't possess much. He was a minimalist, to the max.

For the next five minutes, I searched Tallis's house, and came up empty-handed. Feeling utterly deflated and even more concerned about Tallis's inner battle than before, I collapsed into a heap beside the still man. I felt like crying.

"Where would you keep it?" I asked while shaking my head. Feeling sweat beading on my lower back again, I proceeded to bang my left elbow on the wooden post of the bed as I tried to scratch my back. A sharp pain inundated my arm, but it didn't concern me. Instead, I got onto my hands and knees, and bent over so I could search beneath Tallis's bed; the one place I'd overlooked.

Sure enough, the offensively cruel implement was pushed into the corner, between the bedpost and the wall. Elation suffused me, all the way to my ears as I reached for the thing. Then, remembering what I was about to do, all the elation fled just as quickly as it had come.

You can do this, Lily, I prepped myself. Wrapping my palm around the leather handle, I pulled it out from beneath the bed and faced Tallis, whom I found in peaceful repose.

But I knew better. It was just a matter of minutes before he'd start thrashing back and forth and speaking incoherently. Yep, there was no way around this brutality, and wishful thinking would only cost Tallis and me more valuable time. Sighing, I faced my first challenge—rotating Tallis over since he was currently tied to the bedposts. There was no way I could turn him over in his present state which meant I'd have to untie him ... And that didn't exactly sound like a good idea.

There's no other way! I told myself as visions of Donnchadh attacking me returned anew.

But I was right—there really was no other way.

I leaned down next to Tallis, placing the cat o' nine tails on the floor beside me. I started to untie Tallis's left wrist from the bedpost, keeping an eye on his face the entire time while scanning him for any sign of awareness. But I didn't notice anything. Once his left hand was loose, I retrieved the line of rope. Then holding my sword in place against his chest, I wrapped the rope around his middle, from his chest to his back, and around to his chest again. I knotted the rope and pulled against it as hard as I could to ensure that it was tight and my sword wouldn't budge. I figured since my sword had protected me in the past against Donnchadh, it was the best protection I had now. Especially since I was in the process of untying him …

"I'm not going to untie your legs, just so you know," I said out loud and then wondered why I was basically talking to myself. But not finding an immediate answer, I focused on the task at hand again. I figured Donnchadh would be easier to control with his legs bound; well, that is, if it were Donnchadh that I'd soon be dealing with. And, really, it wouldn't be difficult to flip Tallis onto his stomach with his legs still bound. I just had to be careful to make sure my sword didn't castrate him in the process.

I started untying the rope around his right hand, but not before taking a few seconds to determine whether or not he was still asleep. With his eyes closed and his breathing regular, I figured I was safe. Once both of his hands were free, his body started to slump forward, owing to the laws of gravity. I pushed against him, and kept him in a sitting position to make sure my sword didn't inadvertently geld him. Carefully rotating him until he was lying on his side, I straightened out his legs so his private parts were in no way near the sharp edge of my sword's blade.

"Hmm," I said as I studied his back. I could access it perfectly while he was on his side, so I didn't need to push him all the way onto his stomach after all. That was good news for his nether region. In order to protect his neck and head from the cat o' nine tails, I tucked his head down and forward as far as it would comfortably go. That done, I turned to my next item of business. Glancing down at the cat o' nine tails where it lay on the ground, I picked it up.

Do it, Lily, I ordered myself once it became clearly obvious that I was stalling. 'Course, I'd never so much as held a cat o' nine tails before, so it only made sense for the thing to feel unfamiliar and awkward to me. Imagining that I was standing too close to Tallis, I backed up a few steps and strained to remember the way he'd flogged himself when I'd come across him in the snow.

Stop stalling and do it already! I yelled at myself.

Without another excuse, I raised the hideous object above my head, and brought it down with as much force as I could muster, which wasn't excessive. The braided ends with the razor blades hit Tallis's skin, but barely half of them left a mark. The marks they did manage to leave weren't anything compared to what he'd done to himself in the snow.

There was no response from Tallis at all.

You have to do it much harder, I told myself. I inhaled deeply, recognizing the truth in my words because this first attempt merely left shallow scratches on his back. Only a few of the blades drew any blood, and the few drops of blood they did draw were miniscule, at best. I lifted the device above my head again and brought my arm down as hard as I could. The resulting impact of the leather thongs against Tallis's back made me grit my teeth.

But my extra effort paid off. Each braided end flogged his skin, and more than a few of the blades embedded themselves into his back. When I pulled against them, I found they wouldn't budge. I gently pulled a few more times before deciding my tender ministrations were pointless. So, steeling myself, I yanked on the cat o' nine tails as hard as I could. The handle reeled back at me but all of the blades freed themselves from Tallis's back.

Angry, red lacerations immediately spread all over his skin, bubbling over in seconds with thick, syrupy blood. Tallis's blood was much darker than I expected. In fact, it was so dark, it appeared almost chocolate brown, and was much more sludgy and viscous than human blood should have been.

Donnchadh's contaminants, I thought, figuring the answer made sense.

Rivulets of the gluey stuff began to run down Tallis's back, covering the black ink of his tree tattoo. But I knew this wasn't enough blood to purify him. Nope, I'd probably need to drain as much of the contaminated blood as I could until it started to run red and fluid. Glancing back up at my handiwork, I realized I had a good way still to go.

I lifted the cat o' nine tails up over my head again and brought it down even harder than I had previously. The blades stuck into his flesh as before, but this time, I didn't waste a moment trying to gently extract them. I jerked on them, using as much strength as I could manage and the blades pulled themselves free, leaving deeper and more numerous wounds on his back. The fudge-like, brown blood began bubbling out of the new wounds, resembling chocolate snail trails that snaked to the ground below. Without respite, I flogged Tallis again, hating the sound of the leather when it snapped his bare skin. But I hated thinking about the damage I was inflicting on him even more.

Luckily for me, he didn't make a sound. He didn't flinch. Nothing.

I whipped Tallis with the cat o' nine tails another four times before I felt content with the number of wounds I'd inflicted. The color of the blood that was streaming down his back changed from a deep brown to a lighter, brownish-red and was no longer gluey in consistency. However, it still wasn't moving as freely as it should have. Either way, I was exhausted and doubted if I could ever hold either of my arms over my head again.

"That's it for now," I said, my voice revealing my exasperation and fatigue.

I watched Tallis's blood pool into a large puddle on the dirt floor; and just like the snow I'd witnessed earlier, the earth refused to absorb it. The blood just continued to puddle on the ground until it resembled chocolate Jell-O pudding. Then, all at once, the puddle completely dissolved into the earth without a trace, as if it had never been in the first place.

Dropping the cat o' nine tails, I approached Tallis, stepping over him so I could check his breathing and make sure he was still alive. The expression on his face was just as placid as it had been before I flogged him. His breathing seemed more regular, and less labored. Or maybe I was just imagining it.

Intending to clean up the wounds I'd inflicted on him, I reached for the muslin and doused it in water. I sopped up all the remaining blood that trickled from the various gashes on his back, and observed the wounds already healing themselves. That was one of the benefits of being immortal ... Tallis could heal himself.

I supposed being possessed by an unruly warrior spirit did have some advantages ...

"Near to a fount that boils"
– Dante's *Inferno*

FIVE

Tallis slept for another two days and two nights.

During that time, he continued to toss and turn, thrashing around and mumbling incoherently. But the more time that elapsed, the less frequent were his bouts of unease. By the second day, I figured out Tallis's disquiet was an indication that Donnchadh's pollutants were building up inside his body and needed to be purged. That meant I had to release the impurities from Tallis's body, yep, by flogging him with the cat o' nine tails. Once the lashing was over, he would sleep like a baby.

Tallis's peaceful sleep wasn't the only sign that the floggings were helping him. His blood was no longer coagulated and dark brown like it was the first time I took the cat o' nine tails to his back. Now, it was a bright crimson that flowed freely as soon as the blades of the leather braids tore his skin.

It is Monday morning, Bill's phone announced via a buzzing text message. I was lying on Tallis's bed, the gigantic Scotsman beside me on the floor, snoring peacefully. I had just been about to get some zzzs, myself, before the phone alerted me back to wakefulness. With a grunt, I fished it out from my fanny pack, which lay beside me, and flipped open the top of the phone.

Thanks, Alaire, I texted back clumsily. I'd had to whip Tallis so many times, the palms of my hands were red and blistered. Consequently, I'd wrapped my right hand, which suffered worse than my left, in the muslin after soaking it in cold water. It seemed the muslin was the only thing to relieve the stinging from my chafed and blistered skin.

I daresay you are in the midst of your voyage to meet me at the gates of the Underground?

Not exactly, I typed back, thinking he was probably going to have a big hissy fit once he read the rest of what I had to say. *In fact, I'm running late. Really late.*

There was a ten-second delay before he responded. *Explain.*

I heard myself sighing audibly as I faced the sleeping Tallis and suddenly wished he'd wake up so I could give him a clean bill of health and be on my way back to the Underground City. But that was just wishful thinking … *The nature of the business which called me here requires me to stay for another day or so, which means I probably won't be able to see you until Friday, or maybe even later.*

I shuddered as I awaited his reply because I knew Alaire was used to getting what he wanted and wouldn't be a good sport when he didn't.

This will not do.

I sighed again, frustration growing inside me. I really didn't feel like justifying myself to Alaire at the moment. No, I was exhausted and my hands were still burning as if I'd just plunged them into boiling water. And my arms and my shoulders didn't feel much better—my muscles ached after the numerous floggings I'd had to deliver. I probably needed my sleep as much as Tallis did. *I'm not sure what you want me to do,* I responded testily. *Even if I were to leave at this exact moment, it would STILL take me four days to reach the gates of the Underground from here.*

You are in breach of our agreement, Ms. Harper, Alaire texted back almost immediately. I could detect the anger seeping through his terse words.

My teeth began gritting of their own accord and even though I wanted to tell Alaire where he could shove it, I knew I couldn't. Not while Alaire basically still held all the cards in the deck known as "Lily Harper's Future." *I'm sorry, but it couldn't be avoided.* I decided to add an unhappy face emoticon, hoping it might make Alaire feel sorry for me.

There was another long pause, and I wondered if maybe he was contacting Afterlife Enterprises to make sure I did get the infraction he'd promised to waive. As soon as that thought formed in my head, anxiety started brewing in my gut and I felt nauseous.

Hello? Are you still there? I typed, suddenly scared to death that I *had* just earned my first infraction. One more and I'd be headed to Shade, where I'd have to stay for the next hundred years …

Apologies for the delay, he replied as my heart continued to hammer in my chest. *I have dispatched a guide to accompany you from your current location back to the gates of the Underground City.*

I exhaled a pent-up breath I hadn't even realized I was holding. So apparently Alaire hadn't been on the line with Afterlife Enterprises, which meant I wasn't in jeopardy of earning my first infraction! I could only hope … But that didn't explain the guide he'd dispatched.

Thanks for the guide (I think?), I texted back, my heart climbing up my throat. I was still too concerned about whether or not my neck was still on the line in the infraction department to even contemplate why Alaire would send me a guide in the first place.

You are quite welcome.

Then I thought I probably should inquire. *So maybe I'm missing something, but I'm not sure why you're sending me a guide?*

I must admit my reasons are selfish ones.

His answer managed to clear up nothing so I decided to shelve the infraction-or-not subject for the present and, instead, pondered the subject of a guide. *Selfish? What do you mean?*

Quite simple, really, he replied immediately. *Your trip will be much shorter with someone who knows how to navigate the Dark Wood and knows how to do so extremely quickly. And a shorter trip means I will have the pleasure of your company sooner.*

I was lost as to how a guide could impact the length of my journey to the Underground City and decided to quiz Alaire on that topic. *But how will a guide speed up a four-day journey to the gates of the Underground?* I started, and then immediately added: *And I'll have to wait another four days for your guide to even get here, so I'm not sure why you think I'll arrive any sooner than I would if I came on my own?* Before he had the chance to answer, I typed: *Speaking of, how in the world is your guide planning to find me?*

That was a barrage of questions, he texted back.

I'm confused, I responded, with no amount of apology.

Yes, that is quite obvious, Ms. Harper. I will do my best to enlighten you ... I have located you via the satellite signal on your phone.

I didn't like knowing Alaire could pinpoint exactly where I was because I didn't think Tallis would appreciate him knowing Tallis's exact location. Glancing over at the sleeping giant, I thought to myself that it was time to move on. The last thing I wanted was to endanger Tallis anymore than he already was. And as far as his current level of danger, I sensed he was near the tail end of it. His color, respiration and overall health seemed to have improved substantially over the last day or so. Yes, I probably needed to get a move-on.

63

As to your other questions, Alaire continued, *the guide I am sending is a shade.*

When there were no follow-up texts on this point, I figured Alaire thought his statement was self-explanatory. Well, he might have, but I didn't. *So what does that mean?*

Instead of a return text, the phone rang. I didn't have to wonder who it was. I answered the phone immediately, fearing the high-pitched ringing might wake up Tallis.

"You do not know what a shade is, Ms. Harper?" Alaire demanded, his tone of voice sounding amused, yet condescending all at the same time.

"Good morning to you too, Alaire," I muttered, taking a deep breath. I tried to ready myself for dealing with the exasperating Leader of the Underground City. I much preferred to text him than talk to him over the phone. Texting was more impersonal; and where Alaire was concerned, impersonal was definitely the way to go. "It's like a ghost, right?"

"Quite similar."

Clearly, he wasn't going to offer any other information, which meant I would have to dig. "Okay, so what does a ghost have to do with shortening my journey time?"

"I said a shade was *similar* to a ghost," he corrected me.

"Okay," I responded as I rolled my eyes. "What does a *shade* have to do with shortening my journey time?"

"I am happy to tell you, Ms. Harper," Alaire said and I could hear the smile in his voice. "A shade can move much more quickly than can a human."

"Well, that's fine and good for the shade, but let me remind you that I'm not a shade or a ghost or a spirit or a wrath or a phantom or even an apparition, which means I move as quickly or probably less

64

quickly than the average human," I spat back with little humor.

"A wraith, Ms. Harper," Alaire responded in a patronizing tone that I was beginning to get used to.

"What?" I barked, irritated that I wasn't following him.

"You mistakenly pronounced the word *wrath* when the true pronunciation is *wraith*." Alaire chuckled and the sound caused shivers to race up and down my spine because it was completely void of warmth. The sound was as cold and hollow as the Underground City itself.

"Ugh," I grumbled. "Back to the point."

"The point, my dear Ms. Harper, is that the shade will take perhaps one day to reach you. Once she arrives, she will lead you back to the gates of my city via her own unique brand of travel."

"Then the shade is going to show me a shortcut?" I asked, just to make sure I understood him fully.

"In a manner of speaking, Ms. Harper. I am not certain how better to illustrate the point." I could hear the sarcasm dripping off his tongue and I wanted to reach through the phone and smack him.

"Maybe if you were clearer in your explanations in the first place, you wouldn't have to make so many of them," I responded flatly, not appreciating his comment.

"Apologies, Ms. Harper," Alaire said with another acidic laugh. "Now if you will excuse me, the Underground City cannot run itself. I am a busy man."

That was debatable, but I wasn't about to say as much because I wanted nothing more than to get him off the phone. Any excuse was a good one, as far as I was concerned. "Okay."

"I look forward to seeing you Wednesday evening," he finished just as the subject titled "Lily's near brush with her first infraction" suddenly waved its ugly head.

65

"Um, Alaire?" I started while wondering how to ask what I needed to know without offending him.

"Yes?" he sounded interested.

"Obviously, I won't be able to meet you on Tuesday evening like we originally agreed," I began and then paused as I tried to figure out how best to deliver the rest of my sentiment, "which means I'll be late, and referring to your point earlier, I will be in breach of our agreement?"

"Obviously, yes."

Hmm, if he had any idea where I was going with the conversation, it didn't appear that he intended to make it easy on me. Not that I really expected him to ... "So, um, are you still going to, uh, let me slide on that infraction?" I blurted the remainder of the sentence out in record time.

"Perish your fears," Alaire answered. The irony of his response was not lost on me, given he was the head of the Underground City, one entirely built on fears, but anyhoo ... "I will fulfill my end of the bargain as long as you appear no later than Wednesday."

"Thanks," I said, sighing my relief. "As long as your shade's as quick and good as you seem to think she is, I'll be there Wednesday with bells and whistles on."

"Very good, Ms. Harper," Alaire said and I heard the sound of him tapping his fingernails against his desk which meant he was getting fidgety. "Until we meet again."

"Very good," I repeated before hanging up the phone.

***

I was walking through the Dark Wood all alone. The chill of the cold air caused goose bumps to bubble up and down my arms, but the darkness was the sole reason for my fear. I was surrounded by it, bathed in a

66

pitch that obscured the horrible creatures who lived deep inside the forest. I could faintly recall following the glowing outline of the shade Alaire sent to me, but now, that shade was nowhere to be found. She'd simply vanished, leaving me alone in the darkness, alone in the haunted wood.

Growing more frightened by the moment, I picked up my pace and started to speed-walk as I strained to see any sign of the glowing entity. Not finding her, I remembered Alaire telling me how shades were able to move more quickly than humans could.

Maybe I'd been going too slow for her? Maybe she didn't even realize I wasn't still following her? I started to jog, being careful to avoid the various obstacles cluttering the forest floor—hulled out remains of fallen trees, carcasses of God only knew what, and the bleached bones of other unfortunate creatures. I could hear my heart pounding in my chest and my breath was coming in short gasps.

I increased my speed until I was all-out running through the forest, searching for any sign of the shade. I heard the sounds of branches breaking under the weight of something to the right of me, but when I turned in that direction, I saw nothing except endless rows of dead and rotting trees, the knots in their trunks resembling angry, contorted faces.

The echo of footsteps crunching the forest debris started up again, this time sounding even closer to me than the last time. I pivoted to my left and ran as fast as I could, feeling like something was chasing me, like something was right behind me ...

I woke up with a start and took a few deep breaths to calm myself. I forcefully expelled the images of the haunted forest from my head, and had to remind myself more than once the entire thing had just been a bad dream.

Glancing around, I recognized Tallis's home immediately. When I'd dozed off, the sun was still high in the sky, but it was dark now, which meant I had to have been asleep for a while. I sat up and stifled a yawn just as I felt the heat from Tallis's body directly behind me. It took me a second to remember that I'd briefly woken up a few hours ago because it was freezing. Rather than taking the time to build a fire, I'd opted to cuddle up next to him.

"How loong have Ah been oot?"

My heart flew into my throat as my nerves went on high alert at hearing Tallis's voice behind me. I turned around immediately and brought my hand to my chest to try to calm my frantic heartbeat. Tallis didn't seem to notice that he'd just scared the hell out of me as he pushed himself into a seated position. My sword was still held firmly in place against his chest by the rope I'd tied around his middle.

"Tallis?" I asked, studying him with narrowed eyes as I wondered if he were truly himself, or if I would soon have another fight on my hands.

"Aye," he answered as he nodded his head. He looked like he was exhausted even though he'd been sleeping for days.

"How ... how are you feeling?" I asked, suddenly very uncomfortable with the fact that I'd been snuggled up beside him and from what I could tell, he might have been awake long enough to know.

"Betta," he answered as he glanced down at my sword where it lay against his chest. He fumbled with the knot and managed to untie it rather alarmingly quickly, freeing himself seconds later. He handed my sword back to me before looking at his legs, which were still bound together. He studied the ropes for a few seconds before facing me.

"Impressive, lass," he said and then reached down between his thighs as he began unfastening the bindings.

"Um, how do I know you aren't Donnchadh?" I asked, holding my sword in such a way that I could

68

aim it at him in a quick second if the need arose. Yep, it was pretty disconcerting to find him in the process of freeing himself when I still wasn't convinced he was the real Tallis.

"Ah amnae Donnchadh," he said, but didn't bother looking at me. He released his legs and rubbed his calves, where the marks from the ropes were clearly defined in his skin. Maybe I'd tied them too tightly ... Without another word, he pushed against the wall and stood up, wavering slightly. Even if he was unsteady on his feet, he still towered over me. And while that fact had never made me nervous before, it did now.

"Are you sure you should be standing?" I asked and cleared my throat as I studied him, trying to ascertain if he really was Tallis.

"Doona fooss ova meh, lass," he replied in an irritated tone that definitely sounded like the old Tallis I'd come to know so well. "Ah am fine." Then, without another word, he approached the fireplace and began building a fire with the firewood I'd hauled in from outside. In the reflection of the moonlight, which streamed through the windows, I could see that the wounds I'd inflicted on his back had already healed. "Whit happened?" he asked, not bothering to glance over his shoulder to look at me.

"I was about to ask you the same question," I said, taking a seat on his bed. I wished I didn't feel so inept and awkward. Tallis just had a way about him that made me never feel comfortable. "When I found you here, you were drunk and your couch and a chair were broken."

He didn't seem concerned over the loss of his furniture and simply shrugged, still not bothering to look at me or the contents of the room. "Last Ah remember, Ah came home frae the tavern an' lost mahself in mah whiskey," he said in a low voice. He lit

69

a match on the moss he placed between the logs and a healthy fire erupted.

"Yeah, you lost yourself in your whiskey, all right," I answered with a frown. "When I found you, you were completely inebriated and completely out of your mind. Donnchadh had taken over your body."

Tallis nodded as if it were old news, but he didn't say anything. Instead, he blew on the fire, fanning it with his hand in order to give it more oxygen. Seconds later, a larger flame engulfed the entire stack of logs. Tallis watched the fire burn for another few seconds before he stood up. He turned around to face me, appearing even larger than I remembered. There was an expression on his face which I couldn't read. "Did Ah hurt ye?" The way he asked the question showed no trace of remorse or anger. It was simply a question, requesting a "yes" or "no" answer.

But the lack of emotion in the way he asked it made my throat suddenly tight. It was the type of question that should have been asked with some level of emotion. Instead, Tallis appeared as if he were wearing a mask of indifference, and the answer to the question held no consequence to him.

"No, you, er, Donnchadh didn't hurt me," I replied, but then thinking I was letting him off the hook too easily, I added: "But he tried to."

Tallis nodded as if he couldn't argue with my comment. That same poker face persisted in his features and, truth be told, it was beginning to irritate me. "Ah couldnae control him," he announced as he focused on the palms of his hands, flexing and releasing his fingers as he watched them. "Ah knew ye were here an' Ah wanted tae protect ye, lass, boot Ah couldnae."

"You didn't have to. I protected myself," I said with no amount of apology, suddenly very proud of that fact. I *had* protected myself, well, that is, with the help of my sword.

70

"Ah imagined sooch was the case, given how ye'd tied meh oop," he finished and his eyes met mine. They were back to their midnight blue. I could see the reflection of the fire as it danced along his pupils and gave him the look of a mystical being. "Ye are ah strong, capable lass," he said in a deep voice, his eyes never leaving mine. Neither of us said anything for a few seconds, but we also didn't break eye contact. When Tallis spoke again, his voice was even deeper and coarser than before. "The strongest Ah've ever mit."

"Why did you leave us?" I barked, hearing my voice break as I asked the question. The expression on Tallis's face told me he didn't understand what I was asking. "Back at the tavern, on our return trip from the Underground City," I started to clarify as my jaw tightened at the memory of the incident. "You just up and left Bill and me there … by ourselves." I inhaled deeply. "I want to know why."

Tallis nodded as if my request was expected. Then he dropped his attention to the floor and frowned. "Ahm sorry," he said in a mere whisper.

I didn't say anything for a few seconds because I wasn't convinced he didn't have more to say. But after another four seconds went by, it became fairly obvious that Tallis wasn't going to try to defend his actions, or much less, explain them. "You're sorry?" I scoffed, but the laugh died on my lips as soon as anger overcame me. "You're sorry?" I demanded again, eyeing him furiously. "That's all you're going to say about it?"

"Ah dinnae know whit else tae say," he admitted, his jaw tight. He glanced up at me and held my gaze for a few seconds before he shifted his attention to the window and stared out of it vacantly.

My hands fisted at my sides as my entire body shook with outrage. Needless to say, this was not the response I'd expected.

71

Well, he might not have known what else to say, but I had a whole mouthful of words for him. "After you abandoned Bill and me at the tavern, I didn't let that stop me from coming after you. Knowing you were in trouble, I traveled through the Dark Wood, and I did it by myself."

"Ah never woulda asked ye tae do that, lass."

"It doesn't matter if you wouldn't have asked me!" I railed back at him. "I would have done it a thousand times over because you needed me!" My heart hammered away in my chest and made me feel light-headed, probably because I hadn't had enough to eat in the last ... however long. "The point is that I never abandoned you!"

"Lass," he started, lifting his hands in a play of submission, but I interrupted him. There was no way I was going to end this conversation prematurely—no, not until he understood the full extent of everything I'd done for him. Shakespeare had gotten it right when he wrote "how sharper than the serpent's tooth it was to have an ungrateful child"; only in this case, an ungrateful bladesmith.

"No," I began, my entire body shaking. I inhaled deeply and willed myself not to cry. Sometimes, when I got excessively angry, I would just start crying, which only infuriated me all the more. "When I found you here," I started as I glanced around the room before settling my eyes back on him again. "you were so drunk, you couldn't even stand up straight. And you were completely out of your mind. Well, *you* weren't even yourself. Somehow, Donnchadh was in control of your body, which I only found out the hard way when you nearly raped me. Even after fighting you off, I stuck around for three days to nurse you back to health." My voice cracked again. "What's more, I had to flog you and detoxify you from Donnchadh's pollutants," I continued, holding out the palms of my hands so he could see the open blisters. "And all you can say is *you're sorry*?"

"Whit dae ye want meh tae say?" he demanded, as if everything I just told him had simply gone in one of his ears and out the other.

I shook my head and realized that arguing with him was pointless. He obviously wasn't going to give me what I most needed and wanted—acknowledgement. It became pretty apparently clear to me that Tallis could care less about the fact that I'd just saved him from Donnchadh. And I was beginning to believe that the truth of the matter regarding him leaving me in the tavern was that he didn't care about me and never had. Tallis was a man who was and would forever be ... alone.

"I should have just left you here to rot," I spat back at him. "I should have left you to your fate the same way you left me to mine."

Tallis's eyes narrowed and he crossed his arms against his chest but he didn't say anything. That was when I decided it was time for me to go. Tallis and I were like night and day and we would never understand one another. Maybe it was time to call a spade a spade and admit our awkward friendship was nothing more than a farce since we meant nothing to each other. Well, at least, since I meant nothing to him. Reaching for my fanny pack where it lay on the bed, I fastened it around my waist and faced him. "I guess the biggest idiot in all of this is me," I said, the anger no longer tainting my voice. Instead, I sounded defeated. Feeling the sting of tears in my eyes, I immediately started for the door.

"Besom," Tallis interrupted as I pushed the door open. "Besom" was his pet-name for me and in Gaelic it meant "troublesome woman." As soon as I heard it, my heart grew even heavier in my chest.

"You're good at being alone, Tallis, it's what you do," I responded as I turned back to face him. I'd failed

73

to keep the tears from rolling down my cheeks, but at this point, I didn't even care. I was an emotional person, and there was nothing wrong with that. So what if Tallis couldn't speak my language? He could go on being the apathetic son of a bitch that he'd always been. "So just keep on doing what you do so well."

"Nae," he started, but I was stepping through the door, seeking only to escape.

But what about the shade Alaire sent? I suddenly remembered. *Maybe she won't be able to find you if you leave?*

Alaire said he was tracking you through the satellite signal on your phone, I answered myself. *So I'm sure he and the shade can keep on tracking you no matter where you are.*

Feeling Tallis's large hand on my shoulder, it felt as if my entire body was withering on the inside. I hated to admit it to myself but I loved the feel of his large hand on my skin. At that moment, what I wanted more than anything else was for him to engulf me in his arms.

I didn't turn around although I did stop walking. But that was only because he forced me to. "Look at meh," he demanded.

"What do you want?" I demanded as I turned around and found him studying me intently.

His eyes were narrowed but appeared hollow, as limitless in their deep blue as is the ocean. There was no emotion on his face, nothing to mar the blank mask I was so accustomed to seeing. "Ah left ye aloyn in the tavern 'cause Ah had tae."

"You had to? What does that even mean?" I pressed. Moments later, I shook my head and wondered why we were even going through the motions of he said-she said. It didn't matter anymore. Nothing with Tallis mattered anymore.

"Ah had tae leave because Ah couldnae stay. Ah had tae leave because o' ye."

74

"So it was *my* fault that you abandoned Bill and me?" I tried to make sense of the statement, but found none because there was no part of it that was truthful. How could I have been the reason that Tallis left Bill and me? I laughed for dramatic effect, as I turned my back to him, tacitly conveying that I was giving up on him as well as the conversation. I just didn't have the strength or energy to deal with him any longer.

"Nae," he started.

"There's no point to any of this, Tallis," I interrupted him in a soft, beaten voice. "It is what it is."

"Nae, it wasnae yer fault," he said, blatantly ignoring my attempt to discontinue the conversation. He tightened his grip on my arm so I couldn't go anywhere. "Boot 'twas because o' ye that Ah had tae leave."

"So you've said, Tallis," I nearly whispered while trying to pull my arm away from him. He wouldn't release me, which suddenly infuriated me. The whole situation began to infuriate me. "You win! I don't care anymore and you'll be happy to know that I'm going to leave you alone from here on out! I'm physically and emotionally too exhausted to deal with more of this!"

"Ah couldnae stand tae be near ye," he continued, as though he wasn't even listening to me.

"Great," I said with mock cheer, even though his words had a much more profound effect on me than I let on. Inside, I was shriveling. His words hurt me unimaginably—making me feel like I was buckling, caving in on myself. I clenched my eyes shut tightly to hold my tears back. It became suddenly extremely important that he not see me crying again. "I'm glad to know you think so highly of me," I managed finally, striving to retain my cool in front of him.

He doesn't deserve your tears, I told myself.

"Ye doonae," he started, but I refused to listen. The pain cut too deeply.

"Just let me go, Tallis," I interrupted him, pulling with all my strength to make him release me from his iron grasp.

"Nae," he snapped as he gripped my other arm, holding me in place.

"I've heard enough!" I screamed at him. "I get it!" Although I still struggled against him, he continued to hold me until I realized I was just exhausting myself. "Please," I said, finally, my voice barely a whisper. "You're hurting me."

Those three words were the most honest I'd ever said to him.

"Along a gully that runs out of it"
– Dante's *Inferno*

SIX

Tallis didn't say anything for the span of three seconds. Instead, we just stared at each other as if we'd both been turned to stone and could do nothing else. Well, Tallis might have been stone cold and emotionless, but I wasn't. No, on the contrary, my emotions were engaged on a battleground inside of me, anger and hurt both vying for the starring role. My heart was punctured and bleeding over the injustice of the whole damned situation. I'd stood by Tallis's side and nursed him back to health, and for what? To discover his total lack of gratitude and then I'd had to listen to him admit that he wanted nothing to do with me? A tornado of disappointment, embarrassment, pain and resentment brewed inside me, threatening everything in its path. I felt like I was seconds away from crumbling, breaking apart, and it was all I could do to keep my tears at bay.

And I didn't know if I were more upset with Tallis or myself. As far as Tallis was concerned, it wasn't as though his spots had changed, so why would I have expected him to be anything other than what he'd already demonstrated he was? Why did I suddenly assume he would care about anything or anyone other than himself? I'd always known him as the quintessential loner, one who relied on no one and preferred that no one rely on him. So what could have prompted me to believe that he was really something

77

and someone so different? Deep down, I already knew the answer to the question. I'd believed Tallis was capable of human emotions because I fervently wished he could care for me in the same way I cared for him.

I was a complete and total idiot.

Just because I had feelings for Tallis didn't mean he had feelings for me or was even capable of them. As soon as that thought entered my head, I felt sick to my stomach. I instantly sought solitude, to be by myself, and hide my own humiliation and disappointment in privacy, as far away from indifferent eyes as it was possible to be. "I ... I have to go," I announced, my throat feeling raw. Tears burned my eyes, threatening to roll down my face, but I furiously blinked them away.

"Ye willnae go oontil ye listen tae meh," Tallis answered. I glimpsed determination in his narrowed eyes and the way he gritted his teeth. I didn't understand why, but he appeared unusually driven and purposeful, almost to the point of being angry. I clenched my eyes shut tightly as soon as I felt the sting of my tears.

Don't cry, Lily! I scolded myself. *Don't you dare break down in front of him! Keep yourself together! Whatever it is he has to say, you're going to make it through! Just keep your chin up!*

I managed to force my tears back and sighed in relief. Opening my eyes, I faced Tallis with an expression of impatience clearly conveyed by my frown and furrowed brow. I figured the sooner I listened to whatever he insisted on telling me, the sooner I could be on my way again to being alone.

"Make it quick," I snapped, pleased to appear so cool, calm and collected from the outside, even if on the inside it was a completely different story ...

"Ah couldnae stand tae be near ye because Ah," he started, but the words died on his tongue. All the determination he'd exhibited earlier fled just as

78

quickly as his words deserted him. I silently begged
him to continue because I didn't know how much
longer I could maintain my façade of strength. He
focused on his hands, and seconds later, picked up
the trail again. "Ah hated mahself fer actin' the way Ah
did an' sayin' the things Ah said tae ye," he finally
managed, exhaling deeply. Then he faced me with an
expression of anticipation, as though he expected me
to understand whatever he'd just alleged.

While I didn't fully comprehend his meaning, I
was beyond surprised to hear him say he hated
himself for anything having to do with me. "Acting the
way you did and saying the things you said to me?" I
repeated, trying to be more patient with him because
there was obviously more he wanted to tell me. I could
see it burning in his eyes. "I don't understand, Tallis,"
I managed, matter-of-factly. "Please try to be more
specific."

"This isnae easy fer meh, lass," he confessed as if
I weren't already very aware that Tallis and language
didn't exactly get along. He ran one of his hands
through his short hair and sighed, shaking his head
with visible frustration.

"Just take your time," I offered, trying to be
supportive because it was fairly obvious that whatever
he had to say wasn't coming easily. I glanced up at his
face and witnessed his knotted brows and tightly
drawn lips, which were pressed into a straight white
line. Clearly, he'd been trying to formulate his
thoughts into words for a while. But unlike me, Tallis
had a hard time expressing his feelings. He wasn't
good with emotions; they choked him.

"At the tavern, lass," he continued. I lifted my
eyebrows, urging him to continue being more specific.
"In yer bedchamber," he persisted, clearing his throat
when I frowned at him. But his idea of "specific" and
mine didn't even share the same zip code. He took
another few seconds to spit the rest of his sentence

out. "Ah told ye Ah wanted ye an' ..." he started, his voice dying away again as a red blush flooded his cheeks. I almost wanted to smile, being so unaccustomed to seeing Tallis struggling so hard and looking so uncomfortable. Usually, as the knowledgeable and determined bladesmith, nothing could ever get in his way.

"And?" I prompted him once I worried that the cat really had gotten his tongue.

He sighed again and looked away from me for a few seconds, seeming to gather his words. When he finally faced me again, he wore a look of resolve. "Ah took liberties wif ye that Ah shouldnae have taken." He spat the words out as if they clung to his tongue like drowning victims and wouldn't have come out otherwise.

I swallowed hard, remembering the incident he was referencing. I could still see the tavern in the Dark Wood as if it were only yesterday that we were there.

I'd just finished bathing when I heard a knock on my door. When I opened it, Tallis showed himself in. He'd been drinking and I could smell the whiskey on his breath. Seeing me clad in nothing but my towel, he'd waited maybe two seconds before yanking the towel right off me, without so much as a raised brow to ask if he could. But that was just the beginning of our liaison. Seconds later, he'd slipped his fingers between my thighs. But it wasn't as though I hadn't welcomed his touch. The pleasure I'd received at his masterful fingers was, in a word, overwhelming.

The only reason we hadn't had sex was because Tallis had been too inebriated and I hadn't wanted our first time together to happen like that. I'd imagined having sex with Tallis so many times and, in the course of each waking dream, excessive alcohol and a dirty, noisy tavern never once entered my vision.

Even though I'd eventually turned Tallis down that evening in the tavern, the incident, nevertheless,

80

had burned itself into my memory. And I couldn't say I hadn't revisited the memory on numerous occasions. "Whatever happened, happened, Tallis," I started, wanting to let him know that I was okay with the unpermitted liberties he'd taken with me, and I forgave him. But he shook his head adamantly, indicating he wasn't finished with the conversation.

"Ah have nae business havin' any sort o' feelins fer ye," he admitted staunchly.

"Feelings?" I repeated, stunned. "For me?" I couldn't help the surprise that suddenly overcame me. As a rule, Tallis just wasn't an emotional man, so to hear him admit he had feelings for anything threw me. But to say he had feelings for me? It almost seemed like I was in the midst of a very realistic dream. True, I didn't know if his feelings were simply sexual in nature, or more, but I also couldn't say I really cared. It was enough for me that Tallis thought about me at all, in any capacity. Baby steps, right?

"You can't help developing feelings for people, Tallis. It's natural to get close to someone, especially when we have to rely on each other. It's sort of par for the course, right?" I started, feeling like I was explaining the way life worked to a five-year-old.

But he shook his head again, clearly not buying what I was selling. Then he inhaled deeply, exhaling long and slow several moments later as he faced me with a pensive expression. "Lily ..." he started, but silenced himself again.

It was the first time in a long time that he'd said my name and my eyes widened in surprise. I didn't know why, but I loved the way he said it, how the word dripped off his tongue with familiarity. The way he said my name made it sound like it was comfortable to him, as if it were a name he'd said all his life.

"Yes, Tallis?" I asked, my voice whisper soft.

81

He swallowed hard, piercing me with his eyes as he focused them on mine. His were unblinking. "Ye are the light."

All I could feel was shock. At first. Then after a few seconds, the shock gave way to the most intense happiness that I remembered feeling in a very long time. I was the light? I didn't fully understand what the comment even meant, but the way he said it, and the words he chose were enough to send waves of bliss splashing through me. Reeling inside, amazed and confounded by what Tallis had just admitted, I was speechless. I thought I should probably have said something ... anything ... but words failed me. And, apparently, I wasn't the only one, because we both just stood there, staring at one another as if in a shared stupor.

"Tallis," I said at last, finally finding my tongue. Taking a step toward him, I reached for his hand, but he stepped back from me and pulled both of his hands away, as if the idea of touching me were one that didn't appeal to him in the least. I frowned in confusion.

"There is naethin' boot darkness in meh," he explained immediately, his heavy gaze moving from the hand I'd tried to touch him with to my face. His tone of voice was deep, but pained. "Ah am an aberration, ah sickness, ah plague."

"No," I argued immediately, shaking my head fervently and barely aware of the tears unabashedly streaming down my face. He cleared his throat as if it were hard for him to admit any of this and then he looked away again, almost as if he couldn't bear to look me in the eyes. "No, Tallis, you are none of those things," I started again, but my throat constricted, cutting off my voice, as a tide of sadness washed over me.

How could he think of himself in such a horrible way? How could he call himself darkness and disease?

82

I thought. *Why doesn't he see the man that I see—a hero, my hero?*

"Nae, lass, Ah am whit Ah've described," he said as he smiled sadly, as if to say my words, while they were meant to be consoling, couldn't breach his impenetrable walls. He reached forward and caught my tears on the pad of his thumb, wiping them away.

"Please don't say that about yourself," I managed between the tears that now streamed down my face. "I don't believe any of it for a second," I continued, shaking my head and wiping my eyes with the backs of my hands. "You have no idea what you are to me, or how much I care about you."

"Ye cannae say these things tae meh, lass," he announced, his expression suddenly hardening.

"Why?" I demanded, searching his face for an explanation.

"Och aye," he continued, shaking his head as his eyes aimed for the ceiling only to return to mine moments later. His expression was unreadable. "'Cause ye are the sun," he whispered. "An' Ah am nuffin'."

"Tallis, you are everything," I started, smiling up at him despite the tears that continued to flow from my eyes. A strange mix of powerful happiness and extreme frustration seized me. "And I'm not the sun," I protested as I shook my head, hating the fact that he'd put me on some sort of pedestal. "I'm human and very flawed just like every other person is."

He brought his hands to my face and cupped my cheeks as he stared down at me and shook his head as if I were just a silly girl who didn't get it. When he spoke, his voice was commanding, strong and unrelenting. "Ye are purity, beauty an' innocence," he continued.

"I feel the same way about you!" I insisted.

"Nae," he said and shook his head. "Ah am oogliness," he began as his lips grew tighter. "Ah am the oogliness o' the darkness."

"No," I interrupted, fresh tears of frustration burning me anew. I hated hearing how he saw himself when he was none of those things at all! I just couldn't figure out how to tell him what an amazing person he was, how I could show him the way in which I saw him. For the first time in my life, words actually failed me. "You are beautiful, Tallis," I finally managed, thinking the words paled in comparison to my feelings for him. "I wish you could see yourself the way I see you."

He reached down and took both of my hands, dwarfing them in his. He rotated them around until my palms faced him. When he focused on my chapped skin, which was uneven with blisters, his cheeks began to grow red as he gritted his teeth. "'Twas mah fault that yer innocence was nearly taken frae ye." He glanced up at me with hollow eyes.

"No, I'm not an innocent," I argued, remembering how the handle of his blade hadn't hurt when he, er Donnchadh, had pushed it into me. From what I could recall, I also hadn't seen any blood. "Well, my body isn't a virgin anyway," I rephrased my comment. Technically, my soul still was since I'd never actually committed the deed.

Tallis chuckled before the laugh died and a slight smile took its place. "Ye are the embodiment o' innocence, Besom, nae matter whit yer body may tell ye," he said in a tone that brooked no arguments. A second or so later, the smile vanished from his mouth. "An' Ah am yer protector. Boot ye needed tae protect yerself frae meh." He shook his head again and dropped his attention to my hands, where they still lay clasped in his.

84

"It's true I had to fight you off," I said with a quick nod. "But you weren't yourself, Tallis. I wasn't fighting you; I was fighting Donnchadh."

"We are one an' the same," he argued.

"No," I almost interrupted him. "No, you aren't. Donnchadh isn't you. Donnchadh is nothing like you! And you know I'm right." I paused for a second. "You have to know I'm right?"

"Ye had tae protect yerself 'gainst meh, lass, because 'twas mah fault Donnchadh took control o' mah body in the first place," he answered sternly, as if wanting to ensure that he disproved every nice thing I said about him.

"What do you mean?" I asked, eyeing him with suspicion.

"Ah invited Donnchadh tae take ova," he continued, dropping his gaze to the floor as he exhaled and faced me again. "Afta Ah left the tavern, Ah got mahself as blootered as Ah could because Ah knew 'twould be harder fur meh tae control Donnchadh oonder the influence o' the whiskey."

Frowning, I tried to make sense of his words. "You wanted Donnchadh to take control of you?" He nodded, and I suddenly felt ill. "Why?"

"Because Ah gave oop," he answered simply.

"You gave up because Jason and Alaire didn't grant you the absolution you expected from them?"

He shook his head immediately, letting me know I was far off base. "Nae, Ah could give ah bludy damn 'boot Jason an' Alaire." He took a breath and continued to shake his head. "Ah gave oop because Ah wasnae strong enough tae fight mah evil feelins fer ye, lass. An' havin' these feelins fer ye made meh realize Ah was nae better than Ah ever had been." He chuckled acidly as his midnight-blue eyes met mine. "Ah realized all the time Ah was repentin' was fer nothin'."

"You're a man," I argued, thinking Tallis Black had issues, and then some. "Men have sexual feelings, Tallis. It's completely natural."

"Ah thought Ah was strong enough tae overcome mah humanity," he lamented. "An' Ah thought Ah could be strong enough tae overcome them fer ye."

"What you're asking of yourself is impossible," I pointed out, not understanding how he could even think he was capable of something like that. "Even though you might have the immortal spirit of Donnchadh inside of you, you were, and are, human, Tallis."

"Nae," he started to argue again, but I interrupted him.

"I don't care if you're a Druid and two thousand years old. I don't care if you're possessed. I don't care about your history. I don't care if you're this or you're that. At the end of the day, you're human," I finished. My terse tone warned him not to argue with me. He didn't respond, so I continued. "And," I started, but my voice died away as embarrassment set in. But I had to ditch the sudden awkwardness I felt because I needed to tell Tallis how deeply my emotions ran for him. "And I care about you." I held my chin up defiantly. "I care about you more than I've ever cared about another man and it's important to me that you … know that."

"Lass," he started, exhaling deeply, but I interrupted him by grasping his hands in mine. My blisters burned as soon as I touched him but I ignored the pain.

"I want us to be more than what we are," I explained, suddenly surprising myself for being so direct, but I figured there was no turning back now, so I should say exactly what I was thinking. "I don't want us to just be friends, or whatever we are."

He immediately shook his head. "'Tis wrong tae ever think that ye an' Ah," he began, but his voice trailed away. I could already tell what he was thinking.

"Tallis, you aren't darkness," I declared unwaveringly. I glanced down at his forearms, which were covered with dark, wiry hair that did nothing to hide the sinewy muscles. "You are a good man," I stated simply. When I looked back up at him, Tallis immediately shook his head again.

"Mah past," he started, but I interrupted him.

"So you have a past!" I spat the words out, surprised at the vehemence in my tone. But I was frustrated. It was hard listening to Tallis talk about his eternal faults, and even more difficult trying to convince him that he wasn't the pariah he claimed he was. "So what? You've repented for your past, Tallis. I know you have! And you know you have, too, regardless of what Alaire and Jason Streethorn think! Regardless of what anyone thinks!"

He shook his head more fiercely this time.

"I've seen you repenting!" I protested, the image of him flogging himself in the snow flashing through my brain.

But Tallis refused to change his mind. I could see as much by his stiff composure. "Some things can ne'er be forgiven."

"Yes, they can," I insisted. "All things can."

He dropped his gaze to the floor and inhaled deeply, as if straining for more air. His attention settled on my yoga pants, precisely where I'd stitched them back together after Donnchadh attacked me. "Did Ah?" he started.

"Donnchadh," I interrupted him. "It wasn't you."

"Hoo far did he git?" he asked, his shameful eyes meeting mine.

"I was able to fend Donnchadh off," I answered with a smile intended to convey that everything was okay.

"Whit did Ah do tae ye?" he demanded, his eyes forbidding me from avoiding the question. "Ah need ye tae tell meh, lass."

87

"Nothing regrettable, Tallis," I answered with another consoling smile even though I wondered if I was actually telling the truth on that point. "I'm okay."

His eyes followed the line of my body down to my feet. "Ye'r naethin' boot ah small lass an' ye defeated Donnchadh, the most powerful o' warriors," he said, almost skeptical of his own words. When his eyes found mine, I could see the pride in their depths. "Ye are ah fighter, Besom. Ah hae trained ye well."

"Yes, you have," I immediately concurred. He was damn right; he had trained me well.

We both fell silent for barely a few seconds before he spoke again. "Efter Ah touched ye in the tavern, Ah forced mahself tae leave ye there because Ah was afraid 'twould happen again." He paused temporarily, obviously collecting his thoughts. "Ah left ye because Ah thought 'twas best fer meh ta dae so. Ah didnae want tae, lass, boot Ah knew Ah couldnae troost mahself near ye." He paused for another second. "Ah was able tae keep mah feelins fer ye tae mahself oontil that night at the tavern. Wif the whiskey, Ah had tae act on them."

"I understand why you left us now," I replied as I nodded. "And you were right to think that something … of a sexual nature would happen between us again. I've thought about that, myself," I admitted with a deep breath before I impulsively blurted out the rest of my thought. "But what if I wanted," I started, and quickly corrected myself. "What if I *want* something to happen between us again?"

Tallis immediately shook his head and took another step away from me. "Ye dinnae know whit ye're sayin', lass," he began.

"I do know exactly what I'm saying," I argued, irritated he wasn't responding the way I'd hoped and fantasized he would. I'd already made my mind up that I wanted Tallis—I'd wanted him from the moment I'd met him. Granted, there were times when I'd more wanted to kill him, but the truth of the matter was that those times were few and far between. I had never met anyone like Tallis and I knew I never would. He was my paragon of the perfect man, complete in all his flaws.

"'Twill never happen 'gain, lass."

Instant disappointment snaked through me. I wondered if the reason why it would never happen again had something to do with me being "the light" and him being "the darkness."

"Why not?" I inquired.

"Ah made mahself ah promise."

"A promise?" I repeated, eyeing him pointedly.

"Aye."

"Do you care to elaborate?" I persisted, fully aware that the tone of my voice couldn't conceal my obvious disappointment.

"Ye saved meh frae mahself," he started. I figured he was referring to the incident when Donnchadh took over his body and I helped put Tallis back in rightful control. "Ah owe ye ah great debt."

"You don't owe me anything, Tallis," I replied sadly, but he shook his head in that stubborn fashion of his.

"Ah might not hae been granted the absolution Ah expected from Jason Streethorn an' Alaire; an' now Ah verra mooch doubt Ah will ever see it. Boot Ah hae decided that Ah willnae give oop. Ah will seek the pardon Ah need … through ye."

"Through me?" I repeated, frowning. I didn't like the sound of that at all and, further, I didn't understand how I could offer him an ounce of salvation.

"Aye," he said with a firm nod. "Ye are the best example o' ah human Ah have come across, lass. Therefore, Ah am makin' it mah business tae become yer protector an' tae ensure that nae harm comes tae ye durin' yer missions tae the Oonderground."

"My protector?" I restated, thinking he'd already assumed that role. True, in the beginning he'd said I'd have to pay him for his protection, but it wasn't as though he'd ever come calling for that fee …

"Aye, Ah am forever in yer service," he announced, matter-of-factly.

"But that isn't what I want, Tallis!" I said, glaring at him. "I don't want you to be my protector!" Well, that wasn't entirely true, but I didn't bother to correct myself because I figured he got my gist.

"Ah doonae," he started and it was his turn to frown at me.

"I want us to be equals!" I yelled, amazed at how dense he could be. I'd basically spelled out my wants and needs for him a few minutes earlier. "I want us to be equals, yes, and friends and, um," I started to lose my nerve so I took a deep breath, and stood up taller before forcing the rest out. "I want us to be lovers."

"Lass," Tallis started as he shook his head. He took another few steps away from me as if he were suddenly afraid I might reach out and grab him.

"I have never had sex with a man, Tallis," I explained, dropping my gaze to the ground. Then I remembered that I needed to be strong, and forced my eyes back to his. "I trust you. I feel safe with you and I know you would never hurt me."

"Ah would never hurt ye," he concurred.

"I know," I answered. "And what's more, I'm very … attracted to you. I want my first time to be with you, Tallis, and no one else. I want you to teach me how to please you as well as you taught me how to wield my sword."

It seemed like all the color drained from his face and I couldn't read his expression because there really wasn't one. He just stood there, looking like a statue. My heart pounded inside me and I tried to quell the feelings of humiliation that were already invading and threatening to take over.

90

When Tallis finally spoke, his voice was gentle. "Ah cannae be yer lover, mooch though Ah want tae be." He closed his eyes and inhaled deeply before opening them again and focusing on me. "Ye hae nae idea how badly Ah wish Ah could be yer man, Besom," he said before taking another breath. "Boot Ah can never be. Ye are tae good fer meh," he finished softly.

I never thought in a million years that it could be so difficult to lose my virginity.

"The water was more sombre far than perse"
– Dante's *Inferno*

SEVEN

"Okay," I said with resignation to Tallis.

I'd finally given up our conversation and, in so doing, sounded completely deflated. Yes, the thought did occur to me that maybe I'd given in too soon. And, yes, I imagined there had to be something I could have said that would have changed his mind about how he viewed himself and us ... But after further consideration, nothing came to mind. That was because there really wasn't anything more to be said. I couldn't think of a single thing that could change Tallis's prerogative; and rather than chasing my tail, I figured it was time to concede victory to Tallis. At least, for now.

I started for the door again and couldn't help pausing when I noticed Tallis didn't try to stop me this time. That realization felt like an enormous rock settling right down into my gut.

He's letting me go, I thought. *Just like that.*

"Where are ye goin'?" Tallis demanded as I halted at the threshold of the doorway. My heartbeat was racing and it felt like maybe only mere seconds stood between it simply exploding right there in my chest. In what felt like slow motion, I turned around to face the man who possessed my heart. I didn't say anything right away because I was so overcome with emotion. All I could do was stand there, wishing things could have turned out differently between us.

"Lily?" he repeated my name for the second time in the last thirty minutes, yet it still had the same impact as the first time he'd said it. He took a step closer toward me as he eyed me curiously.

"I'm going to see Alaire!" The words just flew from my mouth as if they had a mind of their own. In fact, I couldn't even remember trying to formulate a response in the first place. As soon as the words were out of my mouth and clinging to the air between us, I knew I'd said them merely to make Tallis jealous. Yes, it was wrong, but I couldn't help being thrilled at Tallis's sudden pinched expression. His eyes narrowed in obvious anger and his breathing instantly increased.

"Alaire?" he repeated, his eyes burning. They were tapered into such tight slits that I could barely make out their midnight blue any longer. "An' whit are ye goin' tae see Alaire fer?"

As soon as he asked the question, I berated myself for answering so honestly in the first place. I'd just opened a huge can of worms. Knowing I was on my way to see Alaire, there was no way Tallis was going to let me go easily.

"I, um, I agreed to have dinner with him," I started. When I noticed the sudden redness in Tallis's cheeks, I realized they probably weren't the choicest of words to start out with.

"Dinner?" he repeated as he glared at me. He didn't say anything more but took another step toward me as I retreated from him, which put me directly on the other side of his front door. He stopped and just stood there like a giant A, his legs spread wide and his enormous arms crossed over his equally ample chest. "An' jist why the bludy hell are ye havin' dinner with Alaire?"

"Well," I started before exhaling the breath I'd been holding. I scoured my mind for a plausible explanation for why I would have agreed to be wined and dined by the equivalent of the devil. Tallis cleared

93

his throat, which made me instantly lose my train of thought. I made the mistake of glancing up at him, only to behold his obvious anger. I tried to smile, but surprisingly, it felt more like a wince.

"Aye, ye were sayin'?" he demanded impatiently as it took me another few seconds to remember what we were even talking about.

"Oh, um," I paused before remembering we were discussing Alaire's dinner invitation. "Well," I started again.

"Aye, ye've used yer fair share o' that word, lass," Tallis ground out. "Nae more stallin'."

"I'm not stalling," I barked and then figured this conversation was now inevitable so I'd better start spitting the words out. "I ... I agreed to have, um, dinner with Alaire after he made it very clear that if I refused, I'd be sure to receive an infraction for killing one of his ... 'employees' during my last trip to the Underground." I huffed out a breath and crossed my arms over my chest, pleased with my response but still feeling defensive, all the same.

"Alaire has nae plans tae see ye receive that infraction," Tallis replied, his eyebrows furrowing in the middle of his forehead as he continued to glare at me skeptically.

"What?" I started, sounding completely flustered. "Of course he'll insist I get that infraction!" I shouted before swallowing hard. "Well, that is, if I refuse to have dinner with him." I was en route to losing all the bravado I'd flaunted a few seconds earlier. In fact, I was more than sure I sounded more sheepish than a sheep itself could possibly sound.

"Alaire will see tae it that ye dinnae end oop in Shade, lass, 'cause if ye do, he loses."

"He loses?" I repeated, eyeing him curiously.

"Aye."

"How does he lose?"

Tallis sighed, shaking his head like I was a little dense or something. "'Tis ah difficult thing tae maintain ah fascination wif someone when the object o' yer fascination exists in ah different world!"

"Oh," I said, letting my shoulders fall as I realized that maybe Tallis did have a point. I mean, if I weren't around, Alaire couldn't exactly make dinner plans with me, could he? "Well, if I were out of commission, I'm sure Alaire would just find some other Retriever for his … muse." The word "muse" actually paled in comparison to whatever odd relationship Alaire and I shared.

"Aye, he would," Tallis agreed with a nod. "Boot he would have tae give oop on ye first, Besom, an' Alaire is accoostomed tae gettin' whit he wants."

I already knew that much was true. But while I could see how it would benefit Alaire to keep me out of Shade if he wanted to maintain some sort of … relationship with me, I didn't dare bank on it. Not where my future was concerned, anyway. "I'm not going to take the chance of pissing Alaire off just to prove you're wrong."

"Ye are puttin' yerself at risk, lass," Tallis ground out, his jaw set just as stubbornly as I'm sure mine must've been.

"Well, there's even more risk if I don't agree to meet him," I rebutted. "If I so much as caught Alaire on a bad day, that infraction would probably have my name on it. And in case you've forgotten, let me remind you: two infractions equal one hundred years in Shade."

"Ah know that!" Tallis yelled at me as he shook his head more vehemently and looked like he was rapidly losing his composure.

"Then you see my point?"

"Och aye," he answered, nodding. I felt my eyes widening with surprise to find him in agreement with anything I had to say where Alaire was concerned.

95

"Boot whetha o' not Ah see yer point, Ah will nae allow ye tae go anywhere near Alaire or the Oonderground City," he finished and held his chin up in such a way that warned me not to argue with him.

"But!" I started, my voice cracking. I shook my head as plumes of anger began blossoming inside me. Just who did he think he was?! Forbidding me to go near Alaire? Granted, he'd taken it upon himself to become my protector, but that didn't mean he was the boss of me! Oh, he and I were going to have a few words about this little arrangement of ours ... Well, after I got back from my dinner with Alaire, anyway.

"Ah will hear nae more aboot it," Tallis finished firmly.

"*You* will hear no more about it?" I railed back. "In case you weren't aware, Tallis Black, I am perfectly capable of making my own decisions!"

"Apparently noot," he answered. I saw a smirk appear temporarily on his mouth even though he still held his arms crossed rigidly against his chest.

"There's no way I'm going to gamble over that infraction!" I yelled at him, shaking my head and throwing my arms in the air until I'm sure I looked like I'd lost my mind.

"Ah will take yer case tae Jason Streethorn mahself tae save ye from troublin' yerself wif Alaire," Tallis replied, any trace of his smile now gone.

"Yeah, and a whole lot of good that's going to do me! Have you forgotten what happened the last time you approached Jason about keeping his end of the bargain after you retrieved your thousand souls?!" I took a deep breath before slamming him with the rest of what I had on my mind. "I know better than to trust Jason to do the right thing because he did absolutely nothing for you!"

Even though it was a low blow, Tallis's expression didn't change. He looked just as furious as he had right before I said anything. "Ye are bein' ah foolish lass," he managed between clenched teeth. "Ye are puttin' yerself right where Alaire wants ye," he continued. "Right in the middle o' the lion's den."

"Don't think I haven't already thought this through," I answered with as much confidence and authority as I could muster.

"Obviously, ye have nae, or ye would've made the right decision."

"One hundred years in Shade isn't an option for me," I spat back, my shoulders rising and falling with my rapid breathing. Even I was a little surprised by how livid I was.

"An' neither should be suppin' wif the devil."

"Alaire is hardly 'the devil,'" I argued with a frown, trying to quell the argument within myself that I often referred to Alaire as exactly that. But, in this case, Lily divided against herself wasn't going to stand, so I decided to ignore my own hypocrisy. Instead, I turned around to search the perimeter for any sign of Alaire's shade, thinking now would have been a great time for her to show up.

"That's what ye think," Tallis replied while spearing me with another fierce glare. "Boot ye dinnae know Alaire like Ah do," he finished, setting his jaw tight. "Ye dinnae know whit he's capable oove."

"Come on, Tallis," I said with a slight laugh that suggested I thought he was overreacting. "What's Alaire really going to do to me? You think he's going to kill me and feed me to his legion of demons?"

"Nae." Tallis's lips pressed into a tight white line, making every muscle in his jaw look overworked. "He is warmin' ye oop tae him," he responded. "He wants ye tae think he is nae so bad in ordah tae drop yer defenses."

"For what purpose?" I inquired, actually intrigued by what Tallis had to say because I had pondered the subject of why Alaire found me so interesting more than once and I always came up empty-handed.

97

"'Cause he seeks tae pervert ye, lass."

"He seeks to pervert me?" I repeated facetiously. My eyebrows reached for the sky in disbelief as the visual of an innocent girl from Po-Dunk, USA, relocating to Hollywood before getting involved with the wrong crowd suddenly interrupted my thoughts like a bad Lifetime movie. "What does that even mean?"

Tallis shook his head as he released a breath filled with obvious frustration. "It means Alaire wants tae rip ye o' yer innocence."

"Ironic to hear there's actually someone who doesn't want to preserve my innocence," I muttered mostly to myself. I couldn't help thinking I wanted nothing more than for my innocence to be ripped right out of me. Well, not by Alaire, of course ...

"Alaire is nae laughin' matter," Tallis said in a tone that failed to mask his annoyance.

"I never said he was," I fired back. "And even if Alaire intends to strip me of my innocence, it's not like he could accomplish that after one dinner!"

"Aye, boot one dinner leads tae two, which leads tae three; an' afore ye know it, ye troost him."

"I will never trust Alaire," I told Tallis, angry that he would ever think I could be so stupid. "So you can stop your pep talk. I'm more than aware of who and what Alaire is. And I'm also suspicious about what he wants from me. But I'm also not a stupid or naïve woman ..."

"Ah never said ye were, Besom."

"Maybe you haven't actually said as much, but sometimes you imply things," I corrected him. "Anyway, it's not like I don't realize I'm dealing with the Keeper of the Underground City, Tallis." I heaved a sigh, now well beyond tired of arguing with him. My mind was already made up. Nothing could change it at this point. I would simply dine with Alaire and save myself the infraction that I was more than sure awaited me if I flaked. "My defenses are up," I said before taking a deep breath. "But I have to play Alaire's game to ensure that I avoid Shade."

"Ye are tae stubborn fer yer own good," Tallis ground out in reply.

"I could say the exact same thing of you."

"Ah am nae the one suppin' wif Alaire!" he yelled at me, shaking his head. "Ye should take heed o' mah advice."

"Thanks for everything," I replied with a counterfeit smile. "But I'm not going to take my chances where Alaire and an infraction are concerned."

"Lass," he started, but I was quick to interrupt him.

"Everything will be fine, Tallis," I said, trying to convince myself as well. "As soon as my dinner with Alaire is over, I'll return to Edinburgh and wait for my next mission from Jason."

Pretty soon this whole conversation will be no more than a thing of the past, just like my dinner with Alaire, I told myself, hoping and praying my words would prove to be correct.

"If ye insist oan goin' tae meet Alaire," Tallis persisted, clearly not interested in anymore debate, "then Ah am goin' wif ye."

I imagined Tallis showing up at my dinner with Alaire for a split second before deciding it would be a very, very bad idea. "You can't do that," I answered in a hushed tone. "You know how that well that would go over."

"Ah dinnae care."

I opened my mouth to argue why Tallis crashing my dinner with Alaire would be a terrible idea when I noticed his gaze moving to something behind me. I turned around and saw a whitish haze materializing in the trees just behind and to the right of me. I glanced back at Tallis in question, but he didn't spare a glimpse at me. Instead, his attention remained riveted on the mist. I turned around again and watched the white fog morphing into the shape of a woman—at least, I could make out the details of her angular face and long, plaited hair. As to the rest of her body, it never quite revealed itself.

"She must be the shade," I said in a quiet, albeit awestruck voice.

As soon as I uttered the words, I realized my mistake. Tallis would have absolutely known why this shade had appeared.

"Nae, lass!" I heard him yell. I immediately looked back at him only to find him lurching for me, his hands outstretched and fully intent on grabbing me. But the shade behind me must have rushed me at the same time because I was suddenly engulfed in freezing cold air. I felt a blast of wind on my face and instinctively closed my eyes.

When I opened them, I was no longer standing in front of Tallis's cabin.

***

It wasn't so much that the shade led me to a shortcut as it was that she was the shortcut, herself. By enveloping me in her cold mist, we both managed to travel ghost-fast, which was exactly that—fast. Every fifteen minutes or so, the shade released me from her vaporous embrace and allowed me to catch my breath. After a good five minutes, my respiration and heart rate returned to normal; and then, without a word, she again enclosed me in her ectoplasm and we'd be off again, traveling as quickly as the wind.

The shade never uttered one word, making it a quiet journey. But I was so enveloped in my own thoughts, which were mainly centered on Tallis, that I welcomed the silence. Unlike most of the creatures from the Underground City, the shade was not at all frightening. She looked like a reflection from a pool of water—constantly undulating. She was also the color of the sky—a light blue, almost appearing clear at times. The lines of her face and body weren't precise, but well enough defined for me to imagine she was probably in her late twenties when she'd died. That is, if she'd died. I didn't really know much about shades, so I wasn't sure if she was actually alive at some point or not. She seemed nice enough—never becoming impatient despite the customary five minutes I needed to prevent our high-speed traveling from doing permanent damage to my heart.

The more I thought about it, the more I realized that this brand of traveling must have been pretty tough on my body in general. The shade probably knew that too, because she was the one who always made sure we rested between bursts of incredible speed.

While we traveled, I could still see the scenery around us, although it disappeared into a blur of color. It was like looking out a car window when you're driving ridiculously fast. And speaking of fast, it took us mere seconds to get out of Tallis's section of the Dark Wood which boasted of sunshine and verdant foliage. Then we were ensconced in the dead section of the Dark Wood, which consisted only of darkness. Whenever we rested in that part of the Dark Wood, the shade placed herself as close to me as possible while swirling around me like a ghostly tornado. I figured that was because she worried the creatures in the haunted forest might decide to make a meal of me. Not to say that subject didn't worry me too ...

After what felt like our twentieth rest stop, the shade snaked around me for the umpteenth time. I caught my breath before she dissolved into me again, surrounding me with icy coldness. I closed my eyes, shutting out the darkness of the woods. I preferred the

101

privacy of my own thoughts because they were much less dark and foreboding than the forest, itself.

A few seconds later, I felt cold air rushing past my face, which meant we were airborne again. I could never tell if we were actually flying. The darkness obscured any chance to see exactly what our, er, *my* feet were doing. But it felt like flying so I was happy to go with it.

As soon as I closed my eyes, my thoughts again returned to Tallis. I recalled the memory of him standing in his home with his arms crossed over his chest, looking, for all intents and purposes, like a terribly upset Zeus. It was a good comparison, since everything about Tallis evoked the King of the Gods, including his temper. And I was more than sure that if Tallis had gotten the chance, he would have gladly snatched a thunderbolt from the nearest cloud and driven it right through Alaire's heart.

The wind on my face began to abate, which meant the shade was about to give me another rest break. Since we hadn't been traveling for very long, I opened my eyes, but only found darkness all around me again. Then the shade turned us both to the right, and I found myself facing the gates of the Underground City.

"Wow, that was fast," I said, shock evident in my tone.

The shade, as usual, didn't respond. Instead, she extended her hand toward me. It looked like she was wearing some sort of long-sleeved dress or robe. I could clearly see the outlines of the cuffs, which hung all the way down to her fingers. One hand was clutched around some sort of a vial. The vial appeared to be real rather than part of her ectoplasm because I couldn't see through it. I could clearly make out that it was constructed from some sort of black material, maybe plastic. There was a red band around the middle. I didn't take the vial right away, so the shade nudged me with her hand.

I eventually accepted the vial and glanced down at it quizzically because I'd never seen it before. With no idea as to why she gave the vial to me in the first place, much less what its contents were, I looked up at her and shrugged. The shade pointed to the Gates of the Underground City, her fingers the color of crystal and nearly transparent. Then she pointed to the vial in my hand and made the motion of drinking it. The purpose of the vial only dawned on me then.

"Do I need to drink it in order to walk into the Underground City?" I continued, guessing the answer as she nodded at me, to let me know I was right on the money. "And Alaire told you to give me this?" I double-checked as she nodded again. "Okay," I finished as I eyed the vial again. The Underground City was basically constructed of pure evil, so if I so much as touched anything in it, I'd start to wither and die since nothing innocent could exist there for long. I knew as much from past experience. "Well, guess there's no time like the present," I finished as I sighed and then uncorked the top of the vial.

The shade nodded in response, her translucent hair fanning out around her as if she were floating in a pool. I said a silent prayer that Alaire hadn't gotten his potions mixed up, and then downed the contents. It tasted strangely like sweet cough syrup—like Dimetapp or something. When I turned around to thank the shade for transporting me, she was gone. Her vanishing act startled me temporarily, considering she'd been standing there only moments earlier, but I steeled my courage and headed for the Gates of the Underground, figuring there was no point in putting off the inevitable.

Then I remembered I didn't have my key to the gates. Bill was the last one who'd carried them. A sinking feeling registered in my gut and just as I was about to whip out Bill's phone to text Alaire, I watched one of the gates open by itself, making a horrible creaking sound as it did so. I glanced up at the sky, and saw the black clouds overhead moving on fast-forward, flitting across the red light, which came from what looked like the moon. The swift black clouds were one of the factors in the Underground City that I found incredibly off-putting, although I wasn't sure why. I mean, most people would have agreed that the demons inhabiting the city were significantly more alarming than the clouds, not to mention Alaire ...

"Oh, fuck!" I whispered with frustration as a terrible thought suddenly dawned on me: I'd left my sword in Tallis's house! The shade was so quick in absconding with me that I'd completely forgotten to grab my sword. That meant I had absolutely no protection in the Underground City ...

Then there's no way you can enter! I yelled to myself as I started to panic.

It felt like the weight of the world had just descended on my shoulders as I stood there, immobilized. I didn't know what to do—whether to cancel on Alaire and run the risk of earning my first infraction or ... No, there was no alternative. I couldn't enter the gates without my sword.

Even though I'd made my decision to retreat, I couldn't turn around. It was as if my feet were rooted in place, subject to my indecision. I found my attention settling on the sculptures that crowned the gates to the city. I'd seen these gates numerous times but that didn't ease the feelings of dread that always settled in my stomach whenever I found myself facing them again. Carved in relief was a woman's expressionless face, some huge spider webs, a few snails thrown in for good measure and two lion heads, flanking both sides of the gates. Each lion head appeared to be swallowing a man's face.

How could you have forgotten your sword? I scolded myself. *There's no way you can enter the Underground now if you can't protect yourself and that means you're going to miss your dinner with Alaire. He's not going to be happy! In fact, he's going to be so unhappy, that infraction is basically yours.*

Before I could decide what to do next, I watched a black sports car pulling up just beyond the gates. From what I could tell, it looked like a Tesla. All of the windows were as dark as the black paint. The rear door on the driver's side opened, but revealed no one inside. That wasn't a surprise though—the last time Alaire summoned me, a driver-less Porsche showed up.

To enter the Underground City without my sword, or not ... that was now the question.

The Tesla honked its horn as if suggesting I was taking too much time in my deliberations, and it had an agenda to keep. I took a deep breath, hoping I would be safe with Alaire. As soon as that thought crossed my mind, I realized how completely inane it was. Still, the threat of an infraction was most definitely still on the table.

I only hoped I wasn't about to make the biggest mistake of my life ...

I stepped foot into the Underground City and was happy to discover that it didn't feel like my insides were in the process of being ripped out. Maybe the little vial was doing its job. Approaching the Tesla, I took a deep breath and prayed for the best before taking a seat on the super soft black leather. The car door closed of its own accord and seconds later, we were driving down the streets of the Underground City, the nondescript city buildings dwarfing us on every side.

I could make out a few Watchers patrolling the streets, but they seemed to be the only creatures out and about. Watchers were like a nightmarish version

105

of businessmen because they always dressed in suits. But that's where the similarity ended. Their faces were creased with lines so deep, they resembled mummies. They also didn't have any hair on top of their grayish heads, just mounds of lumpy striations which looked like spaghetti.

Luckily for me, the Watchers weren't a threat—not physically, anyway. They avoided confrontations because their sole purpose lay in reporting any goings-on in the Underground to Alaire. That meant he was already well aware of my arrival.

We drove through the city quickly, each street looking just like the preceding one. After a few minutes, the Tesla parked in front of the tallest office building that existed in the Underground City—Alaire's. The rear door opposite me opened, indicating that I should use it to exit the car, rather than my door. Trying to calm my heart, which began racing as soon as I recognized Alaire's building, I still couldn't believe I'd actually willingly entered the Underground City without my sword. I was completely defenseless ...

Sliding across the leather seat, I hoisted myself out of the car. I looked first to my left and then my right before deciding the coast was clear. Then I beelined it for the double doors of Alaire's Headquarters. As soon as I entered the building, I felt sick to my stomach. Taking a deep breath, I concentrated on the scenery around me in order to stave off the panic attack that was seconds away from manifesting.

The interior of the building was circular with the floors painted to emulate a checkerboard. There were six concrete columns that formed a circle around the lobby desk, but just like the last time I was here, no one attended the desk, or anywhere else, for that matter. The whole place was eerily quiet. I assumed that was because it was probably difficult to find secretarial help in hell.

Walking past the lobby desk, I found the bank of elevators, and my heart began climbing higher up into my throat with every step I took. The plastic plants on either side of the walkway gave the place an artificial and cheap vibe. And the paintings of blue sky and clouds along the hallway walls made me instantly miss the real things. I hit the button to call the elevator, all the while darting glances behind me to make sure I wasn't about to be waylaid by some hideous creature. The elevator doors opened with a tinny "ding" and I stepped inside. Once the doors closed again, the button for the eighth floor lit up without me even pushing anything. "Okay, the eighth floor it is then," I said to myself as the elevator took off with a lurch.

When the elevator doors dinged open again, I faced a long expanse of walkway, all in dark hardwood flooring. I stepped out of the elevator and heard the doors shutting behind me—which was almost as loud as the pounding of my heart. I took a few tentative steps forward, noting how the yellow lights from the sconces on the walls threw shadows across the hallway that looked like little, frightening creatures that were up to no good.

I took another few steps and watched a heavy wooden door to my right slowly begin to open. As soon as I approached it, I realized it had opened itself because there was no one to be seen anywhere. From where I stood in the hallway, I could make out a bed inside the room, which was covered in a golden silk coverlet, on top of which were countless matching pillows.

I guessed this bedroom was my destination for at least the immediate future, and steeled my nerves with a hearty breath as I entered it. The door immediately closed behind me and locked itself. My heart started beating so quickly, I became dizzy and had to stabilize myself with one of the posts of the black canopy bed while I regained my balance.

If I'd regretted forgetting my sword earlier, I regretted it even more now.

"Alaire?" I called out, but received no answer. I stood up straight and closed my eyes for a few seconds, trying to collect my wits. Freaking out simply wouldn't do me any good. When I opened my eyes, I noticed a fire burning in the hearth which immediately reminded me of the fireplace in Tallis's house. But this fire did nothing to alleviate the coldness of the space. This room wasn't warm and cozy like Tallis's house was. It didn't share the same sweet scent of the earth or the man who owned it.

Focus, Lily, I encouraged myself.

Scanning the perimeter of the room, I saw two boudoir chairs flanking the bed, both of them upholstered in the same gold brocade fabric of the bed's coverlet. When my attention fell on the bed, I noticed an envelope sitting atop it with my name written attractively in cursive writing. I retrieved it and tore it open. The letter was penned on letterhead, proclaiming to have come from the "desk of the Keeper of the Underground City." It read:

My dear Ms. Harper,

Please indulge yourself in a hot bath, which has already been drawn for you in the en-suite. You will also find a change of clothing in the closet. When you are dressed and ready to join me for dinner, please ring the bell atop the fireplace mantel.

I look forward to our evening together.

Best regards,

Alaire

I dropped the letter on the bed and looked for the change of clothing Alaire mentioned. Approaching the closet, I opened the double doors and immediately noticed something white that was hanging on a hanger. Reaching for it, I freed it from the hanger and inspected it carefully, unable to keep from gasping as soon as I realized what it was, or, in this case, wasn't.

"Really nice, Alaire," I grumbled while shaking my head in irritation.

My "change of clothing" amounted to basically nothing. It was entirely constructed of white lace and looked like a body suit since it was one piece. The sleeves and the legs were long, but the entire thing was transparent. I did notice that there was an accompanying pair of lace, thong panties, which couldn't have covered much of anything. On the floor of the closet was a pair of white pumps with heels nearly six inches high.

Yep, Alaire was an opportunist, and then some.

"In company with the dusky waves"
– Dante's *Inferno*

EIGHT

I couldn't deny that the warm, sudsy water felt like the closest thing to heaven that I'd experienced in a very long time. I'd debated whether or not to take advantage of Alaire's offer of a bath, thinking I'd rather just proceed straight to our dinner so it would have been over that much sooner. But as soon as I saw the sparkling water already drawn in the clawfooted tub, the urge to immerse myself in a bath had never been stronger.

I'd rationalized my decision to bathe by telling myself I needed to desperately, but, more so, because I needed to buy more time to come up with a plan. I didn't know how I was going to get myself out of the Underground City after dinner with Alaire was over. Furthermore, once Alaire discovered I was unarmed, I wasn't sure what he'd do, if anything. Either way, it wasn't a position I felt good about being in at all.

The foremost problem with the whole situation was Alaire's unpredictability. And that unpredictability translated to *dangerous*, in my books. Would he let me go without a scene? Or did I have cause for concern?

Reclining in the bath water, I sighed with frustration as I further pondered the subject of Alaire's fascination with me. What did it mean? Was I in danger because of it? Or was it a simple crush? Whatever the answer, I hated being without my sword and, therefore, without any protection.

110

What are you going to do if Alaire doesn't release you? I asked myself. *If he finds out you forgot your sword, you're basically at his mercy!*

I didn't have any answers to my questions, which bothered me more than I cared to admit. Not only that, but every time I attempted to craft a plan of escape in case I needed one, I kept drawing blanks, probably because I was so exhausted.

After dunking my hair in the water, I sat up and noticed a bottle of Paul Mitchell shampoo on the lip of the tub. Reaching for the bottle, I lathered my hair a few times before rinsing it, and following suit with the coordinating conditioner. I couldn't help feeling my spirits lift as I washed the dirt and sweat from my hair and body. I'd already taken it upon myself to launder my sports bra and yoga pants because there was no way in hell I intended to leave here in the getup Alaire provided for me, not without making some much-needed adjustments to it first. I was already trying to figure out how to make the white lace outfit a little less … whorish.

I eventually extricated myself from the warm water, thinking I'd spent long enough lounging in the bathtub. Now I needed to dry off before searching for a brush to take out all my tangles. Only then could I turn to the subject of redesigning the atrocity known as my dinner outfit. Stepping out of the bathtub onto the snow-white bath rug, I caught my reflection in the mirror. I looked just as exhausted as I felt. Dark circles beneath my eyes combined with the hollows in my cheeks, reflected my poor, irregular diet and my lack of sleep for the last week or so. My body looked even thinner than normal, although I couldn't fail to notice I'd put on quite a bit more muscle.

"If only the old me could see the new me now," I said to myself as I shook my head in wonder and reminisced about the former me, the one who'd existed before the auto accident that claimed my life and

111

thrust me into this new one. My old life seemed to have happened so long ago, it was now more like a mere dream. Funny how the days, hours and seconds could distance me so far from my former life.

A surge of nostalgia filled me as my thoughts turned to my mother. A rock lodged itself in my throat while I wondered what she was doing now, and how she was managing to cope with the loss of her only child. I wondered if she'd moved on with her life at all—if she was still working at the title company, or if she'd returned to her weekly AA meetings, or was again laughing with her friends while playing bridge.

Whenever I thought about my mother or my best friend, Miranda, the sorrow and yearning to see them both again became almost too much to deal with. For the first time ever, though, I seemed strangely distanced from that part of my life. It was as if a gigantic wall had been erected between the old and new me and whereas before I ached to get beyond the wall, now I finally accepted knowing that I never could.

I shook my head, forcibly driving the images right out of my mind because they weren't any good to me now. I had to focus entirely on my current predicament to ensure I made it out of the Underground City fully intact. I didn't have time for wistful memories or melancholy thoughts.

There was only now. There was only this very moment.

I wrapped myself in a white towel, which I found hanging on a hook behind the door. It felt like being enveloped in a cloud, the cloth was so soft. Then I traversed the white marble floor until I reached the sink vanity, which was, yes, also glaringly white. In fact, everything in the bathroom was so white as to appear stark and antiseptic, albeit clean. Opening the first drawer, I found a hairbrush and immediately set to work on my tangled locks.

Five minutes and a sore head later, I freed my hair of all the snarls, and it framed my face in silky tresses, which shone in the low light of the fixtures above the mirror. Sensing I needed to get a move on, I plodded into the bedroom and approached the fireplace where I'd hung up my yoga pants and my sports bra after washing them in the bath water. Grabbing my pants to test the dryness of the fabric, I found the legs were tolerably dry, but the crotch was still soaking wet. My sports bra wasn't much better. With a sigh, I approached the bed where I'd laid out the white lace outfit from Alaire. I briefly battled with the idea of tossing the white slutty getup and putting on my wet pants and sports bra again, but the thought of that depressed me so much, I decided to at least try on the ridiculous thing, if only to judge how terrible it really was.

With renewed determination, I slipped out of the towel and reached for the panties. Stepping into them, I pulled them up and settled them in place, refusing to have a conniption when the white square of material barely covered ... anything. Then, I grabbed the lace bodysuit and yanked it up to my waist. With a tiny spark of hope and a prayer that the outfit wasn't *too* scandalous, I glanced down. I wasn't sure if it was the dim light or just my vantage point, but it seemed like the double layers of lace covered my mound and actually did a decent job of keeping everything mostly hidden. Pushing both of my arms into the bodysuit, I smoothed it out over my breasts before looking down again. This time, I wasn't so lucky. The top was completely see-through, as in I could see the pinkness of my nipples right through it.

This would definitely not do.

Seeking a second opinion, I started for the bathroom mirror. When I saw my reflection, I immediately frowned, unable to restrain my irritation with Alaire.

113

"There is no way in hell I'm going to show up dressed like this," I grumbled angrily. "Nice try, Alaire, but it ain't gonna happen."

I decided to check out the rest of my body in the mirror and focused on the junction of my thighs, feeling quite pleased to find it was covered rather well by the two different layers of lace. When I turned around to check out my rear end, however, such was not the case. I could clearly see my butt cheeks which were bisected by a tiny white strap that looked a lot like dental floss.

Just don't turn around in front of him, I warned myself while eyeing my yoga pants again as I considered wearing them. I hesitated for two reasons—first, the idea of putting on the ripped, stained, wet pants again was repugnant. Second, I feared it might upset Alaire if I showed up in my yoga pants and sports bra when he'd clearly intended for me to wear the lace bodysuit. Not that I really gave a rat's ass about what Alaire thought of me in general, but at the moment, I didn't dare upset him—both because I didn't want to earn my first infraction but I also wanted to make sure I made it back out of the Underground City unscathed. Yes, pissing Alaire off was most definitely NOT a good idea.

Glancing down at my trampy outfit again, I noticed the bottoms of both legs flared out into a bell shape.

"Hmm, extra fabric," I said, holding my right foot up and jostling it to see just how much extra fabric I had to work with. The pants were way too long for me, as it turned out, giving me more than enough.

Leaning down and gripping the lace of the left pant leg between both of my hands, I pulled on it until it ripped. Even though I tried to get a clean line around my foot, there were quite a few places where the frayed lace looked like it was bleeding threads. In order to avoid being lopsided, I started doing the same on the other leg.

Once I had both pieces of fabric in hand, I pulled the top of the pantsuit down to my waist. Placing one of the sleeves of lace inside the other, I yanked both over my head as I pulled my arms through the circular opening. Once the pieces were in place, it looked like I was wearing a two-layer tube top. Pleased with my resourcefulness, I smiled at my reflection before putting the rest of the bodysuit back on. When I glanced at myself again in the mirror, I was elated to see I could no longer detect my areolas.

My evening was looking up.

I started for the bedroom again and spotted my fanny pack, which was lying on the bed. I immediately secured it around my waist, figuring I could use every inch of cover-up that I could find. That and it would ensure that Bill's phone was close at hand, in case I needed it. Unfortunately, Bill's phone was the only protection I had to count on.

Once my fanny pack was in place and certainly spoiling my outfit even more than my makeshift tube top, I decided to try on the "shoes" in the closet. I couldn't imagine how it could even be humanly possible to walk in heels so high, but figured if clowns could walk on stilts, I could surely handle some hooker shoes. Slipping my left foot, then my right into the unyielding leather, I was mildly surprised that they fit decently well. How Alaire could have known my shoe and clothing sizes was beyond me, but I had to admit I was decently impressed.

"A man who pays attention," I said under my breath while taking a few steps forward and trying to maintain my balance. I paced the room a couple of times before I felt somewhat comfortable in the ridiculous things. After deciding I'd stalled long enough, I approached the fireplace mantel and picked up the old-fashioned looking bell before ringing it.

One second. Two seconds. Three seconds. Four seconds ...

The time dripped slowly by, and it was all I could do to pace the room, not so much to practice walking in my towering heels, but rather because my nerves were on high alert and desperately needed an outlet. My heart was lodged in my throat and my hands were clammy. I could feel sweat beading along my lower back and I felt like I might throw up. All of this because I didn't know what to expect from Alaire. I was definitely way out of my element, both in terms of my next-to-nothing outfit as well as being unarmed in the Underground City.

The door to the bedroom opened suddenly. As I was beginning to expect, no one opened it. I approached it tentatively and upon reaching the threshold of the hallway, I heard the sound of footsteps retreating from the door and echoing farther down the hall. Still, I saw no one. Sensing my invisible companion wanted me to follow him or her, I fortified my courage and wobbled unsteadily toward the door.

In the hallway, I followed the fading footsteps as they sounded against the hardwood flooring until we reached the end of the corridor. As far as I could tell, the bedroom I'd just been in was the only one off the hallway. I didn't see any other doors. I frowned when I found myself facing a wall, but listened intently for the footfalls on the hardwood floors anyway. I imagined my invisible guide would turn around and lead me back down the hallway.

But I never heard the footsteps after that. Instead, the sound of something sliding behind me grabbed my attention. I turned around to find a door at the end of the hallway, after all. However, it was set into the wall and painted the same shiny gray to blend in like camouflage, which was why I'd failed to see it in the first place.

"Ah, Ms. Harper," Alaire greeted me with a large smile. He was sitting at the head of an extra-long, glossy black table which was occupying the center of the room. Beneath it, a red and black Persian rug looked especially dim against the dark hardwood floors.

As soon as I walked into the room, Alaire stood up. He was nattily dressed in a black suit with a crisp, white shirt beneath the jacket. I wasn't sure why, but he seemed taller than I remembered—maybe six foot five or so. As much as it pained me to admit it, he was truly handsome. His blond, short hair was gelled in place, and his large cornflower-blue eyes seemed all the more azure against his tanned skin. When he smiled, his cheeks dimpled, lending him a candid, boyish charm, something completely ironic when I remembered his job title.

"Hi," I responded tentatively as I heard the sound of the door swishing closed behind me. I didn't doubt Alaire could tell I was way beyond uncomfortable, especially when I began darting nervous glances around the room like a stealthy chicken. Self-consciously clasping my hands in front of me, my awkwardness probably looked ridiculous when the brashness of my outfit was taken into account.

"Please have a seat," Alaire said, holding his arm out, and indicating the seat right beside his. He reached over and pulled out the glossy, black enameled chair, which was upholstered in rich red velvet.

"Thanks," I grumbled, but sat down, my gaze still riveted on the room. The walls were a deep red and interrupted by large paintings every few feet. From my vantage point, I couldn't make out the subjects of the paintings or maybe that fact was due to the dimly lit room. What light there was in the room mainly came from an enormous, gothically styled chandelier which hung above the table. The ten or so ancient-looking

117

wall sconces around the room imbued it with a sinister atmosphere. There were no windows, which made no difference to me since I preferred not to see the streets of the Underground City.

"You look very lovely," Alaire said as he sat down beside me and I allowed my eyes to rest on him. "Well, minus that contraption around your waist," he corrected himself as he eyed my fanny pack with obvious distaste.

"That contraption is called a fanny pack. And 'lovely' isn't exactly the word I would use to describe the rest of the outfit either," I muttered, finally employing my voice as well as my sarcasm.

"Perhaps 'ravishing' would be a better term?"

"I was thinking more along the lines of 'whorish' or 'sluttified,' but whatever," I replied with a frown. The goblet on the table in front of me began filling with a red fluid. "I'm guessing that's wine?"

Alaire simply nodded, but his gaze was so penetrating, I couldn't help but wonder what he had on his mind.

"Can I have some water?" I asked, deciding not to get inebriated. Dropping my defenses around Alaire would be pure idiocy. As soon as I said the words, my water glass filled itself. I watched in awe before facing Alaire again. "How did it do that?"

He shrugged as if the wine goblets and water glasses filling themselves were no big deal. "Some might say it's magic, my dear."

"Is it?"

He shrugged again and reached for a silver bell which sat on the table in front of him. It was an exact replica of the one on the mantel in my temporary bedroom. He rang the bell and replaced it on the table again before turning to face me. "I am sometimes known as the Great Magician."

118

"The Great Magician?" I repeated as I shook my head. "Is that any relation to the Great Pumpkin?" I asked, offering him an unimpressed expression.

"Yes and no," he answered matter-of-factly, not appearing to take offense to anything I'd said. Alaire's narcissism knew no bounds, something I found incredibly irritating.

"Then, maybe I should start calling you Harry Houdini."

Alaire just offered me a smile that said my gruff manner was doing nothing to upset his cheerful mood. "It seems you are something of a tailor, I see?" he said when his gaze came to rest on my bust.

"Even though you were, no doubt, hoping for a cheap thrill, I failed to share your enthusiasm about showing up half naked," I admitted with a shrug. Glancing down at myself, and taking in my scantily clad body, I could only frown again. "Although it looks like I still am."

Alaire laughed, just as the door to the room slid open. A strange creature, hefty and intimidating, shuffled in. As soon as I saw him, I nearly jumped right out of my skin. He was carrying a large, covered silver platter.

"At ease, my dear," Alaire said with a hearty chuckle. "Boris will not hurt you."

"Are you sure?" I asked, settling my eyes on "Boris" as my fight-or-flight response escalated tenfold. Boris was probably eight feet tall, dressed in malodorous fur, and had a generally unkempt appearance. He could've been Sasquatch's cousin. His head was the shape of a pear—narrowing at the top and hairless with a wide, full, cleft chin on the bottom. His nose was broad, but not as wide as his lips which were drawn into a contented smile that hinted at little to no brain activity. His face was comprised of multiple folds of skin, which emphasized his drooping eyes. Warts covered both of his cheeks.

119

He served (well, it's really more fitting to say he *dropped*) the silver platter onto the table right in front of us. Using an enormous hand, he lifted the domed cover, his five bulbous fingers looking like gnarled tree roots.

"Thank you, Boris, I will take it from here," Alaire announced. The giant simply nodded as he turned around, his huge mass looming back toward the sliding door. The wood floors beneath him groaned with every step he took.

"What was he?" I inquired, but only after my heart calmed down and Boris was nowhere to be seen.

"An ogre," Alaire answered casually. He picked up the serving fork and motioned to the plate in front of me. Lifting it up, I allowed him to serve whatever was on the menu.

"I prefer your invisible employees," I muttered.

Alaire didn't respond verbally, but offered me a raised brow, the meaning of which was unfortunately lost on me. I watched him spear a few pieces of what looked like steak before placing them on my plate, along with wedges of potatoes, carrots and broccoli.

"Dare I ask if whatever meat that is came from the Dark Wood?" I asked.

"The Dark Wood?" he questioned me with a raised brow and the expression of distaste in his features. "No."

"That's a relief to know."

"Did you really imagine I could eat anything from the haunted forest?" he continued and shook his head, as if the very idea were completely inconceivable. "I am not a scavenger, Ms. Harper."

"In general, I make it my business not to be in yours," I quipped, even as I wondered if it was a good idea to provoke him.

He didn't act as if my comment offended him though. Instead, he sat back in his seat, placing his black, cloth napkin over his lap and faced me with a

120

seductive grin. "And I make it my business to be in yours," he purred with a practiced smile. Then he took a breath and said, "Bon appetit," before cutting a bite of the meat and tasting it.

My stomach immediately started to growl loudly and I could feel my cheeks heating up with embarrassment. I quickly cut some of the meat, hoping to sate my stomach and keep it from making my hunger so obvious.

"How is it?" Alaire asked.

"Delicious," I answered truthfully. "Tastes like steak," I finished and glanced up at him. "Which I hope it is."

"And if it is not?"

I shook my head. "Don't tell me. I don't want to know."

Alaire didn't reply as he speared a piece of potato. A few seconds later, a slow beat began emanating from the speakers that were hung in each corner of the room. It took me a second or two before I recognized the song as "Desire" by Meg Myers.

"Interesting taste in music," I said before looking at Alaire again. I took a bite of my carrot, which was perfectly cooked. "Did Boris cook this?" I asked, frowning because I couldn't imagine how that would be the case.

"Heavens no!" Alaire laughed and shook his head. "I employ a cook."

"So you do have help?" I asked, after swallowing a bite of broccoli.

"Of course I do," he responded.

"Well, I've just never seen any of your...attendees," I continued, sounding defensive.

"Most of them are not visible by the naked eye."

I nodded as I swallowed down another bite of steak. "That's smart of you—going the stealthy route."

"In general my invisible employees are my most valuable," he finished before his expression changed

121

and I supposed so would the topic. "As regards your observation that I have interesting musical tastes," he started and leaned back in his chair, considering me with an amused smile. "I must confess I quite like this song."

"I bet you do," I agreed, more than aware of the sexual nature of the lyrics. I liked it too, that is, before discovering Alaire did.

After taking another few bites of his dinner, Alaire pushed the plate away, even though there was still a piece of meat and a few carrots left. Then he leaned back against his chair, tipping it up until the legs straddled the air as he began rocking back and forth, never prying his gaze from mine. "I especially like the line where she says 'she wants to skin me with her tongue.'"

I laughed and shook my head before eating another bite of my steak, or what I hoped was steak. "Um, I don't think she's actually referring to you, Alaire."

"How do you know she isn't?" he inquired, the smirk on his mouth growing wider. He brought the legs of his chair back down to the ground and reached for the metal bell on the table, ringing it once.

"I guess I don't," I answered honestly, lifting my eyebrows to indicate he had me at an impasse. Silence ensued for a few seconds as I frantically searched for a new topic of conversation. It was no secret that Alaire made me uncomfortable. "Nice to know you get all the newest music in Hell."

"How many times have I corrected you about terming the Underground 'Hell'?" Alaire replied, sounding slightly put out before sighing dramatically. "And yet, you still continue to call it as such."

"If it walks like the devil, talks like the devil, looks like the devil," I started with a smile.

"Yes, yes," Alaire interrupted as he waved me away with his hand and appeared flustered. "As to your question, you should already be aware that whatever you enjoy on Earth, I can procure in the Underground as well." He cleared his throat and smiled at me again. "I hope you enjoyed your ride here?"

"Are you referring to the shade? Or the Tesla?"

"The Tesla," Alaire specified with a slight laugh.

"Yes, I did enjoy the ride," I answered honestly. "It's also very reassuring to know you're so conscientious about zero emissions and saving the environment." I faced him with an expression that suggested I was pleased with my comment.

Alaire didn't say anything right away as he studied me with unmasked curiosity. "I daresay I have not met a woman like you before."

"I daresay you'd be lying."

He continued to study me, a slight smile pulling on the ends of his lips. "You are an interesting woman, Ms. Harper."

"Not as interesting as the paintings on your wall," I rebutted, honing in on the one directly in front of me. It was the first time I'd paid attention to the subject matter of the wall art since walking into the room. Maybe Alaire and Boris were so overwhelming that I'd failed to notice anything else …

"Ah, Luis Royo."

"What?" I asked, ever so quaintly.

"The artist," Alaire informed me with a grin. "His name is Luis Royo. Have you heard of him? Or seen his work before?"

"No," I answered immediately. I pushed my chair away from the table, placing my napkin beside my plate as I stood up. Then I approached the painting, which hung on the wall directly in front of us.

"That one is my favorite," Alaire commented from behind me. "It is entitled, 'The Hand of Three Circles.'"

"Interesting," I replied as I studied the painting. I was surprised I hadn't noticed it earlier because it was nearly six feet tall and a good four feet wide. It depicted a blond woman with her hair in disarray. She had a chain around her neck and one of her wrists. Her other arm was out of view. She was sitting inside a circular opening in what looked like a wall of iron or some other metal. She didn't look unhappy, but neither did she appear to be especially content. Her white, transparent dress hung in shreds around her small frame, just enough of it left to barely cover her breasts, although her nipples were clearly visible through the fabric. The rest of the dress disappeared between her legs, one thigh obscuring the viewer from seeing anything he or she shouldn't. "Who's the guy in the distance?" I asked.

"Hades," Alaire answered.

"The King of the Underworld," I murmured. Hades was depicted just behind the beautiful woman and was holding the handle to the chains around her neck and her wrist. He appeared as a dark, shadowy figure with glowing white eyes and a face like a monster. His ears were pointy and long and his nose was thick. He was bald on top with long straggles of hair hanging down from the middle of his head. His ugliness was obviously in direct contrast with the beauty of the woman.

"It's an artistic representation of the story of Hades and Persephone," Alaire explained as I turned around to face him. I noticed his attention was fastened on the painting, and I glimpsed an expression of sheer admiration in his eyes. "Are you familiar with that tale?" he asked, resting his gaze on me.

"Remind me," I answered. Although I had heard the name Persephone often enough, I just couldn't remember all the specifics.

"Very well," Alaire replied with a smile. "As you quite astutely pointed out, Hades is the God of the Underworld. He happened to fall in love with Persephone, the daughter of Zeus. She was an innocent, virginal maiden. When Hades stumbled upon her frolicking in the fields, he decided he had to have her for himself."

"So? What did he do?" I asked moments later, growing irritated at myself for sounding so enraptured by his story.

"While Persephone was gathering flowers, Hades appeared in his chariot. It was drawn by four black horses with red, glowing eyes. Persephone, who was petrified, tried to flee from him, but Hades was an omnipotent God and much too powerful for the helpless girl. He simply grabbed her before stealing her innocence by raping her among the flowers."

"Jeez," I started but Alaire interrupted me.

"The Earth responded by opening up so Hades could drive his chariot into the dark chasm, while Persephone cried for help ... in vain of course."

"So Hades won then?" I asked, frowning at him angrily. "What a horrible story."

"If by 'won' you mean Persephone had to stay with him, then yes and no."

"Yes and no?" I repeated, trying not to sound so irritated, but there it was.

"Persephone became the Queen of the Underworld; although, every year, she escapes from Hades and returns to Earth, bringing springtime with her, or so the fable would lead us to believe." He was quiet for a few seconds. "Do you like the painting?"

Glancing back up at it, I studied it as though seeing it for the first time. Somehow, I managed to glean much more from the artwork now that I knew the story behind it. "I don't know," I answered honestly.

"As I commented earlier, it is my favorite," Alaire said as I stared at the painting, still not sure what to make of it. "I believe Persephone looks quite a bit like you."

"Me?" I replied before scoffing and shaking my head to let him know he was way off base. When I turned around to face him again, I noticed at least four more Luis Royo paintings in the room. "Are all of the paintings depictions of Greek mythology?"

"No, not all," Alaire replied with a secretive smile as he leaned back in his chair, and resumed his incessant rocking, back and forth. Finding the paintings easier to look at than Alaire, I honed in on the next one. It portrayed another blond woman with curly hair who wielded an enormous sword. The end of the sword was dripping with blood, which also appeared all over the bottom of the woman's white dress. Her breasts were clearly displayed as she held her hand up to her face, wearing an expression of pity. A hideous creature lay dead or dying beneath her. A few seconds later it dawned on me that her piteous expression was merely a façade since it was obvious she was the one who had dealt the death blow.

"What's the name of this one?" I asked.

"Immaculate."

"Why? What's the story behind it?"

Alaire shrugged. "According to Royo, Immaculate covers herself with her victim's blood. She's a demon hunter."

"Oh," I said before my gaze landed on the creature below her. The horns on its head, and its long, pointed teeth, combined with the talons at the ends of its fingertips and its horned wings, definitely resembled that of a demon.

"Did you notice the demon's erection?" Alaire inquired.

"What?" I hiccupped, feeling embarrassment going all the way down to my core. Forcing my attention back to the painting, I immediately spotted the enormous erection between the creature's legs and wondered how I'd missed it earlier.

"Ironic, isn't it?" Alaire asked.

126

"What?" I asked, the heat of my embarrassment still fanning across my cheeks. When I glanced back at Alaire, I found his attention unapologetically fixated on the painting. "What's ironic?"

"That Immaculate is represented as such a tiny, curvaceous and lovely woman; yet she is the one responsible for slaying the repugnant, dominant beast whose primary intention was to ravage her."

I didn't respond as I approached the next painting on the wall. It was of a woman with enormous breasts, which were obscured by her hair. She stood naked except for a black swath of cloth over the junction of her thighs. The fabric was held in place by a dreadful, winged, black creature that stood behind her. His other hand rested on her thigh, with her hand atop his. It was quite clear that the woman wanted the creature's hand on her—and that the two were involved, in some manner of speaking. "And this one?" I asked.

"The Chapel of Darkness," Alaire responded. "Perhaps a true 'Beauty and the Beast' story?"

I just nodded as I headed for the next painting. I wasn't at all sure about my true feelings in regard to any of the paintings. Dark and frightening, they were also erotic and perplexing. They were paintings that the onlooker couldn't simply look at. They made you think.

The next painting I saw depicted a brunette with one of her breasts exposed, and beads of sweat dripping down her body. "Royo seems to really like enormous breasts," I muttered.

Alaire chuckled. "You will find, my dear, that most males do."

I decided not to comment but chose, instead, to interpret the painting. From the brunette's slightly bent-over position, and her closed eyes, as well as the blissful expression on her face, it was obvious she was in the throes of passion. Behind her, an old, troll-like man with a long cape was having sex with her. He gripped her forcibly by her waist and spittle dripped from his open mouth. The two were surrounded by candles and smoke. It took me a second longer, but I made out the shape of a skull, rising up in the smoke emitted from myriad candles. The sign of the pentagram appeared on the skull's forehead.

"This is my least favorite," I said with blatant distaste as my gaze settled on the old, troll-like man behind the gorgeous woman.

"Furtive Signal," Alaire responded.

"What?" I asked, turning around to face him as I crossed my arms over my chest.

"The title of the painting," he replied with a secretive smile. "Though I prefer to call it 'The Devil's Due.'"

After deciding I'd seen enough dark, raunchy artwork for the evening, I returned to the table. "You have bizarre taste in art," I announced before sitting down.

"Perhaps," Alaire answered, "but of one thing I am certain: I have very good taste when it comes to white panties." He raised a brow and I realized with horror that I'd completely forgotten to hide my backside while viewing his paintings. "And of one thing I am certain, you have a lovely ass, my dear," he finished as he eyed me knowingly.

"Made entrance downward by a path uncouth"
– Dante's *Inferno*

NINE

"Do you care for dessert?" Alaire asked when the sliding door to the dining room opened again. A silver platter of cakes, cookies and pastries appeared in thin air, moving toward us as if being carried by invisible hands, which it probably was.

"No, thanks," I answered, anxious for our dinner to be over and done with as quickly as possible so I could get back to my apartment in Edinburgh. I felt more than sure that Bill was probably beside himself with worry by now. Actually, in truth, he was most likely in a drunken stupor after partying it up for nearly a week.

"No?" Alaire repeated as the tray of desserts arrived at his side. It set itself down on the table in front of him. He scanned the pastries quickly, as if he were counting them, his index finger itemizing each one. Then he glanced up at me. "I'm disappointed in your decision, Ms. Harper. I specifically asked that one of my less fleshy employees serve the dessert course since it appeared you were rather uncomfortable with Boris."

"Thanks," I grumbled, even though I was truly grateful for that. Ghosts were much less scary than Boris, or his equivalent.

Alaire just nodded before anxiously returning his attention to the platter of sweets set out before him. He reminded me of a little boy trying to decide which

129

candy to select from an assortment. He chose a wedge of what looked like chocolate cake by pointing at it. Then a serving knife, that was previously sitting lifelessly, rose up and slid beneath the piece of cake before depositing it on Alaire's plate. "Are you certain you'll not have anything?" he asked, looking at me with an arched brow.

"Yeah, I'm sure," I answered, taking a deep breath as I wondered what might await me at the end of our ... date?

No, this is definitely not a date! I mentally scolded myself. *This is a simple meeting with Alaire in order to keep you from getting an infraction. Don't you dare start thinking of it as a date!*

"I must admit, Ms. Harper," Alaire said, interrupting my internal diatribe as he forked a bite of his chocolate cake and brought it to his lips. He began making all sorts of sighs of pleasure and moans, which, I was more than sure, were intended to punish me for refusing dessert. Not that he was successful in his attempts ...

"You must admit what?" I asked, frowning because he was intentionally taking way too long in finishing his mouthful.

"I must admit that it surprises me to find," he started and then took another bite, taking four seconds to swallow it. "That you did not dig very deeply concerning a few of my remarks earlier. I," he interrupted himself with another bite of cake and another equally long pause before swallowing it. "I thought you would have exhibited more intrigue in our discussion."

"What are you talking about?" I grumbled, irritated when he speared another bite of chocolate cake on his fork.

"What I am talking about," he started again before pausing dramatically again as soon as the cake entered his mouth.

130

"Oh my God!" I rolled my eyes and groaned.

"What?" he asked, looking dumbfounded.

"You and that damn cake!" I replied in a loud voice. "Are you going to keep interrupting yourself by taking bites, which take you way longer to chew than it would take any other person?"

Alaire immediately started to chuckle as he picked up a coffee cup from the table in front of him. Previously, it had been empty. He brought the white ceramic mug to his lips and took a few sips of whatever now filled it. When he put it down again, I noticed it looked like tea. "I apologize if my table manners upset you in any way."

"They don't upset me," I snapped and then thought I should explain myself. "It's just irritating to try and have a conversation with someone who continually interrupts it by eating and taking an extra-long time to swallow!" Inhaling deeply, I realized I had more to say. "And your slurping sounds aren't exactly music to my ears either."

"Anything else?" he asked with a smile that indicated he wasn't offended.

"Nothing that occurs to me at the moment," I replied with a huff.

"My apologies," he said with another wide grin, pushing the remainder of the uneaten cake away from him as if it were suddenly abhorrent. Placing his napkin onto the table, he apparently meant to convey he was finished with his meal. I was more than sure the whole charade was devised to make me feel guilty.

"What was your question?" I prodded him, annoyed that I *did* feel a smattering of guilt.

"With regard to my announcement that the Royo painting titled 'Furtive Signal' should be titled 'The Devil's Due,' you had no comment," he said, eyeing me with interest. "Your reticence surprised me, as I felt most certain my observation should have provoked you in some way."

"Did I have to comment?" I asked, shrugging my shoulders and frowning at him. "Maybe I had nothing to say."

"Certainly, you did *not* have to comment," he started, lifting his eyebrows as he leaned back into his chair and regarded me curiously. "But as to you having nothing to say, I fail to see how that is even possible. You, Ms. Harper, strike me as a woman who must speak her mind. In fact, that particular attribute is the one that impresses me most." I thought that was debatable, given how many times he'd stolen glances at my bust but decided not to say as much.

"Thanks, I guess," I managed.

He sighed and cocked his head to the side, appearing as if he were in deep thought. "Yes, I must admit, I never imagined our conversation would have ended as abruptly as it did," he said as he glanced over at me again.

"We're back on the Royo discussion?" I asked, sounding less than enthusiastic.

"I thought you would have asked me why I supposed Royo's painting should be re-titled 'The Devil's Due,'" he continued, making it clear that he didn't care if I wasn't thrilled about this topic of conversation or not.

"I didn't ask you because I sensed I already knew the answer," I responded dryly, irritated with Alaire's smug arrogance. I'd never encountered any man who was as self-centered and self-impressed as he was; well, that is, if he even were a flesh and bone man ... Now that was a topic I found to be much more interesting.

"Fascinating," Alaire said as he started to bob back and forth in his chair, lifting the chair's front legs in the air again. I had half a mind to reach over while he was mid-rock and offer him a generous push. "And what did you suppose the answer was?"

132

I sighed and wondered when this tedious dinner would end, as well as what would happen to me from there. If Alaire granted my departure, and the Tesla drove me back to the gates of the Underground City, I'd still have to endure a four-day journey out of the Dark Wood, which I'd never survive without my sword. Unless Alaire were willing to lend me the next best thing in air travel, also known as the shade …

"The answer, Ms. Harper?" Alaire nudged me, reminding me that I still hadn't responded to his question.

I cleared my throat and frowned, irritated at having to contribute to his already overinflated sense of self. "Maybe, in some way, shape or form, you identify with each of the male characters in your Royo paintings, which is probably why you like them so much," I began. His eyes widened slightly in surprise as a smile seized his lips. "And as to the painting depicting the devil ravishing the brunette, as the Keeper of the Underground City, I'm sure you draw your own parallels between yourself and the devil."

"Perhaps," Alaire admitted with a slight nod, indicating there was no perhaps about it and I was dead on.

"So you figure the devil should have whatever he wants, just as you, no doubt, should possess whatever you want. Well, in your own mind anyway," I corrected myself, not wanting him to get any ideas where I was concerned. I cocked my head to the side as I further studied him. Judging from the wide smile on his face, and the way he kept bobbing up and down in his chair with excitement, I figured I was right on target.

"And in the case of that particular painting, what is the devil's due?" he quizzed me.

"The beautiful brunette, even if she is decidedly out of his league," I answered immediately. "But I imagine the devil's due must extend beyond sex with the brunette."

133

"Go on."

"I believe you meant it to encompass everything. That is, whatever the devil wants, he gets."

"And whatever I want, I get," he added, his eyes narrowing as he studied me. It was beyond obvious that he was directly applying his comment to me. That grim realization made my throat feel like it was shrinking.

"Or so you hope," I said as frankly as I could.

"You are quite astute, Ms. Harper." Allowing the front legs of the chair to rest on the ground again, he leaned forward, placing his elbows on his thighs as he studied me. "And what of the other paintings? How do you suppose those relate to me?"

"They don't relate to you," I corrected him, my eyebrows furrowing in obvious frustration. Alaire's ego knew no bounds!

"Well, in my own mind, then, how do they relate to me?" he rephrased the question, appearing as eager to discuss himself as a Pointer is anxious to retrieve a dead duck.

"In the example of the black, winged creature appearing behind the blond woman," I started.

"The Chapel of Darkness," Alaire interrupted.

"Right," I continued with little interest. "Anyway, the creature reveals his strength and his possession of the woman by covering her most vulnerable of places with his hand."

"Yes," Alaire said, hinting that I was off to a good start.

"So, again, even though the creature is hideous by anyone's measure, its ugliness is of little concern because it clearly possesses the beautiful woman in some fashion."

"In both instances, you distinguish between the male's ugliness and the woman's beauty?" he asked and I immediately knew where this topic was headed.

"I haven't pointed out anything that isn't already obvious. Royo chose to paint his characters that way."

"But regarding the paintings' associations with me, is it possible you find me as unattractive as the devil and the winged creature?" Leaning back into his chair, he crossed his long legs at the ankles, as if he were eager to show off his entire body to aid in my assessment of his obvious masculine beauty.

"Stop fishing for compliments, Alaire," I muttered as I shook my head and wondered how much more of him I could stomach.

"Fishing for compliments?" he repeated in a tone that said he could never even conceive of such a thing. "I'm not, my dear, I'm simply inquiring as to whether you find me physically attractive. You have never said though I have given you countless compliments."

There was no way in hell I would continue to feed his ego, the enormity of which already had no limits. "Maybe the association between the ugliness of Royo's male subjects and you is not so much skin deep."

"Ah, then does the hideous beast dwell inside me?"

"I would say so." I nodded, all the while wondering if I was taking this whole conversation too far. Maybe I should have just played it safe and fed Alaire the BS he wanted to hear from me. But I knew myself well enough to know that I could never do that, impending infraction or not.

Alaire's expression failed to suggest if he were offended or not. "And 'The Hand of Three Circles'?"

"Is that the Hades and Persephone one?" I asked, to which he nodded. "Then, that comparison is pretty obvious."

"Is it?" he scoffed as if it weren't apparent to him at all.

"Yes," I replied. "You probably have more in common with the God of the Underworld than you do with the devil." Taking a breath, I glanced around myself. "The Underground City strikes me as just another name for the Underworld."

"Perhaps," Alaire answered with a nod that admitted nothing. "And how does Persephone fit into your analogy?"

"I don't know," I answered honestly before an idea struck me. "Maybe she's the tie to the real world that you so desperately wish to return to."

Instantly, the smile fell from his face and I realized I'd struck a soft spot. The slight worry that his sudden ill humor might affect me adversely began to recede the longer he sat still and made no move to kill me or reward me with my first infraction.

"Why do you say that?" he asked after a protracted silence. I didn't answer right away because I had a feeling I was treading very deep water. "Well?" he persisted.

"Persephone represents a woman whom Hades could never fully possess, right?" I started.

"Yes," he responded automatically.

"Well, if Persephone is the Earth and you are Hades, then it goes to follow that you can't have the life you once did just as Hades can't wholly possess Persephone."

"Why not?"

"Didn't you just tell me she returns to Earth every year?"

"Yes," he said and then nodded. "So you believe Persephone is an analogy for Earth?"

"I guess so," I answered. I left out the fact that everything about the Underground City was a blatant rip-off of the earthly plane. From the Tesla, to the buildings, to the murals of clouds and blue sky in the lobby, everything strove to be a version of Earth, and one that paled miserably in comparison.

"Or perhaps it is simpler than that?" Alaire argued. "Perhaps Persephone is you?"

"How could she be me?" I asked while shaking my head. "I'm sure you owned those paintings before I was even a blip on your radar."

"True," he admitted, cocking his head to the side thoughtfully. "But perhaps Royo was merely channeling the future. It could be that the painting was simply a window of a future shared by you and me."

I didn't like the idea of sharing my future with Alaire. I also didn't know how to respond to his observation, so I chose to leave it alone and, instead, changed the subject. "So how does one become the Leader of the Underground City, anyway?"

Alaire shrugged. "I imagine in quite the same way as one assumes any government office."

"What? You're elected?" I asked with a facetious laugh that indicated I found his response ridiculous.

"In a manner of speaking, yes."

"So do all the inhabitants of the Underground City go to the polls on voting day?" I persisted, not concealing the flippancy in my tone.

"No, no, nothing like that," Alaire answered with a smile that indicated his amusement.

"Who makes the decision then?"

"Afterlife Enterprises."

"Jason Streethorn?" I asked, my mouth dropping open with surprise. It seemed everything led back to Afterlife Enterprises ...

"Not quite," Alaire replied with a laugh. "Jason Streethorn is not the highest ranking official in Afterlife Enterprises, my dear. He is merely a manager."

"Oh," I answered, not entirely sure why I assumed Jason was at the top of the totem pole. Of course, in my experience, he was the only person I'd dealt with in AE, so maybe it naturally followed that I believed him to be head honcho.

"The position of the Keeper of the Underground City is the most important job title in Afterlife Enterprises, second only to the CEO of AE, himself," Alaire continued.

"And the CEO of Afterlife Enterprises assigned you as the Keeper?" I asked.

Alaire nodded. "That's so." Then he studied me for a few seconds, a smirk still visible on his lips. "I am surprised your forest Yeti did not explain the politics of Afterlife Enterprises, himself."

"Tallis?" I asked. Since there really wasn't anyone else who could fit the mold of the "forest Yeti," it was a rhetorical question more than anything else. Alaire nodded as I sighed. "Tallis isn't exactly much of a talker."

"That he is not, but he certainly could have answered your questions considering the amount of time he's spent here." The way Alaire said the comment, I could tell he was just begging me to ask the obvious question of why Tallis had spent so much time in the Underground City. But that wasn't a topic I wanted to discuss with Alaire because I was more than certain Alaire would flavor his response with his own personal biases where Tallis was concerned.

"Hmm," I said, searching for another conversational outlet.

"I take it you and Black have yet to discuss his history here?" Alaire continued. Even though he carefully guarded his manner, feigning only slight interest, I knew better. Inside, he was clinging to the question he'd just asked, waiting with bated breath for my answer.

"Like I said, Tallis isn't much of a talker," I repeated, intending to keep Tallis's business just that, his own. I had a feeling that any information in Alaire's hands was a dangerous place for it to be.

"I am not one to offer advice, my dear," Alaire started as I immediately doubted the sincerity in his statement. "But Tallis Black's time spent here in the Underground City is a topic you might very well benefit from discussing with him. Perhaps your mountain man is not the saint you believe him to be."

"I never believed Tallis was a saint," I responded snidely, my heart suddenly feeling heavy as soon as I thought of the hulking Scot. Pushing thoughts of him out of my head, I faced Alaire again. "I know what sort of man Tallis is."

"Very well," Alaire said, nodding in a way that conveyed that he definitely didn't agree with my statement. But, apparently, he intended to leave it alone, all the same.

"So what sort of job credentials do you need in order to obtain the position of Keeper of the Underground?" I continued. I wanted to steer him away from the subject of Tallis in order to learn more about his role in the Underground City. I figured this information was probably good to know. "I imagine your warrior background must've helped you immensely?"

"Of course," Alaire said as he nodded. "But a violent background is merely the tip of the iceberg."

"What else did the job description demand?"

"The most important role for the Keeper of the Underground City is maintaining order in what would otherwise be total chaos."

"And how does one accomplish that?"

"Through fear, Ms. Harper," Alaire replied immediately. His eyes were as cold as stone when they settled on mine. I swallowed hard as any former confidence I possessed suddenly dwindled away to nothing.

"What do you mean?" I asked, my voice hesitant.

"Fear is the highest form of power. Do not let anyone ever convince you otherwise." He continued to stare at me as if he could see right through me. "A leader who inspires fear is a respected leader." He was quiet for a few seconds before he smiled. "Do I frighten *you*, Ms. Harper?"

I wasn't sure how to answer the question, but I dared not feign my bravado, as he would see right through it. "I don't know what to make of you, Alaire," I replied truthfully.

He chuckled softly. "You remain guarded with me," he said after a silence, which lasted the count of four heartbeats.

"Do you blame me?"

"Of course not. You are a smart woman and you trust your instincts," he answered. His eyes perused my face before falling down to my neck, then to my breasts, and ultimately, to my stomach. "Your instincts will never lead you astray."

"Stop looking at me like that."

"My apologies," he responded with a charming smile as his eyes found mine again. "As I imagine you can guess, my instincts demand that I take what is mine."

"I'm not yours," I announced, in a flat tone of voice. An undeniable sense of intimidation began washing over me in icy waves.

"No, not yet."

"Not ever."

"Never say never, my dear," he replied, his tone sounding more playful than it had only moments earlier. "Now, where were we with regard to Royo's paintings?" he said, suddenly changing the subject, and clapping his hands together excitedly. "Ah, yes, two down and two to go."

I swallowed, taking a deep breath before adjusting my mind to the change of topic. Truthfully, it relieved me when Alaire switched the course of our conversation. I'd been on edge at the mention of him feeling entitled to "take what was his." His comment hovered over me like a looming threat, the dread of it difficult to shake.

"The, uh," I started, steering my attention back to the subject of Royo's paintings and Alaire's assumption that they all had something to do with him. "The only painting which doesn't seem to fit the mold of the others is the one of the woman who slayed the demon," I announced. "I think you said she was called 'Immaculate'?" He merely nodded, so I continued. "I'm not really sure how you relate to it, but I must admit, I like it the best."

"Do you?" he asked with a smirk, some of his former candor evident again. "I am not surprised that you like it the best, Ms. Harper. It is the only example of the four that depicts a woman overpowering a man."

I nodded. "But it's really so much more than that. The woman slayed the demon, which, no doubt, symbolizes evil, so I think of it as good triumphing over bad."

"I am not certain Royo sees the world quite as black and white as you may believe."

I shrugged. "Well, regardless, the only good demon is a dead demon, as far as I'm concerned."

Alaire chuckled heartily before allowing the laugh to die when his eyes found mine again. "Perhaps you are Immaculate, herself, my dear?" he asked. "And I am the unfortunate demon whom you intend to slay with your sword?"

"I could only be so lucky," I grumbled but offered him a smile.

"Speaking of swords," Alaire started as he eyed me narrowly, his eyes piercing mine. "May I venture to assume you have misplaced yours?"

I swallowed so hard, I half wondered if I'd swallowed my tongue. I didn't respond at first, but cleared my throat while mentally grasping for the best reply.

"Do not fret, Ms. Harper," Alaire continued in an offhand manner. "I do not plan to extend our little dalliance any longer than was mutually agreed upon."

141

Relief washed over me before I remembered that I this was Alaire I was dealing with, so maybe I shouldn't have been so quick to trust him. "And we agreed to have dinner," I said, making damn sure we were on the same page.

"Yes, just dinner," Alaire concurred with a nod. "But I do hope you will delight me again sometime soon, as I have enjoyed your company immensely."

"We'll see," I answered, desperately hoping I'd never have to see him again, let alone have dinner with him.

Alaire was about to comment further, but the words were snatched right out of his mouth when it sounded like a hurricane suddenly formed right outside the dining room. I heard a roar, which I wasn't even certain was human, and moments later, saw the blade of an axe coming right through the wall beside the sliding door in the room. I heard myself scream as the axe crashed through the wall two more times.

Alaire threw his chair back and immediately stood up, alarm clearly etched on his face. I turned toward the room's entrance and observed the blade of the axe slicing through the wall again before leaving a hole the size of a small child. I heard the axe fall to the floor as, seconds later, two large hands appeared through the hole and ripped the rest of the drywall apart.

"Well, well," Alaire announced in a friendly tone, although his eyes appeared murderous. "It appears we have another dinner guest, my dear." He glanced at me briefly before returning his gaze to the unexpected *guest,* who was just pushing his way through the large hole in the wall. "What a shame I forgot to set a place for you."

If Alaire's gaze was murderous, Tallis's was even more so.

142

"A marsh it makes, which has the name of Styx"
– Dante's *Inferno*

TEN

"Ah am nae interested in conversation, Alaire,"
Tallis ground out, while standing a few feet from us
and shaking with obvious rage. He appeared to be
using every ounce of willpower to refrain from
launching himself at Alaire. He turned the intensity of
his gaze on me and his face turned a few brighter
shades of red once he perused my outfit. "Lily, coome
haire," he managed between gritted teeth.

I stood up, but Alaire immediately barricaded me
with his arm to keep me from walking away. He
cleared his throat, his eyes never leaving Tallis. "I, too,
am not interested in idle conversation with you,
Black." When he took a few steps toward the outraged
Scotsman, I couldn't help noticing how polar opposite
they were—Alaire, dressed in a crisp business suit
with coiffed hair and a clean-shaven face, and Tallis,
clad in a kilt, exposing his massive chest, with our
swords strapped to it, and a large animal pelt draped
across his shoulders. His hair was an inch or so longer
than I remembered, and his cheeks and jawline
showed week-old stubble.

"And as you are clearly crashing an event to
which you were not invited," Alaire continued, "I would
kindly appreciate it if you would turn right around and
crawl back through that fairly large hole you've just
put into my wall." Shaking his head, Alaire muttered

143

something about "employing bodyguards" in the
future.

"Lily!" Tallis yelled at me, letting it be known that
he wanted me by his side immediately. His eyes looked
like they might bulge right out of his head. I took a
tentative step toward him, but this time Alaire reached
out and grabbed hold of my upper arm in an obvious
attempt to keep me right where I was.

"We have not finished our discussion yet, my
dear," he said to me before facing Tallis again. "And,
therefore, this Neanderthal was just on his way out."
Alaire's lips were so tight, they nearly vanished into
his face.

Tallis's eyes were glued to my arm, where Alaire
held me immobile. "Release 'er," he demanded, the
midnight blue in his eyes quickly becoming absorbed
by inky blackness.

"Alaire," I started in a trembling voice. I could see
where this situation was headed and wanted no part
of it. "Let's call it a night." I tried to pull my arm free,
but Alaire's grip felt as tight as a tourniquet.

"No, Ms. Harper," Alaire replied in a louder tone,
his gaze never leaving Tallis. "You and I will continue
our evening as soon as this behemoth learns some
manners and fully understands that breaking and
entering will not be tolerated!"

I definitely couldn't concur with that. As soon as
Tallis bulldozed his way through the wall, I'd felt
nothing but relief because I knew I was safe as long as
Tallis was by my side. My former worries as to whether
or not Alaire would release me after dinner, and how I
could make it through the Dark Wood unarmed, were
no longer a concern to me. Now, the only
unpredictable factor went by the name of Alaire ...

"Fur the lest time," Tallis said in a frosty voice,
enough of a warning all on its own. "Oonhand 'er."

"Perhaps I should remind you, heathen, that you
cannot and will not talk to me in such a manner,"

144

Alaire seethed, his chest rising and falling noticeably. "There may have been a time when you could and did speak to me in such a way but that time is long past."

I was surprised and found myself wondering what the nature of their relationship was in the past, that Tallis had apparently ranked more highly than Alaire when it came to Underground City politics.

"Ah will speak tae ye however it pleases meh," Tallis spat out, his eyes glued to Alaire's hand where he held my arm.

"Does it bother you when I touch her, Black?" Alaire asked. He laughed, and his tone of voice suddenly sounded playful. But beneath his apparent levity was something not quite so humorous. Rather, it was more along the lines of acidic. He continued to grasp my arm as if it were his last lifeline. He walked toward me, but stopped when he stood directly behind me. I felt his other hand wrapping around my other arm.

"Let go of me, Alaire," I whispered. A rash of goose bumps broke out along my skin and I felt a shiver racing up my spine, but neither for good reasons. I didn't like being touched by Alaire. Every hair on my body was standing at attention and my heart felt like it was slamming against my ribs. I started to feel nauseous. Turning my head so I could see Alaire out of my peripheral vision, I attempted to defuse the situation. "You said you would let me go after our dinner was over," I managed before glancing at the table, and spotting the remainder of his uneaten cake. "And since we've finished dessert, clearly, our evening is at its end."

Alaire didn't respond so I tried to shake his hands free, but he clung to my arms like his hands were manacles. Making no motion to release me, he instead started to rub my arms up and down. "I thought you were a man of your word?" I whispered to him, my voice soft but angry.

145

"Did it ever occur to you, Black," Alaire suddenly piped up, obviously ignoring my comment, "that she enjoys my caresses?" I felt my mouth drop open in abhorrent shock because I'd never so much as even suggested such lies to him. Then he chuckled. "Her entire body is shivering, perhaps … with anticipation? Excitement? What would you call it, Ms. Harper?" He eyed me momentarily, but probably realizing what my response would be, didn't allow me to answer the question. "Exhilaration over the thrill of a *real* man's touch?"

"Enuff!" Tallis roared, pulling his sword from its sheath, and wielding it high above his head in a manner that indicated he was finished playing games.

"Please, Alaire, don't blow this out of proportion," I said in a forgiving tone of voice, hoping to talk some sense into him. "Just let me go and we'll discuss all of this later. I'm sure we can reach a compromise that doesn't have to end in violence."

But Alaire didn't spare me a glance. I could see from the corners of my eyes that his attention was riveted on Tallis. "I can feel her innocence flowing through her body, humming in her blood," he teased, making it more than obvious that he was deliberately seeking a reaction from Tallis. Moving one of his hands over my stomach, Alaire fanned his fingers across it. I felt myself instinctively shrinking away from him. Moments later, I was reminded of the Royo painting, the one with the naked, blond woman and the hideous, winged creature behind her with its hand covering her thigh possessively.

"If you're trying to impress me, Alaire, it isn't working," I said, changing tactics because he clearly couldn't have cared less about trying to keep the peace with Tallis. If anything, he was trying to goad Tallis, provoking the larger man to lose his cool. "Alaire," I repeated his name when he didn't answer me. He exhaled a breath onto my neck and leaned down until our heads were parallel, making a big motion of inhaling deeply. "The smell of naiveté and virtue is unparalleled, is it not, Black?" he asked Tallis before standing up again. "Heady and intoxicating. Finer than the most expensive perfume."

"Git yer filthy hands off 'er," Tallis growled, taking a step toward us. It was obvious, though, that he didn't intend to use his sword. He couldn't—not when Alaire was standing behind me, and, basically, making me serve as his shield.

"My filthy hands?" Alaire repeated with an acerbic laugh as he glanced down at his pristine hands, flexing his fingers, the nails of which appeared to be manicured. The laugh died and when he spoke again, his voice sounded almost surly. "What of *your* filthy hands?"

"Alaire, stop," I said in a loud voice as I tried to free myself again. Still gripping my waist, and none too gently, Alaire pulled me against him, pinning me in place.

"Tell me, Black, what part of her uncorrupted body have your filthy hands touched?" Alaire fumed. "And I don't, for one second, believe that you don't feel exactly the same unrelenting attraction to her as I do." Then he laughed again as he shrugged. "After all, you and I are cut from the same cloth, are we not, Tallis Black?"

"Ah am naethin' like ye," Tallis replied, his eyes smoldering. He continued to remain rooted in place though, as if unable to make a move.

"Nothing like me?" Alaire responded with a mirthless chuckle, his eyebrows lifting as if to parody his words. "Am I to understand that you believe we have *nothing* in common?"

"Naethin'," Tallis responded more fervently, his eyes begging Alaire to argue with him.

"Then you don't smell the purity on her skin whenever she happens to stand too close to you?"

147

Alaire inquired, the former flippancy now absent in his tone of voice. "Nor the scent of her youthful loveliness that makes you want to bury yourself as deeply as possible inside her?"

I could see sweat beading along Tallis's hairline, and I watched him swallowing hard for the third or fourth time as he fastened his gaze on Alaire. His shoulders became rigid and his hand was clenched around the handle of his blade so tightly, his knuckles turned white. His jaw clamped down and it looked as if his cheeks might cave in. Judging by Tallis's body language, it was suddenly apparent to me that whatever Alaire was saying must've been closer to the truth than Tallis preferred.

"You don't have to answer, bladesmith," Alaire continued as he buffed his nails against the collar of his shirt. He feigned interest in his fingernails for another few seconds before abandoning his artful show and returning his gaze to Tallis. "I already know the truth," he ground out. "I know there are times when you have to forcibly resist the urge to ravish her, to starve the whims of the demon that lives inside you. And I know there are times when you wish that demon could overwhelm you, and do the things that you, in good conscience, cannot do."

"Nae," Tallis replied, shaking his head. But the way in which he denied Alaire's words only pointed to the fact that he was having difficulty.

"Deep down, you often wonder if the desires of the creature are not the same as your own," Alaire continued, his tone condemning, accusing. "Unlike you, however, I already know the answer to that question." Alaire paused to take a breath and it suddenly dawned on me why he was so inexplicably drawn to the Royo paintings. Alaire was comprised of nothing but demonic ugliness. It cohabited inside a beautiful, yet very deceiving, shell. "Perhaps the only difference between the two of us is that I have

148

accepted the truth," Alaire persisted. "I understand that the demon and the man are one and the same, and neither can ever be divorced from the other."

"Nae," Tallis repeated, shaking his head, but I could see the inner battle playing out in his eyes.

Alaire interrupted him. "I know your struggles, Black. I understand how hard it is to realize you *are* the beast because, as you well know, we both share the same demons."

"What?" I asked incredulously. My stomach dropped all the way down to the floor. But Alaire ignored me, and Tallis wouldn't even look at me.

"So when you say we share nothing in common, you and I both know that is a blatant lie," Alaire finished, his voice wavering in what I presumed was unbridled anger. "It is almost as much of a falsehood as your pretending to be Ms. Harper's guardian and protector." He laughed mockingly then, as if the very idea of Tallis as my protector was a complete farce. "You and I both know you're simply moments away from forcing yourself on the very maiden you claim to protect."

"Nae," Tallis repeated, shaking his head more vehemently this time. But even though Tallis attempted to repudiate Alaire's words, I glimpsed the cold truth of what Alaire was saying in Tallis's haunted expression. It stung me all the way to my core.

It can't be true, I thought. *You know that Tallis isn't Donnchadh. You've seen him fight and subdue Donnchadh. Remember: Alaire is a self-proclaimed master of magic so all of this could be nothing more than Alaire's attempt to make Tallis doubt himself. None of this is actually true.*

"Tallis is not, and never will be, anything like you," I ground out in an angry voice as I pulled against Alaire's hold but he continued to pin me in place. "I

149

refuse to believe any of this for one minute." I glanced at Tallis then. "And neither should you."

"No?" Alaire asked, shaking his head like the joke was on me. I could feel his right hand, which was wrapped around my upper arm, moving across my collarbone. He pushed my head back until it rested against his chest and ran his index finger down the length of my neck. "Then you believe he is a good man, my dear? Is that it?"

"I know he's a good man," I answered honestly, my neck craned in an uncomfortable position. I didn't try to fight Alaire though, and I wasn't sure why. Maybe because he could've simply snapped me in two if he chose to. But that didn't mean I wouldn't assault him with words ... "And whatever parallels you insist on drawing between him and yourself ..." I lost my train of thought when Alaire's fingers traced the floral pattern of the lace just above my breasts.

"Whatever parallels I insist on drawing between him and myself?" Alaire repeated, his fingers coming dangerously close to my nipples.

"Don't touch me!" I seethed.

"This is atween ye an' meh, Alaire," Tallis stated angrily, his eyes plastered on Alaire's fingers as they danced above and around my breasts.

"I do apologize, bladesmith, if the lure to spar with you is less enticing than this pair of large and lovely breasts." He brought his head down again so it was parallel with mine. Then he dropped his gaze to my breasts just as he brushed the fingers of his left hand across my nipple and it hardened instantly. He cupped his hand then and allowed my breast to fill the cavity in his palm before he began palpating it.

"Get the hell away from me," I seethed and struggled against him but he kept me pinned in place.

"Come now, my dear," he started with another acerbic laugh. "You know you love every second of my touch."

"No," I demanded and shook my head, my gaze settling on Tallis who stood completely still, his eyes narrowed on Alaire's fingers where they continued to massage my breast.

"It is pointless denying it because both of your nipples are erect," Alaire continued. I could tell he was watching Tallis. "Perhaps I should touch you between your legs to get a final verdict?"

"Dinnae touch her!" Tallis boomed. "Leave Lily oot o' this! 'Tis 'atween ye an' meh."

Alaire lifted his head to face Tallis. "Very well, I shall leave the lovely Ms. Harper out of our discussion; even though doing so is rather ironic, considering she lies at the very crux of the matter." As soon as he finished his statement, he ran his fingers across my nipples again as I bucked beneath him. "There, there, my dear," he cooed into my ear.

"Ah'm warnin' ye, Alaire," Tallis answered as he hefted his sword high into the air.

"Very well, then," Alaire said with a counterfeit smile as he dropped his fingers from my breasts and allowed his hands to rest on my hips. "Where were we in our discussion?" he asked Tallis eagerly. "Ah, yes, we were comparing notes over the times when you must banish the images inside your head, images such as penetrating the very lady you claim to protect."

"That's enough!" I yelled.

Alaire shook his head and chuckled. "My apologies, my dear, but evidently, any discussion with your mountain man invariably involves you." He faced Tallis again with a frown, but when he spoke, he addressed me. "Perhaps you should seek another protector, my dear. I believe it is only a very short time before you will find yourself demanding protection from this one."

I finally found the usefulness in my hooker shoes and lifted one foot, bringing the stiletto heel down as

151

hard as I could on Alaire's toes. With a squeal of pain, he immediately released me to tend to his wounded foot. Tallis burst forward then, and pushed me out of his way. Tripping over my shoes, I fell against the wall. A stabbing pain in my left ankle made my heel collapse beneath me and I tumbled to the floor. Even though my ankle was throbbing like an SOB, I was more worried about what was going on between Tallis and Alaire. I flipped over and watched Tallis hoisting his sword high above his head, ready to bring it down over Alaire, who lay at his mercy on the ground in front of him.

"Tallis, no!" I screamed, but it was too late. In one fluid motion, Tallis buried the blade deeply into Alaire's stomach. The sound of the blade severing several of Alaire's ribs before penetrating the wood floor beneath him made me sick to my stomach. Alaire's eyes went wide with shock, but strangely enough, only seconds later, a smile danced across his lips.

Tallis didn't say anything as he wrapped his hands around the handle of his sword and stepped on Alaire's chest with his left foot in order to gain purchase before yanking his sword free. Crimson blood dripped off the end of Tallis's sword and spurted from the gaping wound in Alaire's stomach.

"Nicely … done," Alaire managed with a sardonic grin. His mouth instantly filled up with blood, which overflowed from his lips. When he started to cough and sputter, I had to look away.

"Ye will hae naethin' more tae do with Lily from thes point oan," Tallis instructed in a steely voice as he faced Alaire with unmasked hatred. Removing the animal pelt from his shoulders, he wiped off Alaire's blood from the tip of his sword before re-sheathing the sword on his chest. When he turned to face me, some of the anger dissipated from his features. "Are ye okay, lass?" he asked before fastening the pelt around his shoulders again.

I was so flabbergasted by what I'd just witnessed that I couldn't answer. I opened my mouth, but no words came out. Tallis approached me and leaned down to collect me in his arms. Standing up, he carried me to the doorway, pausing only to pick up his axe. I didn't say anything as I glanced back at Alaire. He was sitting up, even though he appeared half-dead with blood still spewing from his mouth.

"We will ... speak soon, Ms. Harper," he called out, mid-gurgle.

I didn't reply because I had no words. Instead, I wrapped my arms around Tallis's neck and enjoyed the comfort of his strong arms as he carried me out of the dining room. Taking deep breaths to calm my frantic heartbeat, I wondered what would happen once Afterlife Enterprises learned that Tallis had murdered the Keeper of the Underground City ... while on my watch.

"I don't understand what happened back there," I said as we started down the hall.

"Ah ran him frough wif mah blade," Tallis answered with a shrug, like killing Alaire was an everyday occurrence and one not worth discussing.

"I got that much," I replied with a frown. We approached the doorway to the bedroom I'd been occupying, and I said, "Stop here." Tallis slowed and bent down so I could reach the doorknob to open the door. Tallis then walked into the room and carefully deposited me on the bed before leaning his axe against the wall. He didn't say anything as he knelt down in front of me and removed the shoe from the foot that wasn't hurting.

"I saw you run him through with your blade," I persisted. "What I can't understand is how he managed to sit up and talk to me with blood pouring out of his mouth. Usually when you stab someone with a five-foot sword, they die."

"Alaire cannae die," Tallis answered matter-of-factly.

"He's immortal then?" I asked and Tallis nodded. "Just like you." Tallis nodded again before he started to remove my other shoe. "So why run him through with your sword in the first place?"

Tallis frowned. "Tae drive mah point home."

"No pun intended?" I asked with a slight smile.

Tallis didn't respond but attempted to pull my other shoe off, just as a sharp pain ricocheted up my leg. I gasped and pulled away from him as he released my foot. "I think I might have broken my ankle when you pushed me away from Alaire."

"Ah'm sorry, Besom," he started, shaking his head as if he were angry with himself.

"Don't be," I replied. He gingerly toyed with the clasp on my shoe before freeing the strap and delicately pulling it off my foot. "You were just trying to get him away from me. You had no other choice."

"Ah dinnae like tae cause ye pain, lass."

"I know, Tallis," I said with a big smile, genuinely happy to see him again.

Tallis flung both shoes into the corner of the room and lifted my wounded ankle, studying it from top to bottom. "Why are ye dressed like this?" he asked in a quiet voice, without bothering to lift his gaze to mine. Instead, he examined my foot more carefully.

"Alaire picked this horrible thing out for me."

"Ah could've guessed," he answered. His dour expression suggested he wasn't exactly happy with the news. "Boot why are ye wearin' it?"

I cleared my throat and wondered how best to answer his question. I could imagine how bad it looked that not only had I agreed to have dinner with Alaire, but I'd also agreed to look like a strumpet while doing

154

so. "Because I was afraid that it might upset him if I didn't wear it."

"Why would ye give ah bludy damn aboot upsettin' Alaire?" he asked with an irritated glance before returning his attention to my foot.

"I was worried that he might not let me leave once he saw that I'd forgotten to bring my sword with me." Then I pointed to my sword, which was still held in place across Tallis's chest. "But you already knew that part."

"Ye moost always keep yer sword oan ye at all times, lass," he ground out. "Ah dinnae know whit would've happened tae ye had Ah not shown oop."

"Neither do I," I agreed, gulping at the thought of what would have happened had I been left to the mercy of Alaire. "I won't forget my sword again though," I added with a sigh, still relieved that Tallis had come for me, which meant I was and would be okay. But that very subject raised some questions of its own. "How in the world were you able to get here so fast?" I asked as soon as it dawned on me that our timelines didn't agree.

"Fast?" Tallis asked and glanced up at me with an expression that said his trip hadn't been fast at all. "It took meh three days tae reach ye, Besom."

I frowned and shook my head, not understanding how that could possibly be true because I hadn't been with Alaire for more than a few hours. "That's impossible."

"Ah," Tallis said and then nodded as if he were making sense of the discrepancy. "Time doesnae pass as quickly in the Oonderground City as it does elsewhere."

"So what was three days to you felt like three hours to me?" I asked but then cocked my head to the side as soon as I remembered it had taken the shade and me a day to reach the gates of the Underground. "Well, a day and three hours?" I corrected myself.

"Och aye," Tallis responded as he began palpating my foot. He pressed from my toes up to my arch and then my heel. When he reached my ankle, he cupped it in his palm and carefully bent my foot one way, and then the other. "'Tis nae broken," he announced.

"That's a relief."

Tallis nodded as he stood up. He spotted my yoga pants and sports bra where I'd left them in front of the fireplace. He reached for both and handed them to me. "Ye moost dress quickly, lass," he started. "Once Alaire heals himself, he willnae be in ah very gud mood."

"Okay," I replied. Tallis walked across the room and closed the door, making no motion to leave or go into the hallway. Instead, he simply kept his back to me, tacitly letting me know he intended to stay in the room while I got dressed.

"You know I don't believe any of what Alaire said," I commented as I removed my fanny pack and placed it on the bed beside me. Pulling the lace bodysuit down to my waist, I yanked the makeshift tube top I'd created over my head. Then I slid my sports bra over my shoulders before repositioning my boobs comfortably, and fastened it in the back.

"Alaire said many things."

"I know, but I was talking about you being like him," I clarified. "I know what kind of man you are, Tallis, and you are nothing like Alaire."

Tallis was quiet for a few seconds. "Mayhap we arenae soo different as ye hae bin led tae believe," he said in a monotone.

"What do you mean?" I stood up on my good leg and pulled the lace bodysuit down before sitting on the bed to push the rest of it off. I left the panties on, figuring it was probably a good idea because who knew how good the mending job I'd done on my yoga pants was?

Tallis shrugged. "Some o' whit he said was true."

156

"What part was true?" I asked, pushing my legs through the pants. I carefully stood and tugged them up to my waist. "I'm decent," I announced. Tallis turned around and lumbered over to the bed where he picked up my socks and carefully slipped them on my feet.

"Some o' the things he said aboot the way Ah feel toward ye," he answered, although evasively. I figured he was referring to the more sexual things Alaire had said about Tallis being my protector, but feeling attracted to me at the same time.

"You know, it doesn't bother me if you're torn about your feelings for me," I said with a sigh. "And whatever ... feelings you may have about me, they don't make you similar to Alaire, or any other man, for that matter."

Tallis nodded as if to say he understood the point I was trying to make, but refused to look at me. Instead, he studied my sneakers more than necessary as he put them on my feet and tied the shoelaces. "It still bothers meh," he answered softly.

I nodded my understanding, figuring this was just another extension of the conversation we'd already had before the shade whisked me off to Alaire's. And it wasn't a conversation I wanted to revisit. I imagined Tallis probably felt the same way so I opted to change the subject. "What was Alaire talking about when he said you and he shared the same demons?"

"Alaire is possessed, jist as Ah am."

"Is that what makes him immortal?" I asked but he didn't say anything, only nodded. "Is Donnchadh a demon then?"

"Nae."

"Why did Alaire say you both have *demons* inside you?"

"Mayhap, Alaire is possessed by ah demon, boot Ah amnae. Donnchadh is an ancient warrior, lass. He isnae demon." He glanced around the room a couple of

times, as though he were looking for something. Then
he motioned for me to loop my arms around his neck.
He lifted me off the bed and deposited me in the chair.
Walking around the chair, he gripped it securely and
pulled it away from the bed another two feet or so.

"What are you doing?" I inquired curiously.

"Ye cannae walk wif yer foot in that condition," he
answered as he studied the poster bed quizzically
before retrieving his axe. He swung it at the base of
the post closest to him and the wood splintered into
pieces, flying this way and that. After two more
swings, the post dropped off the bed and Tallis picked
it up. Then he walked to the corner of the room where
he'd thrown my hooker shoes and selected one.
Gripping the heel, he tore it clean off and threw it on
top of the other shoe. Then he placed the heel-less
shoe on top of the bed post, rotating it until the post
fit inside the shoe snugly. Dropping the narrow end of
the post onto the floor, he placed the other end with
the shoe on it beneath his armpit, leaning on the
temporary crutch, and testing it to make sure it was
strong enough to hold his weight.

Content with his handiwork, he turned to my lace
bodysuit where it lay on the bed. He started twisting
the lace around itself until it looked like a rope. Then
he tied the shoe to the top of the post with the
bodysuit-rope before facing me with a smile.

"Nice work, MacGyver," I said with a laugh. Seeing
his frown, I realized he had no clue who I was talking
about. "Never mind," I hastily added as I stood up. He
supported my arm and assisted me with the makeshift
crutch. Once beneath my armpit, I leaned on it and
took a few steps forward, keeping my wounded foot
elevated. "It works pretty well," I admitted as Tallis
just nodded.

He started for the door and I followed him, when
Bill's phone, which was in my fanny pack, suddenly
vibrated. I paused and unzipped the pack, pulling the

158

phone out. When I flipped open the lid to read the text message, I felt my spirits instantly fall.

"Whit is it, Besom?" Tallis asked, apparently aware of my unease.

I inhaled deeply and glanced up at him. "It's AE," I started. "They've just texted me with my next mission." I exhaled as I considered the dangerous task ahead of me, as well as my present inability to walk.

"Where tae?"

"The Toy Store," I replied, thinking to myself that this toy store probably wouldn't be anything like Toys 'R' Us. Then I glanced down at myself and shook my head before facing Tallis again. "You know I'm in no shape to defend myself."

"Ah amnae worried," Tallis responded and shook his head as if to emphasize the point.

"You aren't worried?" I repeated and frowned at him to let him know I wasn't following.

"Aye," he answered. "We willnae have any trooble in the toy store."

"Down to the foot of the malign gray shores"
– Dante's *Inferno*

ELEVEN

Even though Tallis seemed to think otherwise, I had a feeling that the fourth level of the Underground City would be no less menacing than the first three I'd had the misfortune of visiting. The Toy Store, which was located on the fourth level, was entirely surrounded by the muddy river, Styx. In order to reach its gloomy shores, Tallis stole a small wooden barge, which had been abandoned on the shore on the far east side of the Underground City. The barge was maybe five feet wide and four feet long. Considering it was rotted in places, and altogether missing slats of wood in others, I wondered if the thing would even float in the dirty water of the Styx.

But float it did, and before I knew it, we were sailing down the gurgling current of the muddy river. At least, I hoped the murkiness of the river was from mud and not something more sinister. Even though the water didn't move very rapidly, the current was strong enough to keep us cruising at a good clip. The water was the color of coffee and the small wake, which trailed us, crested in a murky foam.

As we sailed along, Tallis kept the barge from ramming into the banks of the river by steering it with a long, wooden pole he'd found beside it. I sat in the front of the barge with my legs folded Indian-style while Tallis stood directly behind me. He didn't say much of anything, in true Tallis style. Not that I minded—it was enough of a relief just knowing the Scotsman was there.

The scenery around us didn't reveal much other than the hulled-out remains of long dead trees that met the bank of the river, and the dirt terrain below them. The moonlight reflected off the water, revealing nothing in the abysmal darkness beneath the current. I had to wonder what kind of horrible creatures lived deep within the waters of the Styx, if any.

Interestingly enough, as far as creatures were concerned, I still hadn't seen even one inhabitant of the Underground City since starting our adventure, but that was just as well. It wasn't as though I ever enjoyed hobnobbing with the nefarious creatures of the Underground.

"I didn't realize this place actually had natural land inside it," I commented to my mostly silent guide. "I was getting used to seeing nothing but city streets and nondescript buildings."

"Aye," Tallis agreed. "The Oonderground is mostly asphalt an' concrete. Boot the Toy Store an' its surroundin' land is original tae the old city, the one that existed afore Alaire rebuilt it."

"Alaire rebuilt the city?" I asked, unable to conceal my surprise. I'd only ever known the Underground City as it now appeared.

"Aye."

"Interesting," I replied, my eyebrows reaching for the dark night sky. "How long ago did Alaire take control of it?"

"Mayhap ah few hoondred years," Tallis answered. The sound of his makeshift oar when it parted the water was almost soothing.

"So he hasn't managed it for very long," I said, glancing back at Tallis. With his black kilt, the animal pelt over his shoulders and our swords strapped to his chest, he reminded me of some kind of warrior spirit, sent from Valhalla.

161

"Aye," Tallis answered before growing quiet again. As we continued down the Styx, a misty fog began to envelop us. The farther we sailed, the thicker the fog became, circling around us like thousands of ghosts. I started to wonder if the whitish vapor were something that should have caused us unease, but Tallis didn't seem to even notice it, so taking my cue from him, I didn't freak out. Instead, I just turned around and faced forward again, finding it difficult to see the horizon through the milky white haze that obscured it.

But my mind wasn't wholly focused on my surroundings. Instead, I kept thinking back to my dinner with Alaire and his observation that I should inquire with Tallis as to his history in the Underground City. "Tallis?" I said with a sigh, knowing he probably wouldn't like my prying.

"Aye?"

"When I was having dinner with Alaire," I started, but grew quiet once I noticed the sudden frown on Tallis's face. "Um, he uh, he made some comments about you spending quite a bit of time in the Underground City," I finished and hesitated because I knew Tallis was uncomfortable whenever discussing Alaire.

"Whit did he say?" Tallis asked. His tone of voice was curt, to the point of sounding almost abrasive.

"Actually nothing," I answered with a shrug, "and that's sort of the point." When Tallis's eyebrows furrowed, I figured I needed to explain. "He seemed surprised that I didn't know more about your history in this city, since you know it as well as you do. And, I guess, I was surprised that I didn't know more about it too, so I'm asking you now."

Tallis was quiet for a few seconds, the expression on his face revealing nothing. When he spoke, his voice was deep and monotone. "Ah dinnae like tae discooss mah backgroond."

"I know you don't," I admitted with a frustrated shrug. I'd had a feeling I'd come up against a wall as soon as I asked him the question. "But I was hoping you'd open up to me about your history here, just like you've opened up on other subjects regarding your past."

"Ah have buried that part o' mah past, lass, an' Ah will ne'er revisit it," he stated firmly, his jaw set in a stubborn hold.

"Okay, I didn't mean to upset you," I replied, sighing. The moonlight shone directly on him, revealing his narrowed eyes and stiff countenance. His jaw looked tight and the moonlight illuminated the uneven scar that bisected half his face. To me, the scar made him gloriously handsome. "I'm sorry if I brought up any bad memories," I said softly, my heart aching for him. It suddenly seemed horribly unfair that despite basically admitting our feelings for each other, we couldn't act on them.

"Ah amnae oopset, lass."

I was spared the chance to respond when I felt the barge bumping into something hard. When I faced forward, I could barely make out the bank of the river. I glanced back at Tallis, only to find him in the process of mooring the barge in the dense fog. I faced forward and gripped my makeshift crutch, not wanting it to fall into the river. At the sound of something in the water, I glanced to my right and noticed Tallis had jumped into the river and was now pulling the rest of the barge up onto the sandy ground.

"Dinnae lit the water tooch ye, lass," he reminded me. He laid the oar beside the barge and retrieved the crutch from me. I still didn't know why I couldn't let the water touch me, but figured the consequences probably wouldn't be good, so I left it at that.

"I remember," I answered as I held my hands out to him. He lifted me up and deposited me on the bank, a few feet up from where the river lapped at the dark

163

sand. Then he helped me secure the crutch beneath my armpit.

When I looked up again, I could see a large hill directly in front of us. At the top of the hill was a dilapidated, one-story, wooden structure that reminded me of the lean-tos along the river in the Pirates of the Caribbean ride at Disneyland. I was just waiting for two banjos to start dueling.

"Why did Alaire spare this section of the Underground City, but not any others?" I asked in a quiet voice. I wasn't sure if anyone or anything could hear us, but in general, it wasn't a good idea to announce your presence in the Underground.

"He made ah deal wif the owner o' the Toy Store," Tallis answered, pulling the animal pelt from around his shoulders and spreading it out on the barge. Why? I had no clue.

"The owner of the Toy Store?" I repeated quizzically. I thought it odd that there was someone, other than Alaire, who was in charge of a section of the Underground City. "I thought Alaire owned, er managed, all of the city?" I stared down at the pelt covering the barge again. "Why did you cover our raft with your fur?"

"It carries mah scent," he replied, as if that were explanation enough.

"So what if it carries your scent?"

"'Tis mah way o' guardin' the barge, lass," Tallis answered and sounded flustered. "Mah scent is ah warnin' ta others that the barge is olreddy spoken fer."

"Oh," I answered with a nod, before remembering the question I'd asked him earlier. "So going back to Alaire ... So he doesn't own or manage or whatever it is he does all of the Underground City?"

"Afterlife Enterprises owns the Oonderground," Tallis corrected me. He eyed the barge narrowly before looking up the hill at the shanty that stood looming over us.

164

"I know," I snapped, wanting to get to the point. The longer we stood around in the fog, the more nervous I became. "Alaire manages it, or whatever! You get what I'm trying to say ..."

"The owner o' the Toy Store has lived in the Oonderground City longer than anyone," Tallis answered. His crooked smile seemed to be in response to my frustration. "Alaire simply paid 'er the respect she was due."

"But she doesn't really *own* the Toy Store because AE does?" I asked, confused by his words.

"Jenny owns the Toy Store," Tallis reaffirmed as his eyes came to rest on the crutch beneath my arm.

"How is that possible?"

"Ye an' yer questions, Besom!" Tallis exclaimed with a huff.

"Well, if you would be clearer with your answers, I wouldn't have to ask so many!" I said, throwing my hands in the air with frustration.

Tallis didn't respond right away but offered me a quick smile before he faced the hill and looked back at me again, shaking his head. "Ye cannae walk oop this hill yerself," he announced. Then, without so much as a warning, he approached me, pushing the crutch out of my hand, and grabbed me around my waist. He hoisted me over his shoulder like I were a sack of gifts and he was Santa Claus, albeit a much less jolly one.

"Tallis!" I scolded him, or rather, his backside because that was exactly what I was facing.

"Ah'm hopin' all the bluid rushin' tae yer head will keep ye from askin' meh sae many bludy questions!" he answered with a deep chuckle as I swatted him on his butt.

"That's not nice."

"Och aye! An' neither are yer relentless questions!" Squatting down to pick up my crutch, he started to ascend the hill.

"Ugh," I grumbled, not exactly comfortable slung over Tallis's shoulder with Bill's phone jabbing into my stomach from inside my fanny pack.

"Whit now?"

"Bill's phone is jabbing me in the ribs," I grumbled.

Tallis chuckled and smacked me right across my butt.

"Ouch!" I yelled in mock offense. "What was that for?"

"In return fur ye smackin' mah arse."

"That wasn't a smack!" I argued with him, playing affronted. "That was a little tap compared to the number you just did on me!"

Tallis continued to chuckle. "Next time, hit harder."

"I'll remember that," I promised him and started grumbling while his continuing chuckle drowned out my complaints.

"Tae answer yer question, lass," Tallis began in an obvious attempt at a truce. "Jenny owns the Toy Store, boot she does agree tae work wif AE ... well, mostly ..." Then he chuckled again as if the idea of Jenny being in compliance with AE was amusing. I didn't know why but his apparent glee began to irritate me. "Boot Jenny is ah woman wif ah mind o' her own ..."

"She works with AE?" I repeated as we crested the hill and he set me down on my feet. "How?"

"She's in charge o' the fourth level o' the Oonderground whaur she keeps watch over the souls o' the wrathful."

He helped me reposition the crutch beneath my arm again as I faced the shanty and exhaled my pent-up anxiety before addressing Tallis. "You know, I'm going to slow us down; and I can't do much with my sword attached to your chest." I reminded him of the same point I'd made earlier—when I'd received Jason's text informing me about this mission.

166

"Ah amnae worried, lass," Tallis responded, echoing the same sentiment from the first time I'd brought up the subject. "This is the only section o' the Oonderground City where we willnae roon intae any trooble."

Taking a few tentative steps forward, I did my best to place most of my weight onto the crutch, which I found difficult. The bottom of it kept sinking into the soft, muddy soil. Surprisingly, after his statement that there was nothing to be concerned about, Tallis unsheathed his sword from around his chest and held it poised anyway. I figured it was just to be prepared rather than sorry ...

"Why won't we run into trouble here?" I asked before my foot rammed into something that went rolling. When I glanced down, I noticed it was the severed head of a baby doll. Its black hair was matted and there were water stains all over its face. The socket of one of its eyes was broken, which made it look like its eye was dripping onto its cheek. My heart instantly started to speed up as I sincerely hoped that Tallis was right in not expecting any trouble in the Toy Store.

"Jenny is an auld friend o' mine," Tallis answered. I stepped over another doll, this one with clumped, faded blond hair and bright blue eyes. Just like the doll head I'd kicked with my toes, this one was also filthy. Although its torso was still intact, it was missing an arm and one leg. The arm was resting on the ground directly beside the doll, but there was no sign of its leg.

I didn't respond to Tallis's admission that Jenny was an old friend. Instead, I just continued crutching forward, trying not to sink into the mud or trip over the various dismembered toys that littered the ground. A cool breeze blew around us, and the trees in the distance shook their leafless branches, sounding like rattling bones. The smell in the air was one of damp mustiness, not necessarily bad, but not good either.

We reached the front steps of the lean-to, which were constructed from some kind of ancient wood that was now rotting and broken in some areas. Regardless, Tallis started up the steps, so I followed. The wood creaked loudly underfoot, as if it were mere seconds away from simply collapsing.

The shack was surrounded by a three-foot railing. Most of the slats were missing and those that weren't were in clear disrepair. Sitting atop the railing, and leaning against one of the columns that flanked the staircase and held up the overhang, was a toy monkey. It wore red-and-white-striped overalls, which were ripped and falling apart. It held a cymbal in one of its hands, but the other cymbal was missing. Its face was dirty and stained, but its eyes were even more off-putting. Both pupils were painted black with rings of red around the white parts that made the toy look as if it were completely crazy.

We approached the front door of the shack, which was just as faded and worn as the walls and the staircase, and Tallis knocked on it. The paint on the house looked as if it were once white, but now the wood showed through in most places, while in others, the white paint was permanently stained with dirt and age. The front door hinted at shades of pink; but now it, too, was a much dirtier and run-down representation of its former self.

When the monkey suddenly slapped its hand into the cymbal, it made a high-pitched, tinny sound, and I heard myself utter a little cry before nearly jumping right out of my skin. The monkey's eyes started to spin, and the red lines around its pupils looked like they were meant to hypnotize the onlooker. Tallis glanced back at the offensive thing with a frown before he simply knocked it off the banister with the tip of his sword. It crashed into the dirt with another tinny sound from the cymbal.

When he faced forward again, the front door opened, and seemingly of its own accord. Tallis glanced back at me and nodded, tacitly indicating that it was safe to proceed forward. When we entered the room, I was surprised to find it completely empty, as in it was devoid of any furniture or ... toys. There were three doors in the room, but all were shut.

"For a toy store, it looks like your friend could use some inventory," I snickered to Tallis.

He smiled and I couldn't recall a time when he looked more striking. Smiles on Tallis were such rare occurrences, yet he looked absolutely beautiful whenever one happened to visit.

You have to stop thinking like that! I reprimanded myself. *You and Tallis are and only ever will be friends. He's already made that abundantly clear.*

"We hae yit tae enter the store, lass. This is merely the vestibule," he replied as I forced my sudden depression down, refusing to grant it power. Instead, I turned my attention to the paintings decorating the wall farthest from me. The four paintings were assembled right next to one another and were in a single word—odd.

The first one depicted a little girl who was maybe ten years old. She had platinum-blond hair that was cropped to her chin. Her skin was pasty white and her dark greenish-blue eyes were so large, they dwarfed her small face. She wore a birthday party-style hat on top of her head, but the placid expression on her face suggested she wasn't very happy. Her dress was black and white, which contrasted nicely next to the backdrop of green clouds behind her. In her hands, she held a marionette doll, but the doll's head was severed, a replica of the girl's birthday hat also atop the doll's head. The doll's body, which was clad only in pantaloons, lacked one arm, which lay beside it.

169

I couldn't help the dread that settled in my stomach after viewing the macabre painting. The next three pictures featured the same little girl with the same placid expression; and in each instance, she was represented in off-putting ways.

"A huge needle and shears hidden behind the skirts of her dress," I announced, looking back at Tallis with arched eyebrows to say I found the artwork distasteful. Tallis didn't respond so I simply started viewing the picture directly beside this one and continued my commentary. "A pink nurse's uniform, a pig and a bloody knife." Tallis didn't say anything, but shrugged as if to reply he hadn't been the one to choose the artwork, so why was I bothering him about it? "Somehow this one evokes a whole *Fatal Attraction* sort of vibe, doesn't it?" I asked him even though I figured he had no idea what I was talking about.

"Aye," he answered with a firm nod.

"You've seen *Fatal Attraction*?" I asked dubiously.

"Joost because Ah live in the Dark Wood doesnae mean Ah doonae have access tae the ootside world, lass."

"Wow," I answered as my eyebrows reached for the ceiling to show my surprise. I faced the wall again and shook my head. "Nice artwork. Not exactly warm and fuzzy," I scoffed before facing Tallis again, finding him infinitely more attractive than the paintings.

"Naethin' in the Oonderground City is, lass," Tallis answered. I eyed him, only to find him looking at me with a smirk and a drawn brow. As soon as I wondered what we were waiting for, or whom we were waiting on, one of the three wooden doors in the room opened, but there was no one on the other side. Tallis turned toward it and nodded at me to indicate that I should go ahead. I started forward, my heart lodged in my throat, and crossed the threshold into the next room, with Tallis just behind me.

This room was more along the lines of what one would find in a toy store. There were floor-to-ceiling shelves on all four walls and each shelf was overflowing with toys of every variety—from dolls to model airplanes to drum sets. The only problem was that all of the toys were broken, misshapen, or otherwise in disrepair. I felt like I'd just landed on the Island of Misfit Toys.

Although there were no windows to speak of, the wall farthest from me had a door, which I hoped would lead outside.

"Um," I started while whisking Bill's phone from my fanny pack. I needed to check Jason's text to see exactly where the soul that needed retrieval could be found. When I flipped open the phone, the "soul app" was already pulled up on the screen. It showed a red dot, which represented the lost soul. The red dot was superimposed onto a map that was a 3-D representation of each room inside the Toy Store. Looking up at the room around me and then down at the phone again, I said, "Um, it looks like the soul we need to retrieve isn't in here." Then I faced Tallis in confusion. "The way the phone is showing it, it looks like the soul is behind this room, and down a long corridor. Does that sound right?"

Tallis was spared the chance to answer because the door to the room opened, this time, revealing a young woman. She looked like what you'd find next to the definition of "dominatrix." Dressed in a black leather corset and matching black miniskirt, she wore black fishnet, thigh-high stockings that were held in place with garters. Her platform shoes were also black, although the backs of them were bright red. They had the highest heels I'd ever seen anyone wear—something bordering on eight or nine inches. Her hair, too, was black and straight, reaching down to her elbows. It was styled with longish layers and bangs that were cut straight across. She was very pretty with bright red lipstick, and her light brown eyes seemed to glow from within. She wore black gloves on both her hands and a small, black, top-hat fastener with a feather on the back of her head.

"What do you want?" she asked in an Eastern European accent. She faced me, and her eyes drilled into mine. I opened my mouth, but couldn't force the words out.

"We are haur tae see Jenny, Elizaveta," Tallis answered, striding up and standing behind me.

Apparently having failed to realize I wasn't alone, Elizaveta turned her attention to Tallis for the first time since walking into the room. Her eyes glassed over with the briefest indication of recognition, although she didn't smile.

"The bladesmith," she said in greeting as she allowed her gaze to drop from Tallis's face, to his impressive chest and farther still—down to his muscular thighs, which were halfway covered by his kilt. I couldn't help but notice that she stared at his crotch a little too long. Irritated, I cleared my throat, but Elizaveta didn't bother looking at me. Instead, she merely nodded to Tallis before she sashayed back through the door, her hips swaying in time with her gait. How she managed to walk in those heels was beyond me, but I had to admit I was impressed.

Looking back at Tallis only to find his gaze plastered on her ass, I frowned, but he just shrugged his immense shoulders and offered me an innocent expression. "Whit, lass?"

"Nice, Tallis, really nice," I grumbled and shook my head.

"Ah am boot ah man," he announced, his words settling inside of me like an anvil dropped from a fourth story. They were the same words I'd said to him when he'd lambasted himself for his sexual feelings for me. So it was okay for him to recognize his carnal feelings for Elizaveta but not for me? It was a paradox

172

that didn't sit well with me and one I had to abandon because I had more important things to think about, namely my survival …

I followed Elizaveta down the long corridor until we reached a door at the end of the hall. She opened the door and walked in, holding it for me as well as for Tallis. Well, it would probably be more fitting to say she held the door open for Tallis because as soon as he walked through it, she eyed his backside hungrily and then offered him a suggestive smile when he turned around to check on me. 'Course, for all I knew, maybe he was turning around to check on *her*.

Rolling my eyes, I took stock of my new surroundings. Even though we were inside the building, the Styx bisected the room, flowing through one wall and into the other. It was as if someone had deliberately built the structure around the river because the hardwood floors terminated at the sandy banks of the Styx. In the far corner of the room stood a large, golden throne, which was upholstered in red velvet. There were probably another five or more women who were dressed just like Elizaveta. They appeared to be making the rounds inside the room, and most of them were near the river. They all towered over me in their skyscraper shoes. All of them didn't fail to notice Tallis and a few of them smiled at him … suggestively. Others, who were bolder, sashayed right up to him and ran their hands across his chest. Tallis did nothing but stand there, smiling at each one in turn, while I felt like throwing up.

"Nice of you to warn me that the Toy Store is full of the horniest women I've ever seen in my entire life," I grumbled.

"Apologies, lass," Tallis answered with a wide grin. "Boot Ah dae recall informin' ye that we had naethin' tae fear here?"

"Looks like you need to be afraid of getting raped," I responded with a frown as a strikingly tall blond rubbed herself against him.

"'Tis ah fear Ah would gladly face, lass," he answered with a wink.

"Yeah, yeah," I responded and took another few steps inside the room, wanting to get a better picture of what the women were looking at in the river. As soon as I was close enough, I could see countless glowing souls submerged in the murky Styx. Most were stuck in the middle of the river, gurgling, and choking on the swampy water. Some attempted to crawl up the banks of the Styx, using others to pull themselves forward. But none managed to get very far because they would inevitably start biting and striking at one another, thusly falling back into the water again. And if they lingered too long on the banks of the river, one of the dominatrix women simply pushed them back into the river with the pointed toe of her outlandishly high shoes.

"Tallis Black, the only visitor I'm ever actually happy to see." I heard the soft, feminine voice and turned around to find a very attractive woman with long, wavy, black hair approaching us. Even though she was dressed similarly to the other women in the room, i.e., tight black leather pants and a bright red leather corset top, she didn't wear any shoes. Not that she needed any because she was so tall.

"JennyAnn," Tallis greeted her with a genuine, broad smile.

The woman walked right over to him and threw her arms around him, making sure to kiss him on both of his cheeks, as well as his mouth. When she pulled away from him, she ran her index finger down the line of his scar, leaning in to him to kiss the jagged edge that ended at his jawline. Then she whispered something in his ear to which I wasn't privy. He responded with a deep chuckle as he wrapped his arm

174

around her waist and pulled her close, giving her another hug.

I found myself in a sudden ill humor.

"You've come for your soul," Jenny announced, not sparing me so much as a backward glance. She was extremely tall for a woman, maybe five foot eleven if I had to guess, and looked like she must've been in her mid- to late-twenties. I had to imagine, though, in Underground City years, she was much older if it were true that she'd been a resident of the original city, that is, before Alaire rebuilt it. Her green eyes and black hair, made her unfortunately, strikingly pretty.

"Aye," Tallis agreed.

"I've missed you, bladesmith," she said, while running her hands down his chest.

"An' Ah ye, JennyAnn," Tallis responded, looking at her in such a way that told me these two had some sort of a past. Friends schmiends.

"I heard about the decision that Jason and Alaire made, regarding your absolution, and I think it's a horrible injustice and a travesty," she continued, expelling a pent-up breath.

"Aye," Tallis said again, but this time, his composure seemed to ratchet up a bit.

Then a smile broke out across her plump lips. "Of course, your absolution would have meant that I'd never see you again so I can't say I'm *that* terribly upset about it." She ran her hands across his pecs and then clung to one of his enormous biceps. "As it is, I hardly ever see you."

"Ahem," I cleared my throat, deciding to interrupt them before I found myself witnessing a live sex show. I hobbled forward, very aware that I was surrounded by the sexiest women I'd ever seen in my life, and, yet, here I was supporting myself on a poster-bed crutch, wearing a dirty sports bra and yoga pants with crude stitching up the front. Not to mention my fanny pack.

175

Never mind! I yelled at myself while I offered Jenny my most cheery smile, which I'm sure was fake as hell, but I couldn't say I cared. "Hi," I said as I politely extended my hand. "I'm Lily Harper."

Jenny took my hand, but didn't say anything to me. Instead, she glanced up at Tallis with a question in her eyes.

"Ah'm Lily's guardian," Tallis explained. "She is the one retrievin' the soul."

"Lucky girl to have such a guardian," Jenny replied as she offered me a wide smile that made her appear even prettier. Her beautiful features suggested she could have been Native American. "I'm Jenny Harrington, but my friends call me JennyAnn," she finished before winking at Tallis, and letting it be known she considered him a "friend."

"Pleased to meet you," I responded insincerely.

Jenny offered me a quick smile before facing Tallis again as her smile widened and her hands, yep, found his muscles again. Sheesh, this was going to get really old really fast. "How are the Grevels?" she cooed up at him.

"They're ah bludy nuisance, boot Ah havenae killed them … yet," Tallis answered with a secretive smile that appeared to be exclusively for Jenny.

"You know I would have kept them here if I could have," Jenny said apologetically before showing Tallis her pouty face. "You were my last hope."

"The Grevels are yours?" I interrupted, unable to mask the shock in my voice.

Jenny nodded. "Yes, they were mine, but unfortunately, they aren't very good at defending themselves. They were no match for the bigger creatures in the city, so they started to die off. That, and Alaire doesn't care much about endangered species, so I had to find them a new home." She turned to their new home and smiled up at him suggestively. I suddenly wished that instead of Jenny

176

we were dealing with Cerberus or Plutus or maybe even Pinhead, Jason, Freddy Krueger, Michael Meyers, Pennywise the clown, and Chucky and all at the same time ...

"Ah was happy tae help, Jenny," Tallis said warmly.

I was just about to comment when I heard loud voices coming from the room next door. They were swiftly followed by footsteps, and something I can only describe as a commotion. When the door opened, I watched four women, possibly Elizaveta's clones, rushing through the door with ... Bill in the middle of them?

"Babes, babes," he started, shaking his head and holding up his hands in a play of submission as he eyed each one of them. "Look, you're all fine as shit," he said, pointing at one of the women who was wearing glasses. "And because of you, I'm now considerin' myself a spectaphile, 'cause, girl, you got this naughty librarian, geek-freak thing goin' on." The women all started to grab him again, but he shook his head and took turns pushing them away. "I'm sorry, ladies, but Billy can't be your concubone. Not when my craydar's going balls out, which means you bitches gotta be cray-cray." Then he turned around, saw me and a huge smile took hold of his round face. "Nips!"

"People mud-besprent in that lagoon, all of them
naked and with angry look"
– Dante's *Inferno*

TWELVE

"Where the hell have you been?" Bill demanded of
me, rescinding his smile as a frown took its place. "I've
been so freakin' worried about you, I haven't even
been able ta put the moves on Delilah!"

"Where *is* Delilah?" I asked, suddenly worried that
she'd accompanied Bill and somehow gotten lost in the
shuffle of all the women in the Toy Store.

"She's back at our apartment," he answered
indifferently before throwing his pudgy hands on his
equally pudgy hips in an attempt to return to the
subject he was interested in, namely, yelling at me.
Meanwhile, the four women who'd accompanied him
into the room, continued to rub themselves all over
him, like cats in heat. One of them started kissing the
side of his face, but amazingly enough, Bill didn't
seem to notice. Instead, he continued to glare at me.
"Now you wanna tell me where the hell you've been?"

"I've been having dinner with Alaire; and before
that, I was tending to Tallis, just like I told you I
would," I replied curtly. Bill spared a glance at the
Scotsman, apparently not realizing until then that
Tallis was in attendance.

"Dude, I'm even a lil' bit happy to see you," Bill
said in a flat tone. He nodded briefly at Tallis who
nodded back at him, just as briefly. Bill then held out
his knuckles to the much larger man who, by this

178

time, knew how to speak Bill's language. The two of them butted their knuckles before a wide smile broke out across Bill's mouth. "'Kay, Yeti, we can be besticles again."

I figured that term had something to do with best friends and testicles, but being in no hurry to find out, I changed the subject. "How did *you* get here, Bill?"

"How did I get here?" he repeated quizzically. He dropped his head into his hand dramatically before facing one of the women who stood closest to him. "She wants to know how I got here." The woman simply nodded as if she, too, wanted nothing more than to hear his story. Bill faced me again as his smile dropped right off his face. "I'll tell you how I got here! I had to walk for four freakin' days through that evil, hate forest with those freakin,' crazy ass spiders an' those messed up trees. I didn't sleep for even like, an hour." He turned to the woman on his other side and further explained, "'Cause that forest is like, haunted an' shit." Then he cocked his head to the side as he studied her. "But you're, like, Elvira's sister so you prolly get off on all o' that scary Halloween crap." The woman just nodded at him blankly and I momentarily wondered if she spoke any English. "Anyways," Bill continued as he faced me again, "not only did I have ta travel through the scary-ass forest, but I had ta do it all by myself!" He shook his head like it was a huge tragedy, but I could tell he was proud of himself. And I wasn't about to ruin his buzz by reminding him that as an angel, nothing in the Dark Wood could have hurt him anyway.

"Thanks, Bill," I said with a warm smile.

Bill didn't appear to hear me, though, and continued to shake his head and sigh. Repeatedly. "I'm gonna have ta sleep with a nightlight on for, like, the rest of my life," he finished.

"I'm sorry to hear that," I started as more questions flooded my mind. "But how did you even

179

know where to find me in the first place?" I was perplexed and amazed that Bill had not only taken on such a huge task, but actually succeeded.

Bill ignored my question and put his arms around two of the women closest to him as he faced me again. "I swear, I'm so traumatized by the last five days that I can't even focus on my getting laid parade." I assumed that was just another term for his new band of friends who were still in the process of clinging to him, a shocker in and of itself. As a rule, Bill didn't have much luck attracting the opposite sex. Well, that was before his visit to the Toy Store.

"Bill, getting back to my question ..." I prodded.

"Yeah, yeah," he started and frowned at me. "I wanted to call you an' find out where the hells you were but then I remembered you had my phone. Soze I called Jason Skeletorhorn an' told him I lost my AE phone." Regular phones, aka phones not provided by Afterlife Enterprises, couldn't access other AE phones, so it made sense that Bill would have gone to Jason if only in an attempt to get an AE-issued phone. "So the dude actually FedExed me another phone, an' then texted me with our mission." He reached inside his pocket and produced what looked like an iPhone. "So now, I got me ah brand spankin' new smartie phone soze I can take snelfies!" He glanced at the woman to his right and elucidated. "That's when you take a picture of yourself usin' your phone while sneezin'."

"Oh!" she responded and then giggled as she buried her face in Bill's neck and proceeded to give him a hickey.

"You called Jason and got a new phone just so you could find out where I was and then you came all this way to get me?" I asked, tears welling up in my eyes because I actually found it hard to believe. Even though Bill drove me beyond crazy sometimes, he really, truly cared about me and at times like these, the point hit home.

180

"Does the Pope shit in the woods?" Bill replied, shaking his head like I was slow.

I figured the answer was yes. "Thanks, Bill," I said and smiled at him.

"'Course, sugar mounds, you know how much you mean to me," he responded with a smile before flinching. "Ouch, baby," he said to the woman who was still sucking on his neck, while looking at her from the corner of his eyes. "A little less suckin', baby." Then he glanced back at me and erupted into a fit of laughter. "Said no man ever!"

I just shook my head. "I'm still amazed to see you here. I thought for sure you were hungover somewhere."

"Well, don't get me wrong," he giggle-chuckled. "I had me plenty o' Russian mornings." With a shrug, he turned to the woman to his left, the one who wore glasses, and clarified. "That's when you wake up after a night of drinkin' nothin' but vodka." Then he faced me again. "But after I sobered up, I realized Nerdlet still wasn't home, and then shit got real, knows what I'm sayin'?"

"I can honestly say I've never come across an angel quite like you before," Jenny commented. She glanced over at Tallis, ostensibly seeking his opinion, but he just shrugged as if to say he didn't have an explanation for Bill. But then, no one did.

"Damn skippy, baby," Bill muttered as he looked Jenny up and down and then nodded to let it be known he found her attractive. When he looked at Tallis, he inclined his head. "Who's the super hot, super tall, slay mama?"

"The what mama?" Jenny asked with a laugh.

"Just means you're so good lookin', you're like, stabbin' my heart an' slayin' my eyes," Bill explained before inclining his head in the direction of the other women that surrounded him. I couldn't be sure, but it seemed like their number had actually increased by

181

one or two. "You wanna join us, baby?" he asked.
"There's plenty o' angel Billy to go around."

"Um," Jenny took a step closer to Tallis, and
answered "thanks, but I'm happy where I am."

I immediately cleared my throat, wanting nothing
more than to get this show on the road so we could get
the hell off Sexually Frustrated Island. "Maybe I need
to remind all of you," I interrupted while glaring up at
Tallis. He just smiled at me innocently, like he had no
control over what was happening. "... that we are here
specifically to retrieve a soul."

"Okay, bubble butt," Bill chortled, making no
motion to separate himself from his squadron of
women. "Get to it!"

I sighed, glancing down at his old flip-phone in my
hand, where I still clutched it tightly. I checked the
screen and immediately realized that the soul we were
meant to retrieve was directly in front of me. From the
location of the red dot on the map, it appeared as if it
had to be in the river. "It looks like the soul is in the
river," I announced before facing Bill and Tallis,
neither of whom appeared in the least bit interested.

Bill started humming "Sitting On the Dock of the
Bay" by Otis Redding, so I figured that was a hint that
I was on my own. That, and Tallis wasn't budging an
inch from Jenny's side. Irritated more than I cared to
admit over the whole *Tal-Jen* situation, I exhaled
loudly and started for the river. I kept checking Bill's
phone to make sure I was heading in the right
direction.

"Valeria, assist her," Jenny called out from behind
me. I heard the sound of heels clicking against the
hardwood floors, and before I knew it, "Valeria" was
standing beside me. She was dressed in a long, tight,
black leather skirt that looked like a mermaid's tail.
The dress was strapless and her enormous breasts
billowed over the top, looking like fleshy pillows. Her
hair was long, bright red, and parted down the middle,

182

and her almond-shaped eyes were the fiercest green I'd ever seen. She, too, wore outlandishly high heels.

She held out her hand like she wanted something from me. It took me a second or two to realize what she was after, and I offered her Bill's phone, thinking she wanted to know where the soul was located in the river. But she immediately shook her head.

"The vial," she said in the same accent as Elizaveta's.

"Oh," I answered before unzipping my fanny pack and handing her the clear, plastic vial that all Retrievers used to transport souls. Yanking the vial from my hand, she started toward the river, seemingly oblivious that her long, pointed heels were sinking into the mud bank. As soon as she met the water, though, her heels stopped sinking and it looked as if she were actually floating across the water. She kicked a few souls back into the river who were doing their best to climb out of it. How she failed to succumb to the laws of gravity by not sinking into the water, I had no idea, but it looked like she was walking on a sheet of glass.

She paused after reaching the center of the river and looked down at it, watching the waves of souls as they sputtered and choked with little interest. Seconds later, she bent over and plunged her hand into the water. When she pulled it back out, her hand was in the shape of a fist and completely dry. Not even so much as a single water droplet appeared on her skin. She rotated her hand so it was palm-side-up and opened it, revealing a glowing ball, which was the misplaced soul. Then she emptied the glowing soul into the plastic vial and capped the top of it. Turning to face me, she started walking back over the river again. As soon as she reached the muddy bank, her heels began sinking again, but she didn't seem to notice or care. With one last step, she reached the hardwood floors. She handed the vial, with the soul in it, to me.

"Thanks," I said with a hesitant smile. I unzipped my fanny pack and deposited the vial into it. Then I turned to face Bill, who was completely buried amidst the gaggle of women, kissing and feeling each of them up in turn. I shook my head and sighed as I turned to Tallis, not wanting him to get any ideas about Jenny.

"Got the soul which means we can go," I announced.

Jenny immediately plastered herself on Tallis as I wondered how difficult it was going to be to talk him into leaving and, more so, to pry all those women off Bill. I had no idea what it was about this island, but it seemed like all everyone on it (with the exception of me) could think about was sex! Maybe it was something in the water ...

"Now that we've helped you claim your soul," Jenny said, her attention riveted on Tallis, "I hope you both will appease my girls?" I figured she was referring to Tallis and Bill. At least, I *hoped* she was referring to Tallis and Bill. Yes, I was still inexperienced when it came to being with a man, but of one thing I was certain, I wasn't interested in being with a woman.

Jenny ran her hand down Tallis's chest, making it more than obvious that she included herself in her statement. I felt my stomach churn as Tallis's eyes found mine. He smiled, letting me know he was enjoying every second of my disquietude. I scowled at him.

"Mooch though Ah would love tae, Ah have tae git Lily back," he answered with a heartfelt, apologetic smile for Jenny. "As Ah am her guardian, she is mah main concern."

I could have thrown my arms around Tallis and kissed him with all of my being. But I didn't. Instead, I just stood there, leaning on my poster-bed crutch, glumly.

"Oh," Jenny answered with a pout as her shoulders fell. She glanced over at Bill who was basically being overpowered by the horde of women and currently lay sprawling on the floor with them. "Then I hope you'll at least leave the angel?"

Tallis looked at me and tilted his head as if he were asking me what I thought of Jenny's question. I sighed as I observed Bill and figured he was experiencing something that previously only existed in his dreams. Besides, I was pretty sure that he'd never find himself in this situation again, so I figured I'd throw him a proverbial bone. I nodded at Tallis to let him know I was fine with it.

"'Twill take oos some time tae ready the barge fur the three o' oos, lass," Tallis said, implying that we should head back outside, to the bank of the river. That was just as well because the last thing I wanted to do was hang around and watch Bill. Yuck-and-a-half.

"I'll walk you to the front," Jenny offered, taking Tallis's arm before they both started forward, leaving me to crutch my way behind them. I was so ticked off, I started muttering things under my breath, but limped forward all the same.

When we reached the front of Jenny's establishment, she held the door open for both Tallis and me which surprised me because I figured she'd forgotten all about me. Tallis walked through the door first, and once he was outside, appeared to scout out each direction to make sure the coast was clear for me.

"You're a very lucky girl to have the bladesmith as your guardian," Jenny whispered as I walked through the door. I glanced at her and noticed her attention still rested on Tallis, who was now on his way down the hill toward the river.

"Yes, I am," I answered, not really knowing what else to say.

"I don't know what the nature of your relationship is," she continued, not even sparing me a glance as she studied the handsome Scotsman. I took a step forward and she closed the door behind me. "But it's obvious you both have feelings for each other," she finished. "I could see it in the way you look at each other."

"Yes," I said; there was no point in denying it.

"The bladesmith is a stubborn, proud and difficult man," she persisted, her beautiful eyes finally coming to rest on me. "But he's a good one, no matter his history."

"I know," I answered. I was already well aware of everything she was telling me but I was still surprised to hear it coming from her mouth. Especially when only moments earlier, it had appeared as if she were putting the moves on my bladesmith. Maybe I'd misjudged Jenny?

"Just be patient with him," she ended the conversation with a quick, friendly smile. "He needs you as much as you need him."

I was so flabbergasted, I didn't know what to say. But I was spared the need to respond because Jenny simply walked away. She started down the front steps, evidently unconcerned that she wasn't wearing any shoes, while the decrepit, wooden steps looked like five thousand splinters just waiting to happen. Then she ran down the hill and joined Tallis at the bottom where he was busy inspecting the barge and the oar.

Taking the steps one at a time, I carefully navigated my way with my crutch. Once I reached the ground, I took another few steps hurriedly, not happy to find Tallis and Jenny were no longer in my line of vision. I had a feeling I needed to keep my eye on the beautiful brunette.

"What the hell?" I heard Jenny's voice just as I made my way to the crest of the hill. I stopped short, and my heart suddenly lodged in my throat. Jenny and Tallis were at the base of the hill, surrounded by … hideously ugly monsters.

The fierce things were about two feet high and three feet long. Although they looked as if they could have been bipedal, they moved nimbly using their hands and feet. They were completely hairless and their bodies were shaped of lean muscle. Their skin had a leathery appearance, which, in the moonlight, glowed a bright fuchsia-pink. Both their hands and feet terminated into long, pointed claws that looked as if they could do substantial damage. However, their faces were the most repugnant aspect of their bodies. Their mouths remained agape and featured enormous, protruding fangs, set like rows of shark teeth. They kept rearing up at one another, as well as at Tallis and Jenny, growling and turning up their wide snouts to show their undeniably impressive teeth. Their eyes glowed orange and yellow, but their pupils were mere slivers, just like cats' eyes.

"Go! Get out of here!" I heard Jenny yelling at them as she kicked out at one that ventured a little too close to her. She tried to shoo them back toward the river, but the creatures seemed hydrophobic and wouldn't go anywhere near it.

"Tallis?" I called out, not sure if he was going to come up the hill to help me back down it or what.

"Lily, stay whaur ye are!" Tallis roared up at me. He held up his hand to warn me not to take another step. I nodded as I retreated back under the overhang of the Toy Store's front porch, where I didn't expect to be spotted. From my new vantage point, I couldn't see much, so I crutched over to the other corner, where I could just make out the shock on Jenny's face.

"They shouldn't be here," she told Tallis, shaking her head as if she were at a loss. "It's not as though they could have crossed the river either. You know how much they hate water."

"We need tae focoos oan gettin' them back tae the city noo," Tallis replied, apparently more interested in the solution than the problem.

187

"Yes," Jenny said as she nodded. "Alaire is going to hear about this. He knows none of his creatures are allowed to touch foot on my island." Just as she finished her sentence, three of the hideous creatures ran right past her, growling and lashing out at each other. "This is bullshit!" she railed out, shaking her head in obvious anger. "He's in breach of our contract."

"And I apologize for that," Alaire announced as he appeared from around the corner of a long-dead tree and stood directly in front of them. He was dressed snappily in a two-piece, dark grey suit with a charcoal dress shirt. His hair was slicked back, and the moonlight made it appear even glossier. He looked, for all intents and purposes, sufficiently recovered from his encounter with Tallis, when he'd been impaled by the Scotsman's broadsword.

"What the hell is the meaning of this?" Jenny seethed at him, her hands fisting at her sides. I instantly got the feeling that Jenny and Alaire didn't see eye to eye.

"This, my dear Ms. Harrington, is a mere mistake," Alaire answered as one of the creatures ran across his path, in pursuit of another one. "An accident," Alaire finished in that highfalutin tone of his that made me want to smack him.

"I doubt that very much," Jenny hissed, throwing her hands on her hips. "How can Hanuush demons from the eighth level of the Underground make it to my island when they all detest water? There's nothing accidental about that at all!"

"I do not know what to tell you, my lovely neighbor," Alaire shrugged as he shook his head. "It is quite a mystery, is it not?" Then he faced Tallis and smiled broadly. "Ah, Black, so good to see you after the number you did on me earlier, not to mention how you destroyed my Armani suit."

"Why are ye haur, Alaire?" Tallis demanded as he crossed his arms against his chest and regarded Alaire with anger.

"I came to collect my demons," Alaire replied, raising his shoulders as if the answer were obvious. "As you can see, they are most certainly not welcome here."

"No, they aren't!" Jenny yelled at him.

But Alaire didn't spare a glance at Jenny. Instead, he studied Tallis for a few seconds before then looking to his right and his left, as if he were searching for something or someone. "I cannot help but wonder where our dear Ms. Harper has disappeared to?"

"Lily is nane o' yer concern," Tallis barked.

Alaire shook his head and glanced down at his shoes, which were sparkly clean in the moonlight. When he looked back up at Tallis, I could tell he was irritated. "I seem to remember a time when I wanted to make Ms. Harper my business, and you had no quarrel then."

My eyebrows drew together in puzzlement as I wondered what Alaire was talking about. "Ah dae have ah quarrel wif it noo," Tallis replied, crossing his arms over his chest and regarding Alaire with a scowl.

I wanted to make Ms. Harper my business and you had no quarrel then? Alaire's words filled my stomach like a large boulder.

"It bothers you now then, does it?" Alaire repeated before laughing and shaking his head. "It is such a shame when emotions enter the picture. They tarnish one's logic, do they not?"

"Alaire, I want these demons off my property right now," Jenny warned him. "Otherwise, I'm going to AE to file a complaint."

"Ms. Harrington," Alaire started, holding up his hands in a mockery of placating her.

"Don't 'Ms. Harrington' me!" she yelled at him. "You know you're in breach of our contract. This is my island and I don't want any of your city filth polluting it!"

"And here I thought you were an animal lover," Alaire said with a smug smile.

"If you want to take this to the next level, we can," Jenny spat back at him. "I'm not afraid to confront you."

"I am well aware of that, my dear!" Alaire laughed. "You are not afraid of anything! But, perhaps I should remind you that I am the Keeper of the Underground City ..."

"I don't give a damn if you're the CEO of Afterlife Enterprises, himself!" she interrupted him angrily. She took a few steps toward him before Tallis put his hand on her shoulder, apparently to calm her down. "It's okay, Tallis," she said as she turned to face him. Alaire's gaze immediately settled on Tallis's hand and his eyes narrowed.

"It seems I keep losing to you, Black," Alaire commented. He crossed his arms over his chest as Tallis shook his head as if to say he didn't follow. "I can't recall how many times I've attempted to woo Ms. Harrington into my bed," Alaire explained.

"More times than I can count," Jenny added with a deeply set frown.

"And yet, she has never once surrendered to me," Alaire finished. He tsked a few times and shook his head. "And now, Ms. Harper, it would seem, is following the same example." His eyebrows furrowed dramatically as if he couldn't make sense of it.

"That's because we both can see right through you and neither of us like what we see!" Jenny railed at him.

But Alaire didn't seem to notice. He continued to study Tallis. "And yet, both lovely ladies appear to be investing all their loyalty in you, Black, as if you don't share the same dreadful history that I do."

"Tallis Black is more of a man than you will ever be!" Jenny taunted him. "You are nothing but a preening, materialistic, egomaniac! This city hasn't been the same since you took control of it!"

"Don't get so excited, my dear," Alaire said, frowning at her. He sounded put out and waved her outburst away as if she were having a tantrum. "You know your excitement only further stimulates me."

"If you so much as lay a finger on me, I'll have AE down here in two seconds flat," she ground out. "And you really don't need any more trouble with AE, do you?"

"He willnae tooch ye while Ah am haur," Tallis promised her firmly.

"I would not touch her until the time she asks me to," Alaire said with a shrug of his broad shoulders. "After all, if nothing else, I am the quintessential gentleman."

"I will never want you," Jenny spat at him, shaking her head furiously. "Now take your demons and get the hell off my property."

"As you wish, my dear," Alaire said, without making any move to leave. He just stood there, rooted, as if someone had just pushed the pause button on him. Jenny regarded him suspiciously and just as I was going to face Tallis for his reaction, I heard the sounds of heavy breathing right beside my right ear. In slow motion, I turned to face the horrible rows of pointed teeth of one of the Hanuush demons. It stood barely a foot away from me. In shock, I let out a little cry and jumped back as the thing started growling. In my panic, I dropped my makeshift crutch and placed all my weight on both of my feet, the sudden pain in my ankle immediately crippling me.

"Lily!" Tallis called out, but I was too afraid to look at him, and too afraid to turn my back on the hideous creature who was now stalking me.

"Ah, so Ms. Harper is here, after all," Alaire said. I started to back up from my hiding place, keeping my eyes on the creature the entire time. "Do not run from it, Ms. Harper!" Alaire yelled.

I didn't run, because I couldn't. I just continued to limp away, toward the hill, wanting only to be as close to Tallis as possible.

"She's hurt?" I heard Alaire asking the others. Apparently, it didn't slip his notice that I was favoring one side.

"Don't let the demon see you limp!" Jenny called up to me. "They prey on the wounded!"

I felt the lump in my throat doubling in size. Dropping all my weight on both of my feet, I tried to ignore the stabbing pain in my ankle. I started down the hill backwards, with the creature only a foot or two from me. The aberration followed me, continuing to growl as it bared its rows of jagged teeth.

"Go away like a good little demon," I whispered softly, hoping it might like me better if I didn't seem to be a threat.

But it started growling louder, so I immediately shut my mouth and just focused on walking downhill backwards. That wasn't easy to do, especially with a bum ankle. When I felt my foot slip on the loose dirt, I quickly tried to correct it, but my center of balance was already off. I began to wobble, and before I knew it, I was falling backwards, down the hill. I hit the ground hard and then rolled twice before I dug my heels into the sandy earth and stopped myself. When I opened my eyes, all I could see were the jaws of the Hanuush demon as it pounced on me. In an automatic reflex, my hands immediately went up to shield my face as I turned my head away from the creature. I screamed as I felt the demon's teeth sink into my forearm. Pushing against the heavy creature, I tried to kick the thing off me, but it clamped down even harder on my arm. The pain was excruciating and sent waves of ache throughout the rest of my body.

I heard a grunt and then watched as Tallis lifted the horrid thing off me and threw it aside. The creature yelped when it landed against the ground. But moments later it stood up, shook its head and then trotted off into the darkness.

My heartbeat racing, I sat up and glanced down at my arm, only to find the skin shredded and blood pouring from the sizable holes from the demon's fangs. "Dinnae tooch the wound," Tallis instructed me as I glanced up at him and found Alaire and Jenny had joined him.

"It bit her," Jenny announced as she glanced over at Tallis, with a blank expression.

"We moost git her tae the barge noo," Tallis replied. He reached down to collect me in his arms. I eagerly looped my hands around his neck, the pain in my forearm morphing from an acute, localized agony into a long, drawn-out dull ache that affected my entire body, its tendrils of infernal pain reaching all the way to my head.

"You know that won't do any good," Alaire said. His tone of voice was level even as he studied me in a detached sort of way.

"Why won't it do any good?" I asked, my voice breathless and scared.

"Because you, my dear, have been bitten by a Hanuush demon," Alaire answered as if I could make sense of his statement.

"So what?" I asked.

"A Hanuush demon is quite like the Komodo dragon species you have in Indonesia," Alaire informed me while tapping his index finger on his cheek. "They bite their prey only once, and the toxicity of their venom creates rapid blood loss, while inhibiting blood coagulation, leading to paralysis and, eventually, death. At that time, the Hanuush demon returns to consume its victim."

"There's nothing that can be done once one of them bites you," Jenny added as she faced Tallis, the worry becoming etched in her features. "That's why it won't do you any good to take her out of here; but you already knew that, Tallis."

"Aye," Tallis answered, his lips tight as he studied me. I'd never seen fear in Tallis's eyes before, but I saw it clearly now. And seeing it made me realize the gravity of the situation I was now in.

Tallis thought I was going to die. I glimpsed as much in the midnight blue depths of his eyes.

"Tallis," I started, my voice breaking.

"Shhh, lass," he whispered, shaking his head to reassure me not to worry. "Ah willnae let anythin' happen tae ye."

"You can't do much of anything for her," Alaire told Tallis, shaking his head as he shrugged. "But of course, there is the anti-venom ..."

"Anti-venom?" I repeated. "How do I get that?"

"I've never heard of an antidote for the Hanuush demon's venom," Jenny pointed out, eyeing Alaire suspiciously.

"That just goes to show that you, my fair lady, should be more current on Underground City events," Alaire responded loftily. "I discovered an anti-venom only one month ago." Then he faced me and smiled broadly. "And luckily for you, Ms. Harper, the anti-venom is still in my office as we speak."

"Ye bludy bastard," Tallis seethed and I had a feeling if he hadn't been holding me, he would have lunged at Alaire.

Tallis's anger suddenly made sense to me. The whole situation suddenly made sense to me. Not only Alaire's unexpected appearance on Jenny's island, but also the mystery of how and why the Hanuush demons had randomly shown up ... There was nothing

194

random or happen-chance about it. It had all been orchestrated and planned.

"You son of a bitch," I shouted at Alaire. "You planned this entire thing!"

"Those are strong words for a woman who is well on her way to a most painful death," Alaire replied with a frown.

"If anythin' happens tae 'er," Tallis started, his chest rising and falling with his ire, "Ah will find ah way tae kill ye an' 'twill be moost unpleasant."

Alaire shook his head and frowned at Tallis. "Black, when will you get it through that thick skull of yours that you are powerless in this city now? Any former influence or authority you previously had is long gone and has been for some time now."

"Ye dinnae know whit Ah'm capable o'," Tallis responded stonily.

"Stop arguing!" Jenny screamed at them. "She needs that anti-venom, and she needs it now!"

"Ah, Ms. Harrington, always the voice of reason," Alaire said with a smile. Turning toward the bank of the river, he brought two fingers to his mouth and whistled loudly. Moments later, a small boat appeared at the bank, driven by no one. Alaire turned around and headed toward it, with all of the Hanuush demons following him like he was the Pied Piper. "The boat will be the fastest way for us to return to my office," Alaire explained to Tallis and me.

"Well, if I weren't convinced that Alaire planned this whole thing before, I am now," I said in a soft voice to Tallis as he carried me toward the boat which was maybe ten feet long. I watched as the Hanuush demons followed one another, single file, onto the boat before willingly entering a large cage that sat in the rear of the boat.

"Shh, lass," Tallis warned as he looked down at me and smiled consolingly. "Ye moost conserve yer energy."

"Am I going to die?" I asked, visions of one hundred years in Shade already haunting me.

"Nae, Besom," he answered, shaking his head ardently. "As long as thaur is breaf in mah body, Ah will make sure thaur is life in yers."

"They smote each other not alone with hands, But
with the head and with the breast and feet"
– Dante's *Inferno*

THIRTEEN

"Shit, nips, don't look so hot," Bill declared as
Alaire moored the boat in a small inlet of water with a
short wall on either side of it. There was a dock that
ran up to the street and a few poorly constructed
wooden boats moored to the dock. The lights from the
street lamps illuminated the city buildings in the
distance. Tallis stood up, causing the small boat to
rock from side to side.

"I don't feel so hot," I announced, my entire body
clammy with sweat as my heartbeat continued to race.
I was so fatigued, it was all I could do to keep my eyes
open.

"We're gonna take care of you, sugar mounds,
don't you worry," Bill said with a big, albeit uncertain,
smile. Although he meant to console me, his empty
words didn't do much for me. I was more than aware
that Bill had no idea what was happening to me or
what was going to happen to me. In that respect, he
and I were, unfortunately, on the same page.

I'd been in and out of consciousness since leaving
the Toy Store and I couldn't remember when Bill
rejoined our group after his escapades with Jenny's
girls. But I was glad to find him with us now—well, as
glad as I could be, considering it felt like my body was
burning from the inside out. Nausea churned my

197

stomach, and now it was all I could do not to throw up all over Tallis.

As far as I could tell, Jenny had remained on her island because I didn't see her now. But that was just as well because I could honestly admit I had my fill of watching her with Tallis. Not that I was jealous, but maybe a bit territorial ... Well, and maybe a bit jealous ...

"Hey, man," Bill started, addressing Alaire as he reached over and patted him on the back. "She's sweatin' a whole lot and she's, like, really white. Like dead-person white."

"That's because she's dying," Alaire replied succinctly. He jumped out of the boat and onto the dock that led up to the streets of the Underground City. Once he was on land, he extended his hands toward me as if he intended to take me from Tallis and lift me out of the boat.

But Tallis shook his head. "Ye willnae tooch 'er," he stated before nodding to Bill as the much smaller man approached us.

"Really, Black, will you give this hero business a break?" Alaire asked and then rolled his eyes dramatically.

Tallis didn't answer as he handed me off to Bill, bride-style. Bill nearly buckled under my weight, but somehow managed not to drop me. Meanwhile, Tallis hefted himself out of the boat and reached down to collect me back into his arms again.

"You and I are fighting for the same thing," Alaire said to Tallis and turned his head in my direction as if to say I was the thing that they were fighting for.

"Boot nae fur the same reasons," Tallis said while cinching his arms around me protectively. I closed my eyes, feeling like I was about to pass out again. When I felt someone caressing my hand, I opened them and found Bill hovering over me.

"Stay with us, baby girl," he whispered as his lower lip trembled. There were unshed tears glistening in his eyes. "Conan's gonna make sure nothin' happens to you, ain't that right, Tido?" Bill asked. Facing Tallis, Bill's eyes begged the Scotsman to make his words a reality.

"Aye," Tallis answered simply, but his expression revealed nothing.

I couldn't find the strength to formulate any words. A few seconds ticked by before I heard the sound of tires on the pavement. Tallis carried me to what I supposed was a car and Bill opened the rear door for us. Seeing the interior, I recognized the Tesla immediately. Tallis bent down and placed me in the back seat in a sitting position. I couldn't keep myself upright for long though, and eventually, my body slid down the leather seatback. My arms and legs began to tingle like I was being poked by thousands of tiny pins.

I heard the door beside me open and felt Tallis lifting me by my shoulders as he situated himself next to me. Moments later, he allowed me to fall back against him and settled the back of my head on his lap. Looking up at him, I searched his face for any clue as to what sort of condition I was in, but his expression remained unreadable. He glanced down at me and ran his hand over my forehead before his eyes left mine and he settled his gaze on something outside the car window. There was no slack in his jaw.

But I didn't really need to search Tallis's face for the answer to my question. I already knew I was dying. I could feel my body slowly shutting down. With every breath I took, my insides ached. Exhaustion had already claimed me and I wanted nothing more than to close my eyes and fall into the blackness that awaited me. But if I closed my eyes, I'd be giving up. I'd be giving up the fight and accepting death.

And I wasn't ready to die.

Alaire opened the driver's door of the Tesla and seated himself while Bill sat down in the front passenger seat. Alaire put the car in gear, stepped on the gas, and we were off.

Sweat continued to bead along my forehead as the temperature inside my body rose. It felt as if my blood was on fire, transporting itself through my entire body until all my organs were consumed by flames. I scrunched my eyes shut tightly as each wave of pain hit me. All the while, Tallis ran his fingers through my hair, but never said one word.

When our eyes met, he held my gaze only for a few seconds before turning to face the window again. I had no idea what was going through his mind.

The seconds continued to drip by and I wondered when we would reach our destination. With every second that passed, the fire inside of me burned more intensely and more painfully until the agony was too much for me to bear. With tears streaming down my face, I could taste blood. It took me a second or two to realize that the taste was coming from me biting down on my lips every time the searing pain overwhelmed me. I was faintly aware that Tallis was holding me, and every now and then, I thought I felt the pads of his thumbs mopping up my tears.

My eyelids suddenly felt very heavy. Even though my body was an incendiary of pain, the abrupt urge to close my eyes and be swallowed by the agonizing pain gripped me and wouldn't let go. Just as my eyelashes dusted the tops of my cheeks, my entire body started to shake as if an earthquake were erupting through me. My teeth rattled against each other and my vision grew blurry with each wave and spasm that shook me.

"T ... Tallis!" I managed to scream in a frightened voice as my eyes went wide. Then I lost all control and felt my eyes rolling back into my head before tremors shook me.

"Shhh, lass, joost ride it oot," Tallis whispered as he continued to run his hands through my hair and held me in place. "'Twill nae be mooch longer."

"Dude!" I heard Bill yell at Alaire. "Somethin's wrong with her! Why's she shakin' like that?"

"She's having a seizure," Alaire responded in a level tone, sounding almost annoyed. "The venom has poisoned her bloodstream and is now causing her nervous system to shut down."

"So drive faster!" Bill commanded. The Tesla squealed around the turns in the road. "How much longer 'til we reach your place?" Bill asked, alternately checking on me and facing Alaire.

"Mere seconds," Alaire answered and, true to his word, seconds later, the Tesla began slowing before coming to an abrupt halt. Alaire's office building loomed over us, but I wondered if we were too late. My entire body felt like it was quitting, giving up and preparing itself for a death that was inevitable.

"Just hold on, sweetcheeks, we're gonna have you right in no time!" Bill promised. He reached back and squeezed my arm consolingly. But his touch provided little reassurance because I couldn't feel it. I glanced down at my arm, trying to move my head so I could get a better view, but my head wouldn't budge. Starting to panic, I attempted to move my arm, but it, too, wouldn't respond.

"Ah willnae forget this, Alaire," Tallis ground out.

"I don't recall accusing you of having a poor memory," Alaire responded with a quick laugh.

Tallis didn't respond but glanced down at me as I continued to try to move my arms and legs. But, still nothing. I tried to ask Tallis what was wrong with me and why my body was failing to respond, but I couldn't. I opened my mouth to speak, but my tongue couldn't or wouldn't form the words. "Shh, lass," Tallis whispered as he ran his fingers down the side of my face. "Save yer energy. Yer fight is joost beginnin'."

If my fight is just beginning, there's no way I will survive. The thought utterly depressed me and I had to forcibly banish it into the deep recesses of my mind.

I could feel the cold air on my face as soon as Tallis opened the car door. He lifted my head as he stood up and gripped me beneath my arms to pull me out. Once I was outside of the car, Tallis hoisted me into his arms, but I still couldn't feel a thing aside from the chilly air on my face. The rest of my body was entirely numb.

The only good part about the numbness was the absence of the burning agony that previously beset me. Now there was no pain at all—actually, there was nothing at all. No throbbing, no heaviness, nothing. And I still didn't have any control over my appendages. It seemed like my body was on strike and wouldn't do anything my brain ordered it to.

"We must hurry. It doesn't look as if she has much time left," Alaire announced, pulling his attention from me and heading for the entry to his office building. Tallis darted up the curb behind him, nearly on his heels as they traversed the concrete that led to the double front doors of the building. Bill was directly behind us, his eyes wide with fear. I wasn't sure if his fear was due to my worsening condition or because we were in the Underground City. Probably both.

I heard the elevator doors in Alaire's lobby open with a *swoosh* as Tallis carried me inside. Alaire stood on my left and Bill on my right. Alaire pushed the button for the sixth floor and the elevator doors closed as it lurched up.

"I am willing to make you a deal, bladesmith," Alaire started, offering Tallis a cold and calculated smile.

But Tallis wouldn't look at him. Instead, he faced forward, his countenance growing more rigid. "The

202

time fur agreements atween oos is over," he answered in a monotone.

"Oh, I don't think so," Alaire rebutted with a gentle chuckle.

"Ah'm nae interested in makin' deals wif the likes o' ye," Tallis responded, glaring at Alaire with an angry look.

"Well, unfortunately for you," Alaire continued in his pompous tone, "you don't have a leg to stand on. *I* am the one in the position of power here, Black, because I'm the one with the antidote to the demon's bite."

"Whit are ye gettin' at, Alaire?" Tallis inquired, turning to face Alaire with the full impact of his hateful gaze.

"That's better," Alaire said with an impish smile. It was clear that Alaire relished being in a position of power. He enjoyed playing the puppet master to those around him. And knowing Tallis as well as I did, he could never be anyone's puppet. But now that Alaire had the rare position of advantage over Tallis, he intended to take full benefit from it. "If I agree to save Ms. Harper's life, you will agree to honor our original contract again."

Tallis immediately shook his head and his fierce eyes burned in his face. "Nae, Ah would sooner see 'er dead."

At his words, a shiver raced through me.

"Would you?" Alaire asked with another acerbic laugh.

"Well, I would sooner see her alive!" Bill snapped at Tallis. Frowning, he faced Alaire, although both men ignored him. "What are you talking about? Agreement?" he prattled on.

"I wonder what decision Ms. Harper would have you make on her behalf, Black? Would she choose to live or die?" Alaire asked. Eyeing me with mock sympathy, he added, "Perhaps we may never know," and shook his head with a sigh. "Such a shame, really."

"What the hell's he talking about, anyway?" Bill asked Tallis as he threw his hands on his hips. "What contract?"

"It was a simple agreement that existed between the bladesmith and me," Alaire began. The elevator dinged open and he stepped into the hallway, turning around again to hold the elevator door for the rest of us. His eyes fell on mine and he studied me for a few moments, as if trying to ascertain how much time I had left.

"What was the agreement?" Bill persisted as he followed Tallis into the hallway.

"Black was to bring Ms. Harper to me for a proper introduction," Alaire began, leading the way down the darkly lit hallway while Tallis and Bill followed.

"He did that!" Bill argued with Alaire, who started to shake his head. "Dude, I was there!" Bill insisted. "Nips lost her freakin' mind an' pulled her sword on you, remember?"

"Yes, yes, I remember it well," Alaire said, sounding irritated.

When Alaire reached the single door at the end of the hallway, he unlocked it and opened it wide for Tallis and Bill to enter. Tallis carried me inside, and I recognized Alaire's office immediately. I remembered the large, black desk that dominated the room, as well as the charcoal walls. Two black couches sat in front of Alaire's desk and beyond them was a large pool table. It, too, was painted and upholstered black.

"So, what's the big deal then?" Bill continued, throwing his hands into the air. "Conan kept his side of the deal, so that means you gotta give Lily the anti-venom."

"A mere introduction was not the extent of our agreement," Alaire clarified before turning to face Tallis. "Put her on the desk," he instructed. He went to

204

the far end of the room and unlocked a file cabinet with the same key he'd used to enter the room. Tallis laid me on top of the black lacquered desk and studied me for a moment or two, his face a blank canvas, as usual.

From my vantage point atop the desk, I saw three crystal chandeliers that hung in a row above the pool table. On the wall just below them were paintings of 1940s-style pinup girls. I was immediately reminded of the first time I'd visited this room, when I'd pulled my sword on Alaire. Knowing what I did about the Keeper of the Underground now, I half wished I'd run him through when I'd had the chance.

"Dude, you gotta give Lily the anti-venom," Bill anxiously repeated, his eyes pleading.

"I do not *have* to do anything," Alaire replied, sounding offended as he approached us again, a syringe in his hand.

"We dinnae hae time fer idle conversation," Tallis started.

"A good observation, Black," Alaire agreed. Gripping my arm, he held the needle just above it, pausing as he studied me. "Because your bladesmith is less than willing to negotiate a compromise regarding our expired agreement, I must have first your word that if I save your life, you will consent to owing me a favor," Alaire stipulated as he eyed me narrowly.

"What kind of favor?" Bill asked, shaking his head as though he didn't like where the conversation was going. In truth, I didn't like it any more than Bill, but I hated the idea of one hundred years in Shade even more …

"Never mind the nature of the favor," Alaire barked back at Bill before his eyes found mine again.

"Ah willnae allow Lily tae be indebted tae ye," Tallis stated as he stepped in between Alaire and me.

His eyes remained on the syringe Alaire still held in his hand.

"I don't recall including you in this conversation, Black," Alaire responded, sounding pissed off. Tallis took another step toward him, which served as a warning all its own. Alaire stood up straight, his posture going rigid as he hid the syringe behind his back. "Perhaps I should inform you, Black, that there is but one anti-venom prepared at this moment. Therefore, if I feel the need to destroy this one, our dear Ms. Harper's chances for survival will also be destroyed with it."

Tallis immediately stepped away from Alaire as the smaller man smiled in earnest. In response, Tallis glared at him and his chest rose and fell with his increased breathing.

"That's better," Alaire purred as he approached me again. "My dear, you have perhaps a few minutes left of your life. After that, the Hanuush demon who bit you will return for its dinner."

"Yes, she'll owe you a favor!" Bill said, his voice sounding panicked. "Just give her the freakin' anti-venom already! She'll agree to whatever you want!"

"Unfortunately, you cannot answer for her," Alaire informed Bill before turning to face Tallis. "I need a legally sound agreement between us. The two of you will serve as witnesses, and nothing more." Alaire brought his attention to me again and I glimpsed the iciness in his soul through the hollowness of his eyes. "Now, if you should agree to granting me this favor, Ms. Harper, all you need to do is simply blink twice. If you do not agree, blink once."

Of course, it wasn't a good idea to be indebted to Alaire for anything, but I wasn't ready to throw in the towel and accept death. I wasn't prepared to live for the next hundred years in Shade. And as my eyes settled on Tallis, I knew with a calm assuredness that I wasn't ready to never see him again.

206

I blinked once. Then I blinked twice.

"Very good," Alaire observed with a genuine smile. He picked up my arm and rotated it so my wrist was facing him. Just as he was about to stick me with the syringe, Tallis gripped his hand.

"Yer life depends oan hers," Tallis ground out, his eyes furious. "If she dies, ye die."

"Then I had better get to it," Alaire replied, his calm expression reflecting his lack of concern about Tallis's threat. He yanked his hand out of Tallis's grasp and faced me again. With a quick smile, he thrust the needle into my wrist. I didn't feel a thing. Alaire pushed down on the plunger until all of the red liquid inside spurted into me. Once emptied, Alaire pulled the needle out of my wrist and smiled smugly.

"Now what?" Bill demanded.

"Now we wait," Alaire answered as he walked back across the room and threw the syringe into the trash receptacle.

As far as I could tell, I didn't feel any different. My entire body remained numb and I was still exceedingly exhausted.

"So, Conan," Bill started as he nailed Tallis with an expression of curiosity mixed with suspicion. "What was Alaire talking about with that contract stuff? About you agreeing to bring Lily here to meet him or some shit?"

"Ah, that's right!" Alaire called out from the opposite side of the room while clapping his hands together jubilantly. "We never did finish our conversation on that topic, did we?"

"No, we didn't," Bill said, his eyes on Tallis. But Tallis didn't respond. He kept his gaze glued on me and acted as though he hadn't even heard Bill. He lifted my wrist and ran the pad of his thumb over my veins, apparently searching for my pulse.

"Shall I inform them of the terms of our agreement, or would you care to do the honors,

Black?" Alaire asked. His tone made it very clear how much he enjoyed tormenting Tallis. But Tallis didn't so much as turn his head to acknowledge Alaire. Instead, he continued tending to me, watching me with hawkish eyes.

All of a sudden I felt something—pins and needles in the bottoms of my feet as well as my fingers. Little by little, the feeling began to spread to the tops of my feet, traveling up my ankles to my calves, and up my fingers into my hands and wrists. I tried to wiggle my feet and my hands, but to no avail.

"Very well," Alaire continued. "I assume your silence means that you would like me to fill them in on the details." He cleared his throat and faced Bill. "When I requested an introduction to your lovely Ms. Harper, the bladesmith obliged. You see, we had previously agreed that he would bring Ms. Harper to me and ... leave her in my charge."

I wasn't sure if the feeling of shock that suddenly burst inside of me was due to Alaire's announcement that Tallis had consented to leave me with him, or if it was a mere byproduct of the anti-venom as it started to work. I wasn't allowed much time to ponder the subject, though, because Bill was already demanding the answers that I, myself, physically couldn't.

"What does that even mean?" he inquired, shaking his head with a scowl on his face. His furious gaze alternated from Alaire to Tallis and back to Alaire again. "Why the hell would you want Conan to *leave* Lily with you?"

"For reasons of my own," Alaire growled. His eyes warned Bill not to pry into his affairs.

Bill frowned at Alaire and faced Tallis, revealing ire in his features. "Is that true?"

It was the same question I ached to ask Tallis, myself, but was still unable to speak. Tallis didn't take his eyes from mine and I could feel the weight of his stare. Even before he could answer the question, I saw

208

the truth in his midnight blue eyes. It made me sick to my stomach.

"Perhaps you didn't hear the angel's question," Alaire continued, his voice taking on a humorous tone, as if he were thrilled to be leaking Tallis's secret. "Is everything I've just said true, Black? Have I stated the terms to our agreement accurately? Is there anything more you'd like to add?"

But Tallis refused to answer. He wouldn't even look at Alaire or Bill. He and I just stared at each other in silence.

"Well?" Bill prodded.

"Aye," Tallis finally admitted with a defeated tone. As soon as the word left his mouth, he broke eye contact with me and his gaze fell to the floor.

"What?" Bill asked, completely dumbfounded. He shook his head as though he couldn't believe what he was hearing. I could barely believe it myself. I never would have guessed, in a million years, that Tallis's treachery could run so deep.

As soon as Tallis admitted that everything Alaire said was true, I felt as if someone reached inside my chest and pulled my heart out, before crushing it right there in front of me.

Tallis turned to face Bill. "'Tis all true."

"What the fuck?" Bill railed, his voice shaking. It looked like he was mere seconds from crying. "You were going to just turn Lily over to the devil? Just like that?"

"No, he wasn't going to just turn her over to me," Alaire mocked Bill with a frown. "And as I've already clarified to our dear Ms. Harper, I am hardly the devil." He walked over to a black lacquered cabinet against the wall and retrieved a crystal tumbler. Then he reached inside the cabinet and produced a bottle of brandy. He held the bottle up to Bill and Tallis, offering them a drink, but neither noticed. With a shrug, he started pouring himself a glass. "The bladesmith does nothing without personal gain," Alaire continued. He brought the glass to his mouth and studied Tallis with a contented smile. "In return for bringing Ms. Harper to me, I was to grant him absolution, and free him from the torment he endured from the demon lodged inside him." He took a sip of the brandy before placing the glass back on his desk. "All of this was with the endorsement of Afterlife Enterprises, of course."

"But?" Bill interjected, taking turns at spearing Tallis and Alaire with his furious expression.

"But, as you may recall, the bladesmith did not keep his end of the bargain," Alaire continued as I remembered the moment as if it were yesterday. Bill, Tallis and I had been standing in Alaire's office and when Bill and I started to leave, I found Tallis in a heated, private discussion with Alaire. Although I hadn't been able to discern Tallis's words, Alaire had been loud with his responses.

"I'm afraid the answer was no, Bladesmith," he'd said with a shrug. "I did try to argue for you, but alas, Afterlife Enterprises is the ultimate decision-maker on these sorts of things, aren't they? Of course, there has been new ... activity that has quite changed the scope of our original agreement," Alaire had explained, his eyes firmly planted on me. "Perhaps I can pull a few strings if you can manage to pull some of your own."

But Tallis had shook his head immediately, letting it be known that he wouldn't help Alaire.

"You were going to trade me for salvation?" I suddenly blurted out. My voice was laced with torment, the kind that comes from a broken heart.

It seemed like forever before Tallis turned around to face me. When he did, his eyes hung heavy and it appeared to take every ounce of his willpower just to hold my gaze. "Aye," he answered in a voice that was rough, a voice that sounded as if he were choking on it.

"The souls of those whom anger overcame."
– Dante's *Inferno*

FOURTEEN

As the seconds ticked by, I could feel my vitality returning. Now I was able to inhale fully, whereas before, my breath came in short, quick gasps. The former sensation of pins and needles in my appendages slowly gave way to a slight burning sensation and then, a heavy pressure. Shortly afterwards, the pressure blanched and my skin felt extremely tender. The numbness that previously incapacitated my entire body faded, and pretty soon, I felt the cold hardness of Alaire's desk underneath me. When I attempted to wiggle my toes and my fingers, they quickly responded.

"You're a real piece of shit, you know that?" Bill seethed. He glared at Tallis, his eyes spitting fire. "Lily trusted you! And I trusted you!"

"Ah'm sorry," Tallis said in a small voice. It seemed to sap all of his strength just to look the much smaller man in the eyes.

Bill shook his head, throwing his hands on his hips. "You're lucky I'm not a violent dude, 'cause if I was, I'd come over there an' show ya zactly what I think o' you!"

Tallis didn't respond but simply stood there, allowing Bill to abuse him. For myself, I didn't know what to think. I was still astonished by Alaire's account of what had happened; and hearing Tallis's admission of the truth had my head spinning. That,

211

and a bad case of exhaustion had taken hold of my entire body and refused to let go.

Bill turned to face me, anger still contorting his features. Once his eyes met mine, though, a sad smile took hold of his lips. "Guess the joke was on us, Lils."

I didn't know what to say. I was still so stupefied over everything that had occurred in the last half hour that it seemed like my brain had abandoned me, refusing to allow me any more thoughts.

"Forgive me; I must apologize, but I had to reveal the truth regarding the bladesmith's true nature," Alaire told me. If he were doing his best to act disappointed, I knew him well enough by now to see he was secretly gloating over his victory.

"Ye would dae well tae keep yer mouth shoot," Tallis spat out at him, the resentment in his eyes almost palpable. His hands fisted at his sides and I could see him breathing in short spurts.

"Do not blame me for lifting the curtain up on your web of lies," Alaire responded.

"You have no right to say anything," I fumed at Alaire, finally finding my voice again. Rolling over, I pushed myself up on my elbows, and then my hands, panting with the exertion. Tallis and Bill immediately approached me, with worried countenances, but I waved them away, and focused fully on Alaire. The self-impressed smile plastered on his face made me ill. "Your agenda in all of this is plainly clear," I sputtered before taking a big breath and exhaling it. "You got exactly what you wanted."

Alaire chuckled, but didn't argue with any of my accusations. Calmly, he took another sip of his brandy and his eyebrows arched higher. "How nice to see our lovely Ms. Harper responding so well to the anti-venom."

I pushed all the way up from Alaire's desk until I was in a sitting position and no longer leaning on my hands. Feeling dizzy momentarily, I closed my eyes before the light-headedness passed. When I reopened them, I found Tallis and Bill both facing me. They looked anxious as if they were merely seconds away from assisting me.

"I'm fine," I grumbled, refusing to allow anyone in my personal space. What I needed most of all was some fresh air. Not that I would find any in the Underground City ... I took a few shallow breaths and waited for the fogginess to clear from my mind. Then I extended my hand and bent my fingers out in front of me, happy to see the color of my skin quickly returning to normal. I rotated my body on the desk and allowed my legs to drop off the edge while Tallis and Bill stood by. Both looked like they intended to scoop me up should the occasion arise.

"Lils, you need to take it easy, girl," Bill suggested as he took another tentative step toward me. "You were, like, dead about ten minutes ago, so don't go thinkin' you're gonna hop off dickhead's desk an' like, start doin' some twirls or shit."

"I'm fine, Bill," I managed between deep breaths. I extended my legs out before me, taking comfort in knowing that not only could I feel them, but I could control them as well. Bracing my hands on the corner of Alaire's desk, I jumped down and my knees instantly buckled as soon as my feet touched the floor. I gripped the desk before collapsing against it, somehow managing to find the strength to keep myself from falling onto the floor. Tallis was at my side instantly, wrapping his arms around me and lifting me against him.

"You get away from me!" I roared defensively, the emotional pain feeling like a tsunami as soon as he touched me. Gulping visibly, his eyes clouded with what looked like sincere regret, but he didn't release me.

"You heard her," Bill said in a cold tone. He forcibly removed Tallis's hands from around me and

213

pulled me into *his* arms. "You're never gonna ever touch her again," Bill scolded Tallis, his eyes burning with sadness and anger.

Wrapping my arms around Bill, I tried to take a few steps forward, but it was more than difficult because my legs kept wobbling like jelly. Strangely enough, it wasn't my ankle that caused my discomfort. Actually, I couldn't even feel my ankle anymore. It made me wonder if the anti-venom might've, somehow, healed the inflammation and damage from when I'd twisted it earlier.

"I want to get out of here, Bill," I whispered to my guardian angel. The weight of the world suddenly plopped down on my shoulders, or at least, it felt that way. Now I only wanted to get as far away from Alaire and the Underground City as possible. I longed for the comfort of my quaint and cozy apartment in Edinburgh. I couldn't wait to lick my wounds in grim isolation, somewhere safe that would allow me to deal with my broken heart in solitude.

"You got it, baby doll," Bill replied and we started for the double doors leading out of Alaire's office.

"And remember: I will call you for that 'favor' in due time," Alaire yelled out after us. His voice grated on my nerves like fingernails on a chalkboard.

Feeling utterly physically and mentally fatigued, I couldn't even think of an answer, but it turned out that I didn't have to. Bill answered for me when he lifted his left hand high above his head and flipped Alaire the bird.

Alaire only began chuckling, apparently not the least bit offended by Bill's gesture. "You will find the Tesla waiting for you outside my building," Alaire added. "Have a happy and safe trip home, Ms. Harper," he purred. Then he paused momentarily, probably to take another sip of his brandy. "And do strive to keep Ms. Harper alive during your journey through the Dark Wood, angel," he said to Bill before another acidic chuckle sounded through the room. "How ironic it would be if I saved her from the Hanuush demon's bite, only to lose her to one of the nefarious creatures in the haunted wood. Especially knowing that she still owes me a favor ..."

Bill responded by lifting his other hand high above his head and flipping Alaire the bird again. "You're gonna be just fine, baby doll," he whispered to me. "Billy's gonna make sure that nothin' in that evil forest gets you, 'kay?"

I nodded, although his words provided little to no consolation. When it came to fighting off scary things that went bump in the night, Bill wasn't exactly my best bet. But I knew who was ... At the sound of heavy footfalls, I turned and saw Tallis, just as he caught up with us. Walking past me, he opened one of the double doors for us and I hobbled through it. The longer I stood upright, the more I needed to lean on Bill, although I hated to admit it.

"Ye cannae hope tae survife the Dark Wood aloyn," Tallis stated. His eyes were focused on me and his lips were tight. He closed the door to Alaire's office behind us as I breathed a sigh of relief. Now, at least, I no longer had to deal with the Keeper of the Underground City. Well, that is, for the foreseeable future.

"Dude, I made it all the way here without you; soze, don't you worry, I can make it all the way back," Bill answered, without sparing a glance at the Scotsman. Instead, he kept his eyes glued to the elevator at the end of the hallway. "Keep goin', Nips, you can make it," Bill whispered to me softly.

"Ah amnae worried aboot ye," Tallis told Bill as his eyes narrowed on me and I realized he was making a good point. It would be impossible for Bill and me to survive our trek through the Dark Wood when I could barely even walk. What was even more readily apparent? Bill couldn't defend me if he were busy helping me take each painful step.

"We'll manage," Bill said. We made it to the elevator and Tallis pressed the button to call it.

"Lily is in nae shape tae travel through the woods," Tallis insisted. The elevator doors opened and Bill hauled me inside, propping me against the elevator wall while he shook his arm out. He was, apparently, already finding it difficult to transport me which didn't bode well for the four day trip that still awaited us. "She's woonded, an' as sooch, makes an easy target," Tallis explained.

Bill started to shake his head, but I interrupted. "He's right, Bill," I admitted before suddenly feeling extremely dizzy again. I closed my eyes until the discomfort passed and then opened them again, only to find Tallis and Bill studying me. "I'll only slow us down."

"I don't trust him," Bill said as he glanced at Tallis from the corners of his eyes. "He sold us out once before! Who's ta say he ain't gonna do it again?"

"Regardless o' yer failed troost in meh," Tallis interrupted, "lit meh lead ye tae safety. Efter that, Ah promise ye will ne'er see meh agin."

Hearing his words made my stomach churn and tears began filling my eyes. As ridiculous as it sounded, even now, I hated the idea of never seeing Tallis again. I was just as much in love with him as I had always been, despite his plan to sell me down the river.

Yes, but he didn't go through with it! I argued mentally. *Regardless of what his original intentions were, he chose not to hand you over to Alaire! That has to mean something!*

I shook my head, losing the strength of mind and body to continue arguing with myself.

You can't think about it now, Lily, I decided. *The only thing you should be focused on is healing.*

216

Especially if you're going to traverse the Dark Wood for the next four days, or however long it will take us, considering I can't travel as quickly now.

The elevator dinged and the doors opened when we reached the lobby floor. Bill wrapped one of my arms around his neck and hefted me against him again. As the seconds became minutes, I felt my energy waning and found it increasingly difficult to walk.

True to Alaire's word, we found the Tesla parked right outside of the building, its motor running silently. Tallis opened the glass doors and pulled his sword free from its scabbard across his chest. He checked both directions before turning back to Bill with a nod to let him know the coast was clear. Bill started hauling me forward, his respiration increasing as sweat began to trickle from his brow.

Tallis opened up the rear door of the Tesla and Bill crouched down, helping me into the seat. I collapsed into the warm leather, incredibly relieved that my legs didn't have to support me any longer. Bill closed my door and ran around the car to open the other door before taking a seat beside me. "How ya holdin' up?" he asked as he patted my shoulder.

"I'm okay," I replied, watching Tallis sit down in the front passenger side. Once he closed his door, the driverless Tesla smoothly pulled out onto the street. I noticed a few of the Watchers as they patrolled the city streets, each of them paying special attention to us and, no doubt, reporting back to Alaire.

It was maybe five minutes before the Tesla pulled up to the city gates and parked. Tallis opened his door first. He got out without waiting for Bill and immediately opened mine. When Bill glanced over at him curiously, Tallis shook his head. "She needs tae be carried an' ye arenae able tae soopport 'er weight."

Bill appeared ready to argue, but apparently realizing Tallis was right, slowly sighed with a quick

217

nod. He opened his car door and hurried around the back of the Tesla to join us at the gates of the Underground City. The Tesla silently pulled into the street again, disappearing from view only moments later.

Even though I hated to admit it, I was much more comfortable in Tallis's arms. I rested my head against his broad chest as he approached the gates, which opened automatically. We walked through them, none of us saying anything.

As soon as we were fully ensconced in the Dark Wood, and far enough away from the Underground City to where I could no longer see it, I exhaled a sigh of relief. It was a silly reaction, really, because we'd simply leapt out of the frying pan and into the fire. However, being away from Alaire provided consolation in and of itself.

"Ye should rest now, lass," Tallis said in a soft voice, looking down at me while I looked up at him. "Yer body needs tae heal an' the only way 'twill be able tae is if ye sleep."

I didn't reply as I settled my head back against his chest. Closing my eyes, I wished that things between us could have been drastically different.

***

We'd been traveling through the Dark Wood for two days and two nights. The time pretty much passed in a blur because I spent most of it sleeping. True to Tallis's observation, my body needed a lot more rest to recuperate.

"We will stop haur fer the night," Tallis announced when we approached an open clearing in the forest of dead trees. It was, maybe, the fifth sentence he'd said since embarking on this trip, although Bill and I weren't talking much either. A new, but definite, undercurrent of suspicion now colored any

218

interactions Bill and I had with Tallis, an undercurrent of suspicion which had never existed before. Every time I thought about it, the boulder in the pit of my stomach roiled.

Tallis unstrapped both his and my swords from around his chest, and leaned them against a tree trunk that stood nearby.

"It's your turn to be on watch," Bill told Tallis before going over to the hulled-out remains of a long dead tree. He leaned against it, scratching his back on the rough trunk a few times. "You good, nips?" he called over to me.

"Yeah, I'm fine," I answered as I sat up on the makeshift platform Tallis had built for me. Dragging the contraption with me on top of it for the last couple of days, I could only imagine how sore his arms must have been.

Because Tallis and Bill both needed to keep their hands free for protective purposes, neither one could carry me. So, Tallis, always the innovator, had built a platform for me to lie on. In order to build the platform, he'd simply collected some branches from the forest floor and tied them together, using the remarkably strong intestine that came from some unfortunate creature which happened to cross his path. Once he'd built the platform, Tallis topped it with the animal pelt he wore around his shoulders to make sure the branches wouldn't give me any splinters.

"Hey, Conan, I could use some grub," Bill announced before collapsing at the base of the tree. He rolled into a fetal position as he closed his eyes.

I looked up when Tallis approached me and couldn't help but notice that he wouldn't look me in the eyes. He didn't say anything either but just bent down in order to lift me up from the platform. Ignoring Bill, he gently carried me to a tree next to Bill's and leaned me against the base of it. Then he went back and retrieved his pelt from the platform, which he then laid out in front of me. I pulled myself on top of it.

The sound of heavy snoring from Bill's direction made it pretty clear the angel was fast asleep. Hearing Bill's noisy slumber, Tallis glanced over at him from where he knelt in front of the platform, busily checking the intestinal bindings. It looked as though he was making sure they were still intact and strong.

"Are ye hoongry, lass?" he asked, after he caught me looking at him.

"A little," I answered. I was finally feeling surprisingly energetic and somewhat good, considering only a couple of days earlier, I was on my death bed.

Tallis only nodded at me before standing up and reaching for his sword. He started forward and soon disappeared into the dark forest that surrounded us. Barely five minutes later, he returned. His arms were full of dead tree branches, which he dropped a few feet from Bill and me. I watched him place each branch into a pile, tucking a few handfuls of old tree moss into the open crevices of the pyramid of branches. Removing a lighter from the sporran around his waist, he set the moss on fire, which instantly ignited the branches.

"So ... when did you make that agreement with Alaire?" I asked, finally feeling strong enough to deal with the subject of Tallis's betrayal so I could better understand it.

Tallis didn't respond right away. He continued to kneel next to the fire, holding his hands over it in an attempt to warm them. "Efter our first trip intae the Oonderground City," he replied finally, his voice soft and low.

"Did you come up with the agreement? Or did Alaire approach you?"

"He approached meh," Tallis said as his eyes met mine. I could see the sadness and pain in their inky depths. Inside, I wanted to believe his visible regret was sincere, but I couldn't help doubting it. I wasn't able to hold his gaze any longer, so I looked away. "As soon as the Watchers reported tae Alaire aboot ye, he reached oot tae meh."

I nodded as I tried to think back on all the time I'd spent with Tallis, trying to figure out a timeline for every moment we'd shared with one another. I didn't know why, but it suddenly became extremely important to recount which events occurred prior to and after he'd made his decision. "So the time right after our first mission to the Underground City, when you showed up at my apartment in Edinburgh to tell me you wanted to continue my sword-training?" I started but then lost my voice. Tears began filling my eyes, and I furiously held them at bay.

"Aye," he answered simply, letting me know that he had made this horrible decision prior to arriving at my apartment and persuading me to train with him again.

"Was that the reason you came to see me in Edinburgh? Because you wanted to take me back to the Underground just so you could turn me over to Alaire?" I demanded. Waves of anger inside me made me clench my hands into fists at my side.

"Aye," Tallis replied before dropping his heavy gaze to the ground. He was quiet for a few seconds and appeared to be inspecting the terrain in front of him. Moments later, his eyes met mine. "At least, that was the reason Ah gave mahself as tae why Ah shooed oop oan yer doorstep."

"That was the reason you gave yourself?" I repeated scathingly. Then I scoffed as it occurred to me that maybe, he was just trying to avoid making it look like he didn't care about me, and most likely, never had. "What other reason could there have been?"

Tallis cleared his throat, but didn't drop his eyes from mine. "Ah wanted tae see ye agin," he answered

softly. He shrugged his massive shoulders as if to
indicate it was no surprise that he'd wanted to see me
again. "Mooch though Ah didnae want tae admit it tae
mahself, Ah felt drawn tae ye." He cocked his head to
the side and seemed to be in deep thought. Moments
later, surprise was all over his face. "Mayhap that was
part o' the reason Ah was sae determined tae leave ye
wif Alaire, 'cause Ah didnae like how mooch Ah ... that
Ah ... cared aboot ye."

I couldn't comment. Part of me wanted to laugh at
his words sarcastically, while the other part yearned
desperately to hold onto them and believe they were
true. "So the whole time you were training me on how
to use my sword," I began, trying to clarify his intent. I
refused to lose myself in anything pretty that might
emerge from his mouth.

"Aye, Ah had already made mah decision."

Swallowing hard, I closed my eyes and forced the
tears to cease. The last thing I wanted to do now was
cry in front of him. "So why did you bother training
me, if you knew you were just going to turn me over to
Alaire anyway?" I persisted, finally feeling like I was in
control of my emotions again.

"If anythin', Ah wanted tae give ye a fightin'
chance wif 'im, lass." Clearing his throat, he stood up
and began to pace back and forth, rubbing the nape of
his neck. "Let meh make somethin' verra clear tae ye,"
he started before facing me.

"What?" I asked when he appeared to lose his
train of thought.

"Ah didnae want tae give ye tae Alaire," he
answered. His voice sounded more determined, and
almost angry.

"And yet, that's exactly what you were going to
do," I countered. I had to make damn sure I didn't let
him off easily.

"There was naethin' Ah hated more than imaginin'
his hands all over ye, an' heem forcin' himself oan ye,

222

an' hurtin' ye," Tallis continued. His gaze was so intense, I preferred facing the fire instead. "Ah couldnae sleep at night," he explained. "Ah couldnae escape the horrible images o' him wif ye."

"Then why did you agree to the terms?" I demanded, finding no solace in his words. "If you hated the idea of him hurting me and using me, why did you decide to go through with it? Why did you ever allow him to meet me?"

"Because Ah wanted tae believe Ah could do it," he spat back, rubbing the back of his head again.

"You wanted to believe you could do it?" I repeated and shook my head as I wondered how I could have ever been so misled by Tallis. Here I'd thought he was this wounded man who was atoning for a past that bothered him deeply. I'd been so terribly mistaken, so absolutely wrong.

"Ah was the worst sort o' person in mah past," he explained, his voice growing calmer and softer again. "An' Ah wanted tae be able tae find that power inside meh again."

"But when I met you, you were atoning for your wretched past!" I protested before glancing at Bill. I wanted to make sure my voice wasn't so loud that it woke him up. He needed his sleep as much as I needed mine. When I faced Tallis again, I lowered my tone of voice until it was as soft as his. "You were making amends for all the horrible things you did when I met you. You were doing penance. You were trying to become a better person!"

"Aye," he answered but then shook his head as if my point wasn't valid. "Ah thought Ah was repentin,' boot Ah was only kiddin' mahself," he admitted. "Ah knew as mooch as soon as ye came intae mah life."

"Why would my entrance into your life make you decide you were kidding yourself about repenting for your past?" I demanded. I failed to see how I could have had anything to do with his epiphany.

"The first time Ah saw ye, Ah had tae keep mahself frae takin' ye," he seethed at me. "Ah wanted ye frae the verra beginnin' an' it joost got harder frae then oan. When Ah made mah agreement wif Alaire, Ah wanted tae stop feelin' anythin' fer ye, lass. Ah wanted tae free mahself frae the flame Ah carried fer ye."

I swallowed hard because the truth was, I'd also wanted him from the first moment I saw him. But my sexual attraction to Tallis didn't upset or alarm me like his for me obviously did. If anything, his attraction to me was the very thing that spurred him into making such a horrible pact with Alaire. It was almost as if he truly wanted to get rid of me, simply in order to banish his feelings for me. "So ... the whole time we were traveling together, through the sewers of the Underground City, you knew in just a short time, Alaire would demand his introduction to me?"

"Aye," Tallis agreed. "Ah didnae know when, nor how, boot Ah knew Ah was tae bring ye tae Alaire oan that fateful trip."

I was quiet for a few seconds while trying to get my emotions under control. Anger and deep sadness were tearing my brain and insides apart. It was all I could do to take a deep breath and promise myself I wouldn't cry—whether the tears came from anger or melancholy. "So when did Alaire realize you didn't intend to go through with your side of the arrangement?"

"He knew joost afore we arrived at his office."

"How is that possible?" I asked, shaking my head. "I was with you the whole time before we met him! There was no way you could have told him anything."

"Ah didnae tell Alaire," Tallis responded. "Ah told Grashnelle, an' he told Alaire."

Grashnelle was the water creature who'd appeared in the sewers while we were retrieving a soul from Cerberus. Grashnelle had served as a messenger

224

for Alaire, also informing us that Alaire wanted to meet me.

Shaking my head more vehemently, I tried to make sense of Tallis's story but parts of it weren't adding up. "You forget, I was there the entire time Grashnelle was with us! And I don't remember you saying anything to him."

"Aye," Tallis agreed as he nodded. "Boot if ye recall, Grashnelle could also communicate telepaffically, sae Ah didnae have tae rely oan the spoken word."

I didn't answer as I quietly thought about everything Tallis just admitted to me. My head was brimming with too much information that suddenly made me exhausted again, as if all the sleep I'd managed to get over the last couple of days was no more than a mere nap. But, I wasn't finished with our conversation. There was still way too much that I didn't understand, and still needed to know.

"When Alaire approached you with his bargain, what did he say to you exactly?" I asked, eyeing him pointedly.

"Lass, why dooze it matter?" Tallis asked me. Then, he shook his head, as if all of this were wasted breath. "All that matters noo is ta git ye home safely, so ye never haftae see meh again."

"No, that's not all that matters!" I railed back, hearing my voice crack. "What matters most to me is knowing the chain of events in sequence, so I can fully understand how you could ..." I didn't finish my sentence because my voice failed me. I was moments away from unleashing a barrage of tears.

"Alaire said he wanted meh tae bring ye tae heem an' leave ye thaur. 'Twas all he said tae meh."

"What for?" I demanded, renewed anger starting to churn inside me, although it felt better than wallowing in self-pity. "Why did he want you to leave me with him?"

225

Tallis cocked his head to the side. He was quiet for a few seconds before he returned his gaze to mine. "Ah dinnae know fer certain, boot Ah imagine he wanted tae steal yer innocence frae ye."

"You mean, he wanted to rape me?"

Tallis inhaled a long breath as soon as I said the word "rape." When he exhaled, his attention fell onto the robust fire. "Mayhap," he answered in a soft whisper.

"Maybe?" I repeated, shaking my head as the conflagration inside of me started to burn out of control. "What else would his purpose have been?"

"'Twould hae bin more than joost takin'ye 'gainst yer will, lass," Tallis started. His eyes met mine and were suddenly just as angry as I'm sure mine must have been. "He would hae wanted tae keep ye, tae never lit ye go."

Just like Hades did to Persephone, I told myself before facing Tallis again. "And you were willing to assist him in doing that?" I asked incredulously before erupting into an acerbic laugh. "And to think that I trusted you! I always thought you had my best interests at heart!" I fell silent as I took the struggle inward and thought about what a total and complete moron I'd been and was.

Tallis swallowed hard and his attention fell onto the fire again. "At the time Ah made the decision wif Alaire, Ah could only see mah oon freedom, 'tis true."

"You didn't care about me," I said in a haunted voice. "You never cared about me."

"O' course Ah cared aboot ye," he started, spearing me with a persuasive gaze again.

I shook my head fiercely as soon as I started to cave. I so wanted to buy into what he was saying but I wouldn't allow myself. I couldn't allow myself. "Obviously, not enough."

226

He shut his mouth and didn't say anything more. Instead, he just stared at the fire as if he were becoming mesmerized by it.

"So why couldn't you go through with it then?" I demanded, my voice now razor sharp. "Since you agreed to leave me to my fate with Alaire, why didn't you go through with it when you had the chance?"

"Ah couldnae," he answered, his jaw set tight. He refused to look at me.

"Why not?"

"Two reasons," he started, but his voice died away.

"What two reasons?"

"Yer sword was one."

"My sword?" I repeated skeptically. My eyebrows arched up to the sky as the boulder in my stomach continued to roll. I didn't know why but I'd hoped his response would have been something more personal. I wished it were something more along the lines of how he'd grown closer to me, and therefore, didn't want to deliver me to a wolf.

"Aye," he answered. "Ah couldnae leave ye wif Alaire because Ah remembered how, when ye first held yer sword, ye saw Fergus Castle, the one that had bin in mah family fer centuries."

"So what?"

He shook his head, defeated, as if I didn't understand the significance of his point. When he looked back at me, his eyes were deep and hollow. "Ye seein' Fergus Castle, somefin that Ah've always cherished, told meh that ye were pure o' heart, that ye were oontouched by the oogliness that haunts moost men," he answered. His gaze returned to the fire again. "Knowin' ye waur sae pure, Ah couldnae turn ye over tae Alaire."

"But I saw Fergus Castle way before we ever ventured into the Underground City," I argued, violently shaking my head to let him know his

227

reasoning didn't make any sense. "So you knew I was pure of heart long before you agreed to bring me to Alaire."

"Aye," Tallis confirmed as he nodded sullenly. "Boot Ah thought it wouldnae matter tae meh. Ah made mahself believe that whit mattered most tae meh was riddin' mahself o' Donnchadh, an' endin' a life Ah wanted nae part o'."

"So your bargain with Alaire was freedom from Donnchadh?" I inquired, wanting to make sure I fully understood what he was saying. He nodded. "But wouldn't the release of Donnchadh from your body mean that you would die in the process? Isn't Donnchadh the only reason you're immortal?"

"Aye, Ah would've died," he answered simply with a shrug, as if to indicate it was no big deal. "An' Ah would hae welcomed death."

I hated thinking of Tallis dead. As soon as the thought occurred to me, I mentally banished it from my mind. But what bothered me even more was how he seemed to welcome his own death. I hated the fact that Tallis wanted, above all else, to lose his life and himself. His self-hatred ran so deep, it had no bounds.

"You said the first reason you couldn't go through with it was because of your sword," I started, trying to get back on track. I still couldn't fully understand why Tallis had made the decision he had. And in order for me to move on and never look back again, I needed to understand it. "What was the second reason?"

Taking a deep breath, Tallis just stared at the fire for a good four seconds. When he looked up at me again, his eyes appeared heavier than before. Still, he didn't say anything. We just stared at one another as the fire reflected the deep lines of his cheeks and the fullness of his lips.

"The second reason," he began before biting down on his lip. His eyes narrowed as he dropped his gaze back to the fire. I could see the conflicting emotions

228

behind his mournful eyes and in the tightness of his jaw. He looked up at me again and my breath caught in my throat. I'd never seen Tallis look so completely broken, as if he were stripped bare and helpless. I felt like I could see right through him, and glimpse his soul.

"Tallis." I heard my voice, but didn't even realize I spoke his name.

"The second reason was 'cause Ah loove ye."

Don't miss Lily Harper's return in...

PERSEPHONE
AVAILABLE NOW!

Get FREE E-BOOKS!

It's as easy as:

Visit my website www.hpmallory.com

Sign up with your email address

Download your e-books!

About the Author:

H. P. Mallory is a New York Times and USA Today Bestselling author!

She lives in Southern California with her son and two cranky cats, where she's at work on her next book.

Made in the USA
Monee, IL
25 November 2022

18508614R00134